BATTLE OF THE APRIL STORM

LARRY FORRESTER

KU - 192 - 999

WORLD BOOKS · LONDON

First published in Great Britain 1969
This edition published 1970 by
World Books
By arrangement with George G. Harrap & Co. Ltd.
© Entertainment Holdings Ltd. 1969

Printed in Great Britain by Richard Clay (The Chaucer Press), Ltd.,
Bungay Suffolk

BOOK ONE/*'We Sail At 0130...'*

Kiel, Germany/V-E Day + 2

THE 15-HUNDREDWEIGHT lorry with the letters RN sten-
cilled tall on its canvas hood and a paper Union Jack pasted
on a corner of the windscreen picked its way through the
rubble-choked streets of the bomb-broken city towards the
docks, and Campbell could smell the sea long before he saw
it. Five years in prison-camp, locked far inland; shuffling
and prideless years with only the bleak Silesian plain beyond
the wire, and a horizon on all sides barred by straight, still
pines—like rows of sharpened pencils. Now the salt tang in
the morning air whetted all his senses, and the cold little
gulls wheeling and dipping overhead, squeaking for their
breakfasts, were like welcoming bunting.

Beside him McCallion was sitting forward, gripping the
wheel tightly, his boyish face gravely apprehensive. His
Leading Seaman's uniform was so new that its colour seemed
almost theatrical—a schoolboy costumed for the end-of-term
pageant. . . . Against this youthful freshness Campbell felt
like a discarded scarecrow. His cap had lost all shape. His
greatcoat, inherited from a much larger officer who had died
in the prison-camp, hung on him limp as a shower curtain.
There were big patches on the elbows and the material had
worn paper-thin and faded to a denim-like flatness. The
brand-new rank markings of Lieutenant-Commander stood
out like cheap gilt brooches.

The nearer they drew to the docks, the greater was the
destruction. They rounded a raw mound of rubble and
lurched across a littered square. The only structure still
standing was the shell of a burnt-out church, its shattered
steeple limned sharp and black against the pale sky.

A little way past the church an old man and a very small

boy, ragged and dusty, were fossicking in the ruins of a tenement. They straightened and turned blank, wrenched faces to watch the vehicle grind by, bumping in slow swerves down the ruptured roadway.

Further on, workers were clearing a path through a buried side-street. Some wore the tattered remnants of German uniforms. One had an Afrika Corps badge—dirty and drooping now. McCallion had to slow up and the workers stood silent, staring with that same blank, wrenched look.

Another square, with the rubble already cleared and a huge crater filled in. In the centre: a large, freshly painted signboard, put up by the First Canadian Army, giving them their route for the dockyard. McCallion accelerated past an Emergency Rationing Centre where women waited in a long shabby queue, their faces small and sharp in the tight frames of headscarves, the dulled eyes swinging round to follow the progress of the strange truck. Some had small children with them and one little girl waved and jumped up and down. Her movements accentuated the terrible stillness of this shocked, smashed city.

Campbell shifted his weight in the seat. His gaunt body ached, the tiredness was like cold iron rods through the marrow of his bones. He could feel nothing else.

The main gates of the German naval base, buckled and splintered by bomb blasts, had been lifted aside and propped against the cracked and pitted walls. A temporary barrier with a boldly striped boom had been thrown across the roadway. As the truck lumbered to a stop a Canadian sergeant ducked under the boom and came round on McCallion's side, a clipboard in one hand. He took the driver's identity card and then tilted his head, almost insolently, looking past McCallion at the figure hunched in the other seat. His cold policeman's eyes flicked over the rumpled, threadbare clothing, held for a moment, unimpressed, on the new half-ring, then came up to study the thin, pinched face—and Campbell met him with a calm, patient stare. The sergeant fanned at his brow in a grudging, desultory salute. Campbell acknowledged this and handed over his identity card. The sergeant checked the name against a prepared list on the clipboard.

" 'Tenant-Commander Campbell . . . Nope—don't seem to have you listed."

Campbell fished an envelope from an inside pocket. The sergeant took it, opened the unsealed flap, unfolded the single sheet of notepaper and scanned it, his lips moving silently. He refolded the paper carefully and his voice had a different fibre now.

"You'll find her in the North basin, sir—that is, what's left of her. . . ." Campbell nodded and McCallion took back the cards and the letter. "All the way down the end, turn right."

They began to roll forward. The sergeant threw a much crisper salute. As the boom glided back down into place he stood very still, staring after the truck. One of the guards drifted over to him.

"You ain't never gonna tell me that's the official delegation?"

"No. He's *un*official."

"Yeah? So what's he want?"

"Dunno, exactly. But that letter was signed by God!"

The listing hulk of the great ship, black-licked by fire, was leaning against the quay wall at an angle of more than thirty degrees. She threw a huge, sharp morning shadow over the broad, blast-fissured asphalt, the tottering dockyard sheds and the little group of German naval officers waiting by the blinded pillbox, smoking cigarettes and talking solemnly. The dead ship dwarfed and darkened everything, like the carcass of some slain monster.

McCallion stopped the truck in the loom of the canted bows, just off the black carpet of shadow. Both men got down and stood a moment staring up at the awesome steel wall. Ten thousand tons of her, rusting and rotting at her moorings here in the port she had limped back to more than five years ago, with the black blood flowing from the great wound in her side: never to venture out again—to die in bed, shamefully, with only fretful resistance, under the attacks of the RAF heavies. . . .

McCallion turned to look across at the German officers. Five of them, very stiff and straight now, staring towards the truck. Their caps were hard, wired high at the front; their uniforms immaculate.

"Sir . . . looks like you got y'self a reception committee."

Campbell half-turned, hands deep in baggy pockets, and glanced at the Germans, cool and indifferent—"Wait here."

McCallion, stern with apprehension, edged back to stand, legs astride and arms folded, squarely in front of his vehicle almost as though expecting to defend it. Campbell started forward slowly, keeping close under the tilted hull, wading through the deepest shadow. The German officers watched him, motionless, but he did not look at them again. Just abaft the fo'c'sle break he paused. Despite the blast and fire damage, the rust and the fading flaking paint, he could distinguish the scar, he could see where the new plates had been fitted to close the huge wound in the hull. He stood for almost a minute staring at the mark, shivering slightly, remembering once more and with the same overwhelming clarity the instant when the wound was smashed open, and how the metal screeched amid the smoke and the steam, and how the black blood came oozing, gurgling out. . . .

The retinae of his mind held the picture, so vivid in every detail. And the emotions it evoked were as confused and conflicting as ever. . . . Why am I here? What am I doing? I wasn't a part of it, not really, truly a part of it. I was the outsider—a joke, a weird accident—and not one of them was my friend. ... Out of all the group—Fielden, Hellbound Harry, young Rosinsky, Wreyford himself—why is it me standing here now? The one with the least right ... ?

He turned and paced on, heading now directly towards the Germans. As he drew nearer he could see their faces: aloof masks of resentment and incredulity. He realized they must be waiting here for the official Allied delegation and he grinned to himself—so, he was just in time, he'd got here first. ... But these didn't look like beaten men: all tarted-up and well-pomaded, it was plain they felt insulted by the appearance of a single, scruffy British officer of lowly rank. Yet as he walked unhurriedly towards them he felt no discomfort, all at once he was utterly devoid of emotion.

He passed within a few feet of the Germans. He didn't look at them. Their proud pale eyes locked on him as he climbed the steep, narrow gangplank on to the derelict's crazily tilted deck and began to pick his way through the mangled debris towards the Bridge. Then the senior German, a slight greying figure wearing a ceremonial sword and full Admiral's braid, spoke in curt command to his aide, a young and very tall Lieutenant. The Lieutenant clicked his heels, strode to the gangplank, and began to climb.

Up on deck everything was at a mad angle. Jagged holes and great patches of rust, buckled bulkheads, weirdly bent and riven superstructure—it was like the scenery in some unpleasant dream. Not far from the lower Bridge, on a bulkhead directly behind a wrecked gun position, Campbell noticed a small bronze plaque, discoloured by smoke and corrosion. He hauled himself up to it, rubbed away a patch of soot and rust with his sleeve. At the top of the plaque was a handsomely engraved eagle insignia, over laurel leaves and a swastika. He started to read the orderly German script beneath.

11

An diesem Geschütz
fiel der mech. Gesr. (21)
JOSEF RITTER
für sein Vaterland...

Before he could read on he felt a movement behind him, glanced round. The Lieutenant came up the deck and stood staring at the plaque. His bony face shone with defiant reverence. He spoke English as if it hurt his mouth. "At dis gun . . . fell Ordinary Gunner Yosef Ritter, aged twenty-von. . . . Died for his Vaderland, April 8, 1940. . . ."

Without moving from the plaque Campbell said in German, "Yes, a lot of good men fell that day."

The German regarded him in mild surprise, trying to measure his mood.

"You have very good German, Herr Kommander."

"I had plenty of time to learn. Five years in prison-camp."

Campbell turned his back and made his way on along the tilted deck, into the Bridge. The Lieutenant hesitated a moment, then followed.

The Bridge was severely damaged. Nearly all the perspex had gone and what remained was starred and blackened. The padding of the big conning chair was split and mildewed. Campbell shoved the chair with his foot: it spun around once, giving out a shrill rasp of protest. He moved on, heading aft. The German watched him start down towards the quarter-deck, and followed again.

The ladder was warped and several rungs were missing. Descending carefully, Campbell looked down over the rail, almost vertically: on the quayside far below the Germans' upturned faces were tiny white blotches.

The bell was undamaged. It hung as he had last seen it, not even tarnished, in its fine ornate frame in the centre of the Quarter-deck. A richly engraved ship's bell weighing, he guessed, close on three hundredweights—he saw at once he would have to take the frame as well. And his own coolly practical thought startled and jarred—so this is the reason, this is why I've come, to collect this bell! Not for myself. For them. For the others, who were not my friends. . . .

And then for a floundering moment he was filled with uncertainty. Was this a pointless, empty, sentimental gesture? —or worse: had he let himself be driven to it by some deep sense of inadequacy? Failure? Guilt? Over his years as a captive, had the whole thing festered in his mind?

Until this moment he hadn't known clearly what he'd come here for. Had he gone to such lengths, talked the Americans into flying him up to Bremmerhaven, persuaded a Rear-Admiral to write a special pass and supply transport the rest of the way, out of a purely selfish notion that collecting this trophy would somehow absolve him, like a holy pilgrimage? Suddenly he was foolishly, hideously aware of his scarecrow appearance, his aloneness; the trembling in his hands, the coldness in his bones. . . .

But he had come this far, he would go the rest of the way. He clawed up the incline and stood beside the bell. The clapper and its trailing cord were swinging very gently. After a moment he reached out and gave the cord a little push. The clapper struck out a soft mournful note that echoed away through the empty shell of the derelict.

He became aware of the Lieutenant behind him, felt the pale eyes on his back. Without turning, he gruffed out the German words—"I want this bell. I'm taking it with me. In my truck."

Several seconds of silence. He heard the Lieutenant edging closer.

"But Herr Kommander, what is your authority?"

Campbell wheeled to face him. "Get a working party up here, Lieutenant! Find some hacksaws!"

The German held Campbell's look only for a moment. The very dullness there, the total dissociation with the tone of command, chilled and confused him. He gave a small, awkward bow and made his difficult way back down the deck.

Campbell turned back to the bell. He pushed the clapper cord again—harder, this time.

On the quay below, the solitary, uneasy McCallion, standing by his truck, and the party of German officers near the foot of the gangway, heard the ghostly note vibrate through the gutted wreck. No-one moved or spoke. The sound was still floating in the still air as the Lieutenant appeared at the top of the gangway and started down.

Campbell sat on a ripped and rotting life-raft and his hands still shook as he fumbled out a tin of cigarettes— why am I here? Why am I doing this? God knows I haven't the right, and was never one of them. . . .

As he lit the cigarette, through the quivering match flame the great bell shimmered and rippled. And the last fading echo of its chime seemed to hover . . . to stir an answering vibration in the locked and aching chamber of his skull. Then the smoke rose like mist, thickened and turned into grey, dismal banks of cloud and shrouds of rain sweeping in over the island of Hoy and the cluttered roadsteads of Scapa Flow.

1530 hours
Scapa Flow/6 April 1940

SCAPA FLOW was filled with an urgent clamour on that cold, dank afternoon—the whir and clank of winches and steam capstans, the putt-putt of tenders' engines, raw voices bawling orders on more than eighty ships of war. A lighter was hammering its way out through the swell to the "G" class destroyer *Glowworm*, her deck stacked with crates of supplies and sacks of mail for all of the 1st Flotilla. Squatting down among this cargo, sheltering from the bite of the rain, the men of *Glowworm*'s returning shore party were wet, weary, and wordless.

Wally Hobson and Nobby Clark sat with their backs against a swaying, creaking wall of ammunition boxes. Clark opened and closed his mouth, tenderly fingering the fresh bruise swelling on his cheekbone—he was beginning to feel it now in the chill, penetrating air. Hobson was nursing grazed knuckles, picking little strands of skin from them, and peering through the curtain of drizzle at a short, thin figure standing close to the bows, exposed to the weather, staring intently ahead. The figure wore no hat, no coat. The fine rain's myriad droplets glistened on the brand new Midshipman's serge and the bright brush of yellow hair. One hand gripped the rail, the other a large fibre suitcase of jarring green.

Hobson nudged his mate, nodded at the Midshipman. Nobby scowled, sniffed wetly, and spat expertly downwind.

The Midshipman was shaking with cold. He gripped the rail, his light eyes eager-straining to pierce the drizzle. The curtain thinned, parted, and gave him his first look at the ship of war in which he would begin sea service. A long, low, grey shape riding at anchor in the roadsteads between the islands, not far from the main shore establishment and the floating dockyard at Hoy. HMS *Glowworm*, one of the most modern destroyers in service with the Royal Navy: 1345 tons of powerful, complex machinery, designed and built to hunt and kill. . . .

As the lighter curved in closer he could see men in working rig moving about the destroyer's decks—toiling over her four 4·7-inch guns, the torpedo tubes amidships, the racks of depth-charges at the stern. Others were painting super-

15

structure, funnels, and hull. Amid the sullen greyness she bustled bright with activity.

The Midshipman gripped the rail tighter and took a long breath of the cold, damp air.

Ossie Knowles was Petty Officer of the Watch, waiting as the lighter edged alongside. The Engineer Officer, Harry Trenton, came clanging out of a hatchway to join him. Harry's overalls were a wild abstract in oils, grease, soot, and paint, and he was wiping his big hands on a hunk of cotton waste. His eyes fastened hungrily on the lighter.

"About bloody time! See that my stuff comes on first, will you, Knowles?"

"Yessir. If they got it all."

"They better have—those pump spares especially!" He glowered at his big, steel-cased wristwatch. "I've got just about nine hours left to get this bloody ark back on top line."

Ossie sniffed, gave him a sidelong glance. "It's true then, sir? We're putting out again tonight?"

Trenton hesitated, realizing he shouldn't have let it slip. Then he shrugged, made his voice casual.

"Well, that's the buzz."

Together they moved to the side as the lighter made fast. Trenton saw the Midshipman, with his big green suitcase, picking his way along the small craft's cluttered deck towards the destroyer's ladder.

"Hello—that must be our new Snotty."

Ossie peered down and his broad, brine-scarred face filled with dismay.

"Gaw lummy, ain't big enough for the Brownies! Where do they get 'em? Whip 'em outa Sunday Schools, do they?"

The lighter's deck was rolling, rising and falling several feet, and it was clear to all those watching that if the boy tried to cross on to the ladder with his giant suitcase, almost certainly he would wind up in the water. Ossie chuckled plumply, in wicked anticipation.

The Midshipman stared at the ladder gravely, then glanced upwards. He was aware of the many eyes upon him. He turned his head slightly and saw a line dangling from the destroyer's deck. He moved along to it and with a swift half-hitch secured the suitcase. He looked up at a seaman by the rail directly above, cupped his hands and called confidently, cheerily: "Ahoy there! Haul away, please!"

Leading Seaman Longmore—at 39, *Glowworm*'s oldest rating—blinked in surprise then took the line and began to haul. The big suitcase fairly leapt upwards; it seemed light as a balloon.

The Midshipman walked back to the foot of the ladder, judged his moment correctly and came nimbly up to the destroyer's deck. He stood to attention and started to salute. Then he remembered he had no hat. Confused, he lowered his right arm, turned to face Harry. Despite the engine room grease and dirt, he recognized an officer.

"A'ternoon, sir. I'm Rosinsky."

The voice startled Trenton—it had a bite of East End. He nodded slowly, still wiping his hands on the cotton waste. The boy made a small, uncertain movement indicating his bare, soaked head.

"I ... got no 'at, sir."

"So I see. What happened to it?"

The Snotty's pale eyes were steady, utterly serious.

"Matterafact, sir ... I stuck me 'ead out the train window and it blew off." He paused, then added brightly: "I've left word with the Lost Property people."

Harry and the Midshipman stared at each other for a long moment then simultaneously they began to chuckle. Ossie Knowles, standing a little to one side, rubbed at his chin, grinning in spite of himself—where do they get 'em? Dear God, don't they know we're in a war now? A small ship can't be a bloody training school. It's rough an' it's dirty

17

an' we need men, not 'alf-grown sparrows. . . .

Ossie turned away slowly and in that instant saw the Captain striding towards them from the Bridge. He stiffened to attention and cleared his throat loudly to warn Trenton and the Midshipman. Too late. They were still chuckling as the Captain stopped a yard from them and coughed sharply. They wheeled to him.

The Captain was carrying a black briefcase under his left arm. His cap was stiff and straight as a bandsman's and his expression was austere. He glanced briefly at the hatless Rosinsky, then faced Harry. His voice, like everything else about him, was controlled, correct, precise.

"Do tell me, Mr Trenton—what's the joke?"

"Nothing really, sir. . . . It's just Midshipman Rosinsky, here. . . ." Lamely. "He's lost his hat."

Wreyford turned back to the Midshipman. The boy pulled himself even more rigidly to attention and met the Captain's cold gaze with frank eyes.

"Did you lose your coat, too?"

"No, sir. I 'aven't had m'clothing and equipment allowance, sir—'asn't come through yet. I bought what I could afford, sir. The rest'll just 'ave to wait."

The boy's candour, his complete lack of embarrassment and the unexpected East London accent all were disarming. The Captain grunted, surveying him from toe to crown.

"On an efficient ship of war every man must be correctly equipped. Petty Officer Knowles will take you to the First Lieutenant. If we can't kit you out somehow, you'll go back ashore."

The pale eyes clouded in an almost childish hurt—"Ay ay, sir."

The Captain looked at Trenton again, scanning the grimy overalls. Then he strode on towards the top of the ladder, beckoning. Harry moved swiftly to his side.

"From now on, Mr Trenton, while we're in port you

18

will not come on deck in working rig."

Trenton held the piercing gaze for a moment, back teeth clamped, then nodded down towards the lighter and the supplies being hoisted from her deck in nets. Among the loaders he spotted one of his ERAs,* Hobson. The big seaman pointed at some crates rising in one of the nets, grinned, and hoisted a thumb assuringly.

"My spares, sir. I thought I ought to come up and check 'em."

"It takes only a minute to change. And you will please wear your cap at the proper angle." Harry took a slow quiet breath and adjusted his cap, setting it almost square on his head, like the Captain's. "I should not have to tell *you*—personal appearance is the key to discipline and competence. I look to my officers to set an example."

The Captain consulted his watch and glanced along towards the stern of the lighter. Riding there now was his pinnace.

"I'm going over to *Renown*—Flag Officer's conference. When I get back I shall expect a full maintenance report from you, *and* from Guns."

"Very good, sir."

The Captain faced outboard, saluted with parade-ground punctiliousness and started down the gangway to the pinnace.

Trenton and the Midshipman stood watching the little pinnace pull away through the grey swell. Harry gave a raw growl and pushed his cap back, halfway to its old angle.

"Full maintenance report, he wants. More bloody paperwork—we're buried in bumph and bullshit!"

The Midshipman grinned blandly. Harry found himself grinning back. "What's your first name?"

"Jackie."

"Haven't you even got a duffel?" The boy shook his
_____
* Engine Room Artificer.

head. "Overalls?" He shook his head again. "Christ all-mighty . . . Knowles—find the First Lieutenant and see what he can scrounge for him."

Rosinsky reached for the big green suitcase. As he lifted it the catches twanged and the lid sprang open. One small item fell to the deck—a toothbrush. Trenton saw that apart from this the case was empty.

The boy picked up the toothbrush and for the first time since setting foot on board, looked self-conscious. Then that broad, open grin came again.

"If somebody could lend me some toothpaste . . . ?"

The spares and stores were stacked on the Quarter-deck. Daddy Longmore, Eddie Nisbett, and the Jockey were clearing and stowing the nets and lines. Ossie Knowles paced up and watched them for a moment, then moved on towards the stern and peered after the Captain's pinnace: already it was being swallowed up in the writhing gauze of the rain. He lifted his head and sniffed. The wind was coming now in spiteful jabs and beneath his feet the moored ship was stirring, heaving restlessly—poor old bitch. . . .

Soon the sky would choke up completely, it would come down and touch the water—and we're puttin' out again, t'ain't right, it's bloody madness. Jesus, don't they know the state we're in? On war stations right since the Spanish do—over three years now, 'thout a break. . . . If we'd seen a bit of action—just one real scrap—it'd be a whole lot different, then they'd let us rest, patch up proper. But it's been nothin' but a dirty, dreary slog all the way, with a right load-a stinkin' luck an' all. Three collisions and one runnin' aground—Gaw, what a mis'rable record! This is a good ship, too, one of the most modern we got in service, but she's old 'fore 'er time, that's what. She's been kept goin' too long with just temp'rary repairs, we can't go on patchin' 'er up . . . And the crew are shagged out, they oughta 'ave proper shore leave . . . We was so dead sure of it this time too, Skipper good as said so. We was goin' down to Pompey, to the yards —oh Gaw, I 'ave to write Ruby! I gotta get it off 'fore that lighter leaves—not too much longer now, honest love, it can't be, it can't. . . .

He turned and started quickly for his quarters. But the shore party were coming up from the lighter and the first to reach the deck tried to hurry past Ossie, keeping his face averted. Why . . .? It was impossible not to recognize the biggest man on board, a giant Yorkshireman.

" 'Ey, Lump!"

The big man stopped but didn't turn round. Ossie paused, suspicion growing.

"I'm talkin' to you, mate. C'mere!"

Reluctantly Lump swivelled round and lumbered nearer. One eye was completely closed—a classic shiner. Ossie regarded him grimly for a moment then wheeled to face the others as they came trooping, silent and shame-faced, up the ladder. Every one of them showed signs of battle— bruised lips and cheeks, bloody noses, stained and torn uniforms. They shuffled themselves into a rough line beside Lump—young Tinker Bell, Wally Hobson, Nobby Clark, Grannie Smith, Keelie Grant. . . .

Ossie paced slowly along the line, lips moving soundlessly as he studied each battered face. Then he stood back, shook his head in slow disgust.

"Oh yeh, great, great . . . We ain't got problems enough. One-eyed gunners and look-outs, that's goin' to 'elp a lot, that is!"

They looked at each other mournfully and then Grant, the burly, gentle Glaswegian, scuffed his feet sheepishly—"We didna start it."

"You been fightin' the Highland Light Infantry again?"

Grant shook his shiny bollard of a head—"We run into Knocker White's crowd, from *Grafton*."

Hobson edged forward—"And some from *Grenade* joined in an' all. It were three to one, Ossie."

"I see—fightin' the rest of the Flotilla now, are you? Bloody bright that is. . . ."

"God's truth, we didna start it," Grant insisted. "We hud to wait for the spares. They wusn't ready at the depot so we went fur a jar at the NAAFI, but we'd hardly got in the door when Knocker an' his mates started on takin' the piss. Y'know—gettin' at *Glowworm*, sayin' how we always turn back, an' how as the only things we've hit are coal-barges an' harbour walls, sort o' style. . . . Well, we couldna jus' stand there, could we, eh? I mean, ye got to stick up fur yer own ship, Ossie."

Behind Grant young Tinker growled low and fierce— "Even if it *is* a lousy swill-tub!"

Ossie shot him a warning look. The youngster snorted and turned away.

"You didn't 'ave the crushers down on you?"

"No, no," Hobson said quickly. "It were all over in three or four minutes, honest. Keelie fixed Knocker—"

"I gi'ed him the heid—fuggin' shitpot!"

"—an' laid him out cold. Then we fought our way out."

"There weren't all that much damage," Grannie said mildly. "Just the one window, and a coupla tables went over. . . ."

Ossie heaved a long, wearied sigh. There was no anger in him. He moved up to Grant.

"What about them razor blades, Keelie? They with the stuff for the canteen?"

Grant's face fell and he spread his big hands in apology. "Och, I'm awfa sorry . . . Wi' a' this carry on, y'see—it went right out o' m' heid. . . ."

Ossie scowled fiercely. "Bloody marv'llous, innit!" He surveyed the rest of their sorrowful faces then gruffed— "Good job the Old Man didn't see you just now, that's all.

Get cleaned up, and stay outa 'is way!'"

He jerked his head in dismissal and they slouched off. He stood watching them go and was suddenly very tired. Slowly he started for his quarters.

Glowworm's pinnace was swinging in alongside *Renown*. The Captain stood with the drizzle numbing his face, looking up the glistening grey wall of the cruiser, telling himself again that this time he must convince Whitehorn. And once more running over in his head the things he would say—adamant things, undeniable facts. It would have to be *after* the conference, of course: he would get Whitehorn alone, when the others had gone.

As the boathooks probed out, he glanced at his watch.

In a large, quiet, oak-panelled cabin in *Renown* sixteen officers were seated round a conference table covered with charts. At the head of the table, presiding over the briefing, was the Flag Officer, Admiral Jake Whitehorn, a tiny, gnomish figure, grey and slightly bent. His lean and corded neck didn't quite fill his collar and one could imagine a wispy body rattling about inside the magnificent, heavily braided and beribboned uniform. He turned a silver snuffbox over and over, caressingly, in small, slender, bone-pale hands and glanced slowly around the table while his secretary, Sub-Lieutenant Tim Trotter, fussed nervously with folders and reference books.

Apart from young Trotter everyone at the table was a destroyer skipper. Whitehorn had been a small-ship man himself once, and as he squinted from under his bushy white brows at these young commanders he decided the old saying still held good—destroyers were not so much a branch of the Service as a state of mind, a way of living. . . . These men were a breed apart, each one a distinct individual; and some, with their lush, piratical beards and heavy sweaters, were overtly, proudly flamboyant—in the way that the Air Force's fighter pilots had developed their own private, privileged cult. Despite his own weariness, and the crushing grimness of the news received from Admiralty just a few hours before, Whitehorn felt a steeling glow, a lifting of the spirit. He wished only that he had many more such men, and the ships to give them.

One chair was still empty. He frowned at it, opened the snuff-box and rammed a fiery pinch up his nostril.

"*Glowworm*—not here?"

George MacVean studied his wristwatch, took the big pipe from his mouth. A bright grin split the mask of black ringlets.

"Still thirty seconds to go, sir. You know Garry Wreyford —*he* won't be late!"

Across the table Peter Evans, youngest skipper in the Flotilla, gave a short soft laugh—"Bet he walks in dead on the dot!"

A faint chuckle all round. Whitehorn grunted, applied snuff to the other nostril. Evans held up his arm, studying the big second hand on his watch.

"I make it—fifteen seconds."

"No-one's taking you on, Peter," said MacVean. "We all know Garry far too well!"

Evans smiled sarcastically. "Good old Rammer Wreyford! Wonder if he's hit any coal barges lately?"

Whitehorn's head jerked up, the small eyes drilling, but Evans seemed unaware of the disapproval.

"Eight seconds. . . . Seven . . ." From outside: footsteps. Measured, regular strides. The Royal Marine sentry opened the door wide and stood to attention. Evans, his back to the door, continued to count off the seconds—silently now, shaping the numbers with his mouth.

Precisely on "Zero!" Wreyford entered the cabin. He halted facing the Admiral, straight and grave.

In this colourful company Graham Wreyford's ordinariness made him the oddity: everything about him—uniform, bearing, expression—was so correct, so stiffly serious. He was older than any of the other skippers, yet still a Lieutenant-Commander—the only one in the Flotilla passed over in the New Year promotions list.

Whitehorn felt uneasy. He liked Wreyford, instinctively, but he could never quite make him out. The fellow was a first-class sailor—that was the astonishing thing, when you came to think of all those bumps, the silly mishaps, and the infuriating breakdowns. Still, all the various official inquiries, including those into the more serious collisions and the running aground, had proved conclusively that the incidents were not Wreyford's fault and had absolved him of all blame.

The deep, superstitious streak in all seamen led Whitehorn to conclude that it was just plain bad luck—this fellow had a 'jinx'. But at the same time he was practical enough, and fair enough, not to overlook the fact that *Glowworm* had taken a long and brutal battering on dreary, dirty duties, without respite, and without once being involved in actual combat. He was, he admitted to himself, unhappily confused about the man, and about the ship. But the next few days should finally clear up the problem, one way or the other. . . .

He snapped the snuff-box closed, nodded affably. "How are you, Garry?"

"Quite well, thank you, sir."

Wreyford as he moved to his place was vaguely aware of young Evans' self-satisfied smirk and a certain, slightly awkward atmosphere. He sat down and with deliberate movements opened the black briefcase and arranged some papers and a thick notebook before him.

"Get all the spares you needed from the depot?"

Wreyford hesitated, brow pleating. "Yes, sir. Everything *immediately* essential, that is. . . ."

Whitehorn's shaggy eyebrows lifted. "Yes? Should've thought by now *Glowworm* had enough spares to build herself a sister ship!"

Some gentle laughter from the others—even MacVean joined in. Wreyford glanced round their faces, puzzled, a little shy, and then he too grinned.

Whitehorn gestured to his secretary. Trotter helped him unroll a big chart. In the expectant stillness, from outside and from overhead they heard the chill moan of the rising wind.

"Now then, gentlemen, let me tell you right away—what the newspapers have chosen to call 'the phoney war' is over. Intelligence informs us, quite definitely, that the German land forces are about to launch Operation Weserubung—the invasion of Denmark and Norway." He paused, let the low stirring die down, then dropped his voice a couple of keys.

"Both countries will fight, of course. As best they can. . . . And every day they can hold out will be valuable to us. Because, you may be sure, France and then Britain will be next in line."

His gimlet eyes swung round the table. No-one spoke, no-one doubted him. He picked up some papers and placed his other hand, small and dainty, on the big chart.

"The Home Fleet will put to sea, tonight. *Renown*, with the First Destroyer Flotilla, will be a unit of that force." His hand began to move in elegant sweeps across the chart.

"Now, we know that the first assaults will be made by airborne and parachute troops, but the enemy will have to land *some* forces from the sea, to seize installations and occupy vital bases—such as Trondheim, Narvik, Bergen, and Stavanger. And I don't have to tell you, that means some of his big ships will be out."

Excitement rippled stronger this time. He glanced up and saw their eyes fired with eagerness as they exchanged looks. It gladdened his heart—yet now he had to bridle their aggression, disappoint them, hold them to the specific role for which they had been chosen. . . .

"But this squadron will not be concerned with intercepting the enemy Fleet. We won't be hunting. We have another, vital job to do."

Their faces fell. Evans sat back and thrust his hands into his pockets in a petulant gesture. Only Wreyford remained impassive.

"It won't be dull, I can promise you that. Our objective will be West Fjord . . . the approaches to Narvik. We're going right into the Fjord and we're going to fill it with mines! I need hardly tell you, the enemy will be expecting some such move. So we can count on the U-boat packs showing up in full strength, and the Luftwaffe too—if the weather lets 'em."

The secretary, Trotter, rustled a sheet of paper. "Met reports on our side, sir. Big fronts moving in. Up to Force 9 winds predicted, rain and sleet. Quite extraordinary—I mean, for April. . . ."

"It's splendid!" Whitehorn declared. "Exactly what we need—bags of low cloud, and a steady-blowing gale!"

All round the table, grudging murmurs of agreement. MacVean reached out a big hand and Trotter handed him the Met report. Bill Maitland leant over MacVean's shoulder to scan it with him.

Wreyford was the only one that didn't seem keyed up. He sat stiff and straight in his chair, and frowned at the charts. After a moment he lifted his head and looked across at the large oil painting of George VI fixed to the panelled wall.

1645 hours
Kiel Naval Base/6 April 1940

THE PANELLED WALL of the main cabin in *Admiral Hipper* was bare except for a big gilt-framed photograph of the Führer. Beneath the portrait six officers were grouped around a long table littered with charts, files, and papers. Mann was talking, one hand spread upon a chart, the other holding a weather report.

"And if these conditions last there should be no difficulty. We will slip through the Skagerrak without risk of being spotted."

General von Falkenhorst took the cigarette from his mouth and nodded. "The Luftwaffe will be standing by to give you cover—if there *is* a change."

"And you will have U-boats screening you to the West, sir!" Lieutenant Eberhardt added in his eager, muted bark which made the simplest remark seem an exclamation. Mann glanced over at him: plump, balloon-faced, glinty-spectacled, pale-skinned as a fish's belly—a walking cliché, almost absurdly typical of the new Party-men being insinuated into Intelligence. Facts, figures, questions, answers, fierce spurrings of dogma; but no deep feeling for the Service, no true loyalty or pride or understanding. Ever officious, never off duty. He looked at Eberhardt and imagined thousands of tiny silent wheels whirring inside the casing of lard, lubricated by a colourless, cold, viscous fluid.

"I presume we will be keeping watch on Scapa Flow?" the Admiral said. "Whatever the weather does?"

"Yes, yes certainly, sir: a special low-level reconnaissance has been planned for tonight. It will look like a bombing attack, but flares will be dropped and photographs will be taken!"

Von Falkenhorst glanced at his watch, picked up his cap

28

and said with tired assurance: "Don't worry. You will know if the British Fleet moves out. If there are no more questions, gentlemen?" He glanced round their faces: no one spoke. "Then I wish you a successful trip, Admiral."

"Thank you, General."

"Heil Hitler!" yapped Eberhardt, stabbing at the ceiling. Zeltmann, the SS Colonel commanding the landing force, gave a rapid echo and the General responded automatically, almost absently. Mann thanked God that the Navy was excused this juvenile ritual and retained the standard salute. He turned to Zeltmann—"You can start getting your men on board now, Colonel."

Zeltmann's heels thudded and he hurried after von Falkenhorst. Eberhardt was last to go, anxiously stuffing his bits of paper into a huge, shiny document case.

Mann looked at Stenz and von Scholtz, and after a moment without knowing why they all smiled softly.

"So at last, sir, they permit us to put to sea," von Scholtz said at length, in his slow aristocratic cadences. "If only as troop-carriers."

"Once we are out, Max, anything can happen. We must hope the British come after us."

Zeltmann walked with the General to his staff car, through a chill drizzle. They did not once glance at the 1200 shock troops lined up further along the quay with full equipment, waiting to be embarked on *Hipper* and the four escorting destroyers. Von Falkenhorst did not speak until he was seated in the back and the Corporal-driver got ready to slam the door. Then he bent forward and made the words clear and separate as pistol shots.

"Give me Trondheim, Zeltmann! Quickly, and with the harbour intact!"

"Yes, sir!" Trondheim—Narvik—Tromso: secure those in the first hours and Quisling's underground columns would

29

take over civil administration everywhere else, all of Norway would be subjugated in a matter of days. "We will carry out our orders, General."

"They will try to scuttle ships, destroy the power station."

"We won't give them time. I intend to have my men in control of the entire port area within forty-five minutes."

Von Falkenhorst gave Zeltmann one of his rare, thin smiles and the car moved off, tyres hissing over the wet asphalt. Zeltmann pulled up the collar of his leather topcoat and started along the quay towards his waiting troops.

Sergeant Ernst Neuhofer tossed away the end of his sodden cigar and called gruffly to the three men of his special demolition squad—"Move yourselves! Here we go. . . ." They hefted their equipment and shuffled into line. Little Metchik scowled after the departing staff car.

"So—the Herr General isn't coming with us."

"Back to his warm bed," young Schiller growled, and his sneer was grotesque because his teeth were chattering with cold. "With some patriotic Fraulein." Metchik gave his hard, snarling laugh and Stummer leered lugubriously.

"That's enough!" Ernst barked, with the special ferocity of a newly promoted commander. "Face front!" There was no more talk, but Metchik swung him a measuring look. Ernst knew the hour would come when the Corporal would talk back, and he hoped it would be soon. This little destruction machine of his—these three specialists, with their new plastic explosives—must be tuned to perfection, tuned to run smoothly, automatically, mindlessly, before he took it into action.

Despite all the tough training and testing—a fourth man had blown himself into a mash on the final exercise—Ernst knew it still had a fault: Metchik was the suspect part, threatening to upset the timing and balance. Metchik, the most experienced of the trio, the undersized ex-shot-firer from the Ruhr coalfields, with his black heart and his deep, deep envy and his hacking, sweating, tearing greed. Metchik, who'd been with him in Poland, who'd helped him destroy the bridge at Rudna to cut off the retreat of a whole Polish regiment. Metchik stuttering profanities all the time in the dark, delirious in a fever of fright, yet holding his clammy hand on the plunger a full twelve minutes, delaying the blast until the last instant, until they could hear the hollow thunder of the escaping cavalry on the bridge. And then Metchik screeching in terrible joy as the pieces of men and horses rose in the red glare with the chunks of masonry and thudded down on the bank around their hide-hole. . . . Metchik, the most natural destroyer of them all, the most wanton, and the least brave—a scrawny little soul that lived in blind smouldering malice and fed on violence and ugliness.

The weak link could not be replaced at this late stage, but it could be repaired—stripped down and beaten into shape. But Ernst would have to wait for a definite loss of control, a failure to respond—then he would go to work with the heavy hammer.

So far as he could tell, after the days on the cold, crawling train and the hours standing here in the chill drizzle staring at the great grey cruiser and the destroyers rocking and straining at their moorings and at the big green rollers shouldering into the harbour from the vast and gloomy sea; after all the rumours and guesses about where they were going—to the best of his sombre judgment the other two members of the team were showing no more than normal strain. True, Schiller's handsomeness and gaiety had faded: the young Bavarian looked pinched and paler and smaller: he seemed to feel the cold much more than the others and it froze his whole spirit so that even his grousing grew unconvincing. Well, the heat of battle would cure all that.

For Schiller had an innocent, boyish craving for excitement, perhaps even secret dreams of glory which, while they lasted, and so long as Ernst kept a tight rein, would make him a responsive and reliable part of Neuhofer's Mobile Destructor. He has so conceited, so proud of his nineteen-year-old physique, his prowess as an athlete and as a callous seducer. Shining, smiling Johan Schiller, who could swim a hundred metres underwater with goggles and a nose-clip, sprint and leap and throw with deadly accuracy, murmur warm words to a pretty girl and be in bed with her an hour later, wear a dirty steel helmet like a prince's crown and, with his God-given talent for all things electrical, rig a radio or fix a time-fuse or tap a telephone line in minutes out of the imbroglio of wires, old valves, taped-up transformers, leaking batteries, cutters, screwdrivers, and soldering irons that filled his dented tool trunk.

And Stummer—the thick-bodied, thick-headed Austrian cat burglar and safe-blower released from Hamburg Jail for special Army service was an automaton, operated by drills and commands. He wasn't bright enough to be afraid, and too eager to justify his parole to think of desertion or questioning an order. He handled cordite, dynamite, gelinite, cyclonite, TNT and the new plastic compounds with a sublime contempt, and possessed an uncanny instinct for judging the precise charge needed to provide a required effect—he could blow a steel door off its hinges without scorching the frame.

Totally unimaginative, he had become a criminal for the same reason that motivated his every action in life—because someone had told him to. Someone, no doubt, who knew that this heavy, slow man in fact was the son of an Innsbruck mountain guide and could climb cool and sure as a fly on a window pane, and that his docility and oafishness were matchless assets when it came to scaling a cliff or edging along a twelfth-story ledge with a pot of jelly in his pocket. . . .

32

1700 hours/Scapa Flow/6 April 1940

Over on the left an officer bawled an order. The advance company began to file up the cruiser's gangplank. Ernst told himself it must be France. A raid on one of the Channel ports—or the naval base at Brest? Five ships of war, 1200 troops, and probably U-boats and aircraft in support—the one certainty was that it was going to be something big.

1700 hours
Scapa Flow/6 April 1940

"SOMETHING BIG comin' off, you'll see!" Tinker Bell grated. "Why else would they be sendin' us right back out again?"

He winced and spat an oath as Daddy Longmore applied the sponge once more to his swollen and discoloured eye. For a glum moment none of the others spoke. They were sprawled in their hammocks, or hunched around the big messing table, reading newspapers and magazines or writing letters. *Gloworm* heaved and creaked restively in the roughening sea. The Jockey, squatting in a corner, was breathing soft, quivering, aimless chords out of his mouth organ.

Scowling, Tinker surveyed their faces—mugs, all of 'em, dead dim an' docile as lambs. . . . Can't think for 'emselves, they 'as to be told what to do—Gaw, what a shower-a faggin' deadbeats! Still, reckon the Navy's better'n Maidstone Jail—I'd've gone ravin' bloody bonkers there, belted a screw most likely, like I done in Borstal, an' landed up in solitary, or maybe even gettin' topped. . . .

'Em bastards from New Cross 'adn't shopped me, I'd be down the Elephant with the lads tonight, or up West with some bint blowin' the loot from the ware'ouse job—I'd be fixed up with reserved occupation down the docks an' all, casin' the cargoes by day an' me an' Archie knockin' 'em off nights. . . . That faggin' New Cross mob, turnin' me in just 'cos that bloody night watchman got coshed—'ow the 'ell was I t'know 'e was somebody's old man? Silly old perisher 'ad used 'is loaf an' looked the other way, I shouldn't've 'ad to go on the trot, an' join up when it got too 'ot—shouldn't be cooped up now in this stinkin' tub with a load-a bleedin' mugs, waitin' our turn to get shot up the arse. . . .

Tinker pushed Daddy's ministering hand away, leant forward and thrust his harsh voice across the table at Keelie Grant—"They got no faggin' right sendin' us back out, shape we're in! Faggin' disgrace, that wot!"

Keelie put down his pen and regarded him mildly. "I don't see what ye got to moan about, son. Ye've only been aboard a month."

"Six weeks, mate! And two month on a minesweeper 'fore that, mind."

"Six weeks . . . Listen, Flower—d'ye know how much shore leave most-a this crew's hud in the last three year?"
nothin' else since I come up that gangplank!"

"Yeh, yeh—forty-eight hours. Gaw save us—I've 'eard

"Aye, well it's fact, mate. . . . Less'n any ither ship in the Navy. Forty-eight hours in three year."

"Faggin' disgrace, *tell* ya! Somethin' oughta be done about it. Skipper oughta be 'auled up. If we was to write to the papers. . . ."

Others glanced up. The Jockey's playing faltered and Daddy dropped the sponge on the table and said with morose fatalism, "Got nothin' to do with the Skipper. He's had no more leave than the rest of us."

Tinker gave a short, bitter laugh—"Aw now give over, Dad! What would 'e want goin' ashore, eh? 'E ain't bleedin' Gawd A'mighty there! 'E's only 'appy when 'e's aboard 'ere, faggin' us about with 'is peacetime bull—givin' us penny lectures, fillin' up 'is forms and makin' blokes write reports in bloody triplicate. Tell ya, 'e runs this boat like a bloody bank manager!"

The Jockey stopped playing. The silence was truculent. Then Keelie said firmly, "Just the same, ye canna blame the Captain—he's no' the one that's stoppin' leave. Ye know fine he wants the ship in dock—complete overhaul. He's said so often enough—ask Ossie Knowles. Any Skipper would—Fur Christ's sake, we been on active duties, solid, right since she was commissioned—right since the Spanish do, and that's four year ago now! It's nae use blamin' the Skipper for that. It's the brasshats in Whitehall ye should blame."

"*And* faggin' Hitler!" Daddy grumped. Tinker sniffed, unconvinced, but said no more.

Lump concentrated again on the postcard he was writing —laboriously, with a stubby pencil. His lips moved slightly, silently. After a moment he paused, nudged Nobby Clark.

" 'Ow'd tha spell 'stinkpot'?"

"Eh?" Nobby blinked at the wavery scrawl on the card. "Who you writing to, then?"

"Me mum."

"Lumme—y'can't say a thing like that to her, Lump, lad!"

The giant blinked his mild eyes. "What?—not even 'bout rotten article like Knocker White?"

Nobby's hand involuntarily went up to his bruised face. "That's different, that is ... I'll give you a better word, mate! Write this—g'on. ... 'B–A–S–T–A–R–D. ...' "

The conference on *Renown* was over but Wreyford lingered on. Whitehorn's secretary, young Tim Trotter, gathering up the maps, files, and papers, eyed him with veiled protective hostility. The Admiral was having a final word with Evans whose ship, the *Grafton*, was to be loaded with special mines. As Wreyford made his way towards that end of the table MacVean stepped into his path, smiling gently.

"Coming, Garry?"

"Er . . . not just yet, George. I want a private word with the Old Man." MacVean's smile became a little uneasy as he glanced towards the Admiral. "By the way," Wreyford said easily, "congratulations . . . *Commander*." MacVean was flustered. "Oh—thanks . . . Hard luck *yours* didn't come through."

"Didn't expect it to," he said calmly, his eyes clinging to the Admiral.

"Dammit, it's a bit much, y'know. You've got more service in than most of us."

"It isn't the time you put in that counts. It's what you do with it."

"Not your fault you've had those breakdowns and—er, mishaps. Just damned unfortunate, old chap."

"Yes, perhaps. But it makes a pretty dismal record, y'know. All bumps and scrapes and patching up—no action to justify it." Evans was taking leave of the Admiral now. Wreyford slapped MacVean's arm and pushed past him. "Remember me to Peggy?"

"Yes, of course. And Susan? The little chap?"

"Both well, thanks. Excuse me, George." He hurried away, stepping neatly around the guardian Trotter and cornering the Admiral.

"Sir, I wonder could you spare me just a minute or two?" Whitehorn took a slow breath and regarded him with dulled eyes.

"All right," he said, in a tone that suggested he knew exactly what was coming. "What's on your mind now, Garry?"

"I'm worried, sir. Extremely worried. So little time. . . ."

"We sail at 0130," the Admiral droned flatly. "And if I could get 'em started earlier, I would."

"I have to be frank, sir. In my view *Glowworm* won't be in proper shape for full sea duties until she's been dry-docked. She'll be constantly racked by breakdowns, in every department. And the men are worn out."

"Yes, yes, I know all about that—"

"I feel I must ask you to release us from this operation, sir."

"Out of the question! Look here, I've been given a bloody difficult job to do, and damn' few units to do it with. In fact, I'm hard put to make this look like any sort of show at all. So long as you can keep up with us, I need you."

"Sir, I can't guarantee—"

"That's final, Garry!" The small, tired eyes flashed a plain warning. Wreyford sighed, nodded surrender.

"Very good, sir. I—simply felt it my duty to inform you of the position. . . ." The Admiral pursed his lips, fished out his snuff-box, frowned at it and spoke in a gentler tone.

"I know. I know *Glowworm*'s well overdue. With any luck, after this one we'll be able to send you South for full overhaul and a decent rest. But just now—we sail at 0130."

"Ay ay, sir."

"I'll do my best not to put any strain on you. You needn't carry the mines." The deep lines softened puckishly. "Just stay afloat, Graham. Keep up with us, and try not to bump anyone."

Wreyford flushed slightly. "Goodnight, sir." He took his leave in scrupulous regulation manner.

Ossie Knowles was standing in the tiny, pipe-festooned slit of a cabin he shared with two other Petty Officers, in his undervest, scraping at his face with a hopelessly dull blade. He could feel *Glowworm* lurching, swinging heavily under his feet in the lifting swell and he heard the icy howl of the raiding wind.

Hard to believe it was April. He thought of his small

rectangular garden at Waterlooville, just outside Pompey—down there the daffs would be out now. Ruby would keep things tidy, Ruby liked gardening and she knew the daffs were his favourite. And all around on the Hampshire dunes and coastal flats the gorse bushes would be bold-spiked, clamouring yellow. Suddenly he had a fierce and dreadful longing to tread still, solid earth and see proud, straight daffodils and curved-cup tulips and gorse and trees and rich kind grasses. And to smell, touch, fall into the warm softness of Ruby—gentle, patient, unafraid Ruby. All of that, all of his true and natural world, only seven hundred miles from this cold and ugly place—but it might as well be seven hundred light years. . . .

The door exploded inwards and Bunty Baker came staggering in with a freezing gust that hardened the lather on Wally's face. It took both of them to get the door closed.

"Jesus," Bunty hissed, shaking sleet from his clothing, "this lot's comin' straight down from the ice-cap. Cuts right into you, feels for your bloody bones."

"Gawd 'elp all poor sailors on a night like this," Ossie intoned, dabbing on more lather. "Old Man back yet?"

"That's what I come to tell you—just leavin' *Renown.*"

"Right—I'd better get on deck, then." He scraped away at his chin with renewed fervour.

"Ossie—did Keelie get them blades?"

"No, bugg'rit! Silly sods got in a scrap, soon as they went ashore. And 'e clean forgot the canteen's list."

"Blimey—I been usin' the same one for three months, now. Tearin' me face off. I got a good mind to ask permission to stop shavin'."

"Har!—some 'opes! You know 'ow the Old Man feels about that."

"Yeh, well this must be the only tin can in the Navy without one honest set a-whiskers. No wonder the others reckon we're a shower a-poofs."

Ossie grinned sadly, wiped away the remains of the lather. "A wonder we ain't, after this long!"

"There's one or two I wouldn't risk bending down front of, ta very much."

"Yeh ... still, I dunno, Bun. Skipper's got a point. 'E reckons when a bloke stops shavin' in the mornin' that's the start of gettin' lazy. Somethin' goes, see? And before long 'e stops washin'."

"Now ain't that typical? More a-Wreyford's peacetime bullshit!"

Ossie started pulling on his heavy sweater. "Don't you reckon you need a bit o' bull in wartime an' all? This old tub's about clapped out right now, but there's not much wrong with the crew."

"What? They're on their knees, Ossie—and dead chockered we're not goin' on leave."

"All right, but they're still about the best in the Flotilla. I'd stake me number one boots on that. And it's all Rammer's doin'. Make no mistake—but for 'im they'd a-been finished, useless, long 'fore this. 'E knows 'ow to run 'is ship, does the Old Man."

Bunty moved to help Wally into his oilskins and his voice curled— " 'E knows 'ow to run—period!"

Wally froze with one arm in a sleeve and stared hard into his friend's small, lined wedge of a face. "And what's that supposed to mean?"

"Work it out for y'self, mate. Best crew in the Flotilla, eh?—and the only ones who ain't fired a shot in anger yet! Look at the times we've turned back."

"Come off it! You can't blame Rammer for that."

"Me—I'm just tellin' you what some a-the lads are sayin', that's all. He may be a good peacetime skipper, but we still got to find out what he's like in a fight. That's what the lads are sayin'."

Ossie turned away, pulled the oilskins around him and

snatched up his cap. Bunty opened the door and together they pushed their way out against the wailing wall of the Nor'-Easter.

The wind was coming now in spiteful, screeching jabs, driving blasts of sleet and hail across the heaving water. Standing on deck, watching the Captain's boat struggle alongside, slamming the fenders, Ossie found himself thinking of the old days when Wreyford had his private sailing yacht, *Felicity*—of the numberless times he'd stood here on this same spot and watched her curve in, hull hissing handsomely through kindly seas, with the Skipper at the tiller in white sweater and fluttering silk scarf, crisply calling orders. He glanced along the rail towards the place, on the quarterdeck, where the private craft had been kept: occupied now by Carley life-floats, a graceless stack in the swirling gloom.

Felicity had been a delicate creature of light and play— whenever there came a break in the monotony of peacetime patrols, and the sea and wind agreed, the Skipper would have her over the side and often Ossie would crew for him. Sometimes they would race her against other boats, yacht club boats at Cowes or Gib or Alex, or boats owned by other skippers, like MacVean's scuddly little dinghy—Gawd, I can still 'ear the slap of 'er boom and feel 'er lean and swing as we took 'er through the wind's eye ... And 'ow the Skipper could 'andle 'er: born seaman, the Old Man, no doubt about it, and 'e handles *Glowworm* just as sweet—it's not learned that, it's lived, it's like women cookin'. . . .

Funny, when you come to think of it—a Skipper who can work a ship like 'e can, runnin' us aground and collidin' with bloody coal barges! Well just stinkin' luck, that's all —'as to be, else they'd've court-martialled 'im, wouldn't they? Still, there's somethin' to what Bunty says—or what the lads are sayin'—about 'im bein' a peacetime skipper. . . . Gentleman yachtsman type, RN College bull an' all that.

But now—now *Felicity*'s been stowed away ashore, now that there's a war and killin' goin' on and we're right up against it—what sort of Skipper is 'e now?

We can't tell—nobody can tell, 'til we stop fallin' out and turnin' back . . . 'til the day when we're right up there when the bricks start showerin' down and we stay and get stuck in. I mean, that's what we're 'ere for, innit? That's what this ship was designed an' built for and everythin' we've been doin' up to now's just preparation, a big rehearsal. This next outin' could be it—the real thing, this time, I got the feelin' some'ow. *This time we're goin' to find out. . . .*

Wreyford came up the rolling, pitching ladder, steadied himself and solemnly saluted. Fielden, the First Lieutenant, moved to him, spoke a few words Ossie couldn't catch and then they started for'ard together—two tall, bulky figures in duffels and hoods, like priests in habits. Ossie came to attention as they passed him and Wreyford looked over and called, "Knowles—tell Lieutenant Campbell I'd like to see him on the Bridge. In fifteen minutes, please."

"Ay ay, sir."

Campbell, shirt-sleeved and red-eyed, checked his communications and the range-finders for the tenth time. The links were still faint and fuzzy but they would have to do—until the whole system could be replaced. Every piece of equipment in the Transmitting Station—TS—was in urgent need of overhaul, but Campbell had neither the time nor the facilities to do more than patch up.

It was fiddling, frustrating work. He felt like a builder called in to repair a doll's house, or a plumber mending watches. The whole issue could have been fitted into the gunnery spares room in his last ship, a cruiser—he mourned for the gleaming, solid, spacious dignity of his Director Control Tower there, where he'd sat in his big steel and leather chair in the upper tier, with three Petty Officers beside him and a whole squad of trained ratings on the tier below; each man with his own piece of machinery and his own specific responsibility, and all Campbell had to do was take their readings and speak his orders into the telephone which linked him with the quite separate TS and the big gun turrets. All the calculations were made by machines in the TS, in another part of the ship—averaging out and collating all the readings passed to them and automatically aiming the cruiser's guns. . . .

But here, in this cramped killer craft, designed to chase U-boats and destroy them with depth charges, and to attack surface vessels with torpedoes, the guns were of secondary importance—everything was sacrificed to speed, power, and storage space for the 'fish' and 'dustbins'. Living and working room for the men who sailed and fought the ship was kept to the absolute minimum, and there was no Control Tower, the whole system was jammed into this miniature TS amidships. And on *Glowworm* at the moment the Gunnery Officer was also responsible for the torpedoes, carried on racks on the deck and aimed and fired from sighting positions on either side of the Bridge—an entirely separate operation.

Apart from a secondary armament of machine-guns and hopelessly outmoded Lewis guns, all of which fired independently, *Glowworm* had just four 4·7-inch guns controlled by the TS—'A' and 'B' for'ard, 'X' and 'Y' aft. There were no turrets—the gunners were protected only by shields, and the whip and whine of a stiffish wind was enough to make communication with the gun-crews difficult. In the din of battle Campbell feared it would be impossible.

He turned to the two technicians re-assembling the inclinometer, having replaced faulty and worn components with the new parts brought out by the shore party. Their faces were blurred and stubbled, their eyes soured with fatigue, and the job was still only half done.

Petty Officer Knowles appeared, dripping and breathless
—"Lieutenant Campbell, sir."

"Yes, Petty Officer?"

"Captain's back, sir. 'E'd like to see you up top, fifteen
minutes."

Campbell sighed, reached for the sheets of paper on which
he'd scrawled his report. Three copies. He prayed he'd put
the carbons in the right way—he was too tired to check. . . .

"Righto, thank you, Knowles."

"Sir!"

Ossie left and Campbell growled at the toiling technicians.
"This going to take all night?"

Leading Seaman Kernohan stopped work and emptied
his hands before looking up. There was an edge to his voice.
"Another half-hour, sir—we don't hit more snags, that is."

"Make it twenty minutes. I'll want to test run 'B' and 'Y'
again, soon as I get back." He plucked his heavy jacket from
the chair and moved out, rolling down his shirt sleevs. As
soon as his back was turned the technicians exchanged resentful glances.

"Tell you somethin' for nothin', Knob," Kernohan offered.
"I don't like that bastard."

"Naw. Not one o' us."

"Not a small-shipman."

"Never!"

"Stuck up bastard. . . ."

In the Captain's cabin the sounds of wind and sea were
subdued to a faint moan and comfortable creaks. Wreyford
sat down at his large desk and began to unfasten his briefcase. Arranged in precise tiers on one side of the desk were
metal trays, each with a label: 'Immediate', 'Most Immediate', 'Maintenance', 'Admiralty', 'Personal', 'Defaulters',
'Signals (Code)', and 'Signals (Plain Language)'. On the
other side stood a large, leather-framed photograph of his

wife, Susan, a slender, dark girl with a fine brow and large smiling eyes, holding a very small, white-swathed baby.

Fielden hung up the two damp duffels, crossed to the old armchair over by the big bookcase—weighty volumes of naval history, regulations, seamanship—sank into it, stretched his long legs, and wiggled his toes. He had a secret elegance in his manner, a way of moving unhurriedly yet definitely and cleanly, without fuss or flourish. There was a sense of quality and crispness about his clothes, and yet an air of casualness.

"So—Norway and Denmark, eh?" His voice was as relaxed and genteel as his thoroughbred body. "Rolling up the top corner of the European carpet." Wreyford nodded glumly without looking up.

"Holland next, then France, Belgium . . ." He extracted some papers from his case and began to sort them out into the trays. Fielden glanced at his watch.

"We sail at 0130. . . . That means some of the men will go without sleep."

Wreyford nodded again, without a flicker of sympathy. "Oh, most of them ought to manage about three hours." He fished a chart from the case, began to spread it on the desk. Without thinking, Fielden took out his cigarette case. Wreyford heard the click of the opening catch and his eyes came up.

"Sorry," said Fielden, "forgot!" He closed the case— Wreyford hated cigarette smoke, especially in his cabin. But suddenly the Captain softened, smiled.

"It's all right, David. Go ahead."

"No, no—I really don't want one just now. Sheer habit."

"That's my objection to it. It's a habit."

"Certainly. But I find it good for my nerve-ends."

"Nerves—you, David?" Wreyford chuckled very softly. "Smoke if you want to."

"No, I'll be strong." He slipped the handsome gold case

back into his pocket. Then after a moment—"We all have habits, you know. We're creatures of habit." Wreyford gave him a blank look. Fielden waved languidly at the desk. "All this—the way you fuss with those tin trays. What do you call that?" There was a gentle twinkle in his pale blue eyes: no-one else on the ship could talk this way to the Captain.

"I call it—method. Organization." Wreyford was a little hurt. "I honestly believe it's far less effort to be tidy."

A knock on the oaken door. Wreyford folded the chart in two, hiding the markings and data, and called: "Yes?" Valentino, the Maltese steward, entered and seeing Fielden hesitated a moment before he faced the Captain.

"Sir, the new Midshipman is waiting to report."

"Ah—Rosinsky, yes. . . ." The Captain turned to Fielden. "You met him yet?"

"To my cost." A wry grin. "I made a hefty contribution to his wardrobe collection." The Captain didn't smile. He opened a drawer in his desk and lifted out a slim file.

"Got his report here." He flicked through it. "Not the usual type, but he did well at Dartmouth. Very well, in fact." He closed the folder. "I'll see him now, Valentino."

"Very good, sir." The steward hesitated, shot another quick, unhappy glance at Fielden, then—"Captain, sir . . . could I speak with you, please?"

Wreyford's craggy face hardened very slightly. "What's the trouble this time?"

Valentino fumbled a letter from his pocket. "It is my sister, Captain sir—my *only* sister. She has never been strong. Now she is very ill—dying."

Wreyford took the letter, read part of it, lips compressed. "Last time, if I remember correctly, it was your wife, Valentino. But when the Welfare people went to your home she'd made a quite remarkable recovery."

The steward's dark sherry eyes couldn't hold the flinty stare that Wreyford now raised. Fielden turned away to hide a sad ghost of a grin. Suddenly Valentino broke into a loud, sobbing torrent.

"Sir, please—I am not a sailor. I am a Maltese civilian, employed by the Royal Navy as a steward. So I have the right to give in my notice!"

Wreyford nodded gravely and answered with cold precision. "You have that right, certainly. But for various reasons I can't put you ashore now. And even if I could, you'd have a very hard time getting back to Malta."

"Sir, it is not fair! I have four years working in the Officers' Mess at Valetta, and I am very happy there. Then your ship comes to our harbour for a visit, and because I wish to earn a little extra money I come to you, because your own steward is sick in the hospital—the position is temporary, and the ship is staying in the Grand Harbour. But one morning I wake up and the ship is at sea, there is a war! I am carried off, a prisoner here—for seven months now. It is not fair!"

Wreyford looked at the letter in his hands. Valentino sniffed wetly. Fielden lowered his head and wiggled his toes again.

"Yes ... You're quite right, Mr Valentino. It *isn't* fair. But there's absolutely nothing I can do about it at the moment. Please show in Mr Rosinsky."

Valentino wavered only an instant, then slouched to the door. Wreyford sighed, carefully placed the letter in the 'Personal' tray.

"Poor devil," said Fielden.

"He gets his relatives to write those things, you know that?" Fielden nodded. "He doesn't seem to realize—I censor the outgoing mail. . . ."

The door swung wide open and the Midshipman gusted in, whipping off a borrowed cap and tucking it under his left elbow—"Midshipman Rosinsky, sir! Good evening."

Wreyford wheeled to behold a truly startling figure. The

46

diminutive Jackie was wearing a duffel many sizes too big for him. It reached halfway down his shins and he'd turned up the sleeves, making thick, cumbersome cuffs. Fielden swallowed a gurgle of laughter. Wreyford approached the boy in slow wonderment, then extended his hand.

"Good evening. How do you do?"

Rosinsky blinked in pleased surprise, grinned winningly, and clasped the proffered hand.

" 'Owjido, sir! Pleasure. . . ."

A soft rustle. Something was sprouting sinisterly from inside the borrowed cap beneath the boy's arm: a spiral of rolled up newspaper—like an uncoiling bedspring. Wreyford regarded it for a moment in silent fascination.

"What's that?"

The boy looked down, made a frantic grab.

"Oh law! It's a bit on the large side, y'see, sir," he panted, thoroughly flustered. "I 'ad to pad it out. . . ." Unable to stuff the paper back in place he crumpled it hurriedly into a ball and rammed it into a pocket. "Sorry, sir."

Wreyford cleared his throat, walked round his desk and fingered the folder containing Rosinsky's personal report.

"I didn't expect you until the tenth. You're early. Three days early?"—cadenced as a question.

"Yes, sir, 'ope you don't mind. I got—well, a bit impatient."

"I see. It's very—irregular. But perhaps it's just as well. We'll be putting out in a few hours—you know that?"

The thin, pink face lit up. "I—did 'ear we might be, yes sir. Lucky I came today, isn't it, sir?"

Fielden's chest was weighted and drawn by some nameless grief. That such children should come here, into this ugliness and drudgery and ever-present dangers was a wholly uncivilized thing. Unreasonably he felt a personal guilt, as if it was partly his failure that had brought this boy here, so unready and unaware and pitifully willing.

47

"They've given you a very favourable report," said Wreyford.

"Thank you, sir."

"Don't thank me, I didn't write it. . . . I don't think we'll put you on regular watches right away. You'll need a little time to find your way about the ship. Besides—officially you're still on leave."

"If it's all the same to you, sir, I'd like to get to work just as soon as possible. Fact is y'see, I feel I know the ship quite well already."

"Oh you do, do you?"

"Yes, sir." He inhaled, straightened, and then fairly rattled off specifications—"Length overall, 323 feet—breadth at maximum, 33 feet—'ull depth, 19 feet and 3 inches—tonnage, 1345 displacement—top speed, 35 knots—armament, four 4·7 guns, eight 21-inch torpedo tubes . . ." He paused, suddenly mournful. "The secondary armament—afraid I'm not too sure about that, sir."

"Seven machine-guns," Fielden heard himself say. Rosinsky thanked him with a quick, nodding smile.

"You've done your prep I see," said Wreyford.

"Chap ought to know something about the ship he's going to serve on, sir. Don't you think?"

"Er—yes, of course. Very good." He thought for a moment and a sardonic fibre entered his voice. "Then you must know something of *Glowworm*'s history?"

"Bit sir, yes," Jackie answered instantly. "She's been on active service ever since the Spanish Civil War."

"Quite so. Active service—but we haven't seen a lot of action, you know. We've had one or two . . . umm, unfortunate accidents. Missed out."

Rosinsky nodded cheerily. "So I 'eard, sir. Rotten luck—all those collisions and that. . . . But you can't be unlucky all the time, can you? Our chance will come, sir—bound to!"

Wreyford peered at him for a long moment but there was no doubting his utter sincerity. "Yes . . . well, report to the Bridge in the morning. I dare say we can find something useful for you to do. Better get a good night's rest."

"Ay ay, sir. Thanks."

"Carry on, then."

Rosinsky wheeled, marched to the door and put his cap back on. Without the paper wadding it came well down over his jutting ears, and he had to hold it with one hand to see his way. When the door had closed behind him Wreyford chuckled tiredly. "Young—my God, he's young."

The First Lieutenant smiled with one cheek. " 'Look how the youths are coming, lightly up they spring!' " Wreyford raised an eyebrow and Fielden shrugged apologetically —"Catullus."

"Thank you. So long as we know. . . ." It was a standing joke between them, Wreyford's way of trying to discourage Fielden's quotations. If anything, it encouraged them. "I can't believe I was ever that young."

"I never was," said Fielden. "I was born old and cynical."

The Captain checked his watch, folded the chart. "Let's get up to the Bridge."

Harry Trenton and Jim Campbell were waiting with their reports. Both looked extremely tired but they were very correctly dressed. They saluted. Wreyford acknowledged and his eyes flicked over each man from toe to cap. He walked up to Campbell.

"Lieutenant, please don't think I'm being hypercritical. But there's a right way and a wrong way to salute, you know." Campbell stared, unbelievingly. "Discipline is founded on many small things. If we ignore these, we weaken the whole fabric—you do see that? Now then, let's see if we can get it right. Once more, if you would?"

Campbell stood very still and his face crimsoned. Then

49

he raised his arm again. Wreyford stopped him as the hand touched the peak of the cap—"Ah, I thought so! You're curving the hand, you see?" He reached out and took hold of the wrist. "Wrist and fingers straight—and keep the thumb flat against the first finger. There—that's much better, isn't it?"

"Yes, sir."

Fielden watched this performance, amused and yet uncomfortable. Trenton's handsome face mirrored his thoughts all too frankly. At a nod from the Captain, Campbell lowered his arm and took a long steadying breath.

"Maintenance reports?"

Each of them took an envelope from his pocket and Trenton betrayed his impatience in the clumsiness of his movement. Wreyford regarded him sternly.

"Thank you." Harry held the Captain's gaze. "Even at times like this we have to keep proper records."

"Yes, sir, of course." The very faintest curl in Trenton's voice. Wreyford regarded him for moments more then began to open the envelopes, using a pencil, in small saving movements.

"A ship," he said, "is a self-contained community. And like any other community it has to be administered, Lieutenant Trenton—boring though that may seem to you. You can't run it with an oil-can and a spanner." Harry said nothing, but Fielden saw his nostrils twitch.

In silence the Captain extracted the two reports and read the top copies carefully, licking his fingertips before he turned the pages. Then methodically he detached the other copies and handed them to the First Officer—to be filed away later in his battery of trays. Trenton brought out a tin of cigarettes but Fielden caught his eye, made a tiny shake of his head. Harry glowered, put the tin back in his pocket.

"We sail at 0130, gentlemen."

Campbell jolted forward and exchanged a dazed look with Trenton. "In that case, sir . . . it's my duty to tell you, I just can't guarantee anything like reliable gunnery control! The TS—"

"Why not?" Wreyford asked temperately, tapping the Gunnery Officer's report. "You got all the spares you asked for, didn't you?"

"Spares—well yes, sir. But all I can do with these is patch up. That whole TS is a tired-out hunk of machinery. I need time—two, three days."

"Lieutenant Campbell . . . we haven't got the resources of a cruiser or a dreadnought, you know."

The crimson flooded back into Campbell's cheeks. "I realize that, Captain. But there's a limit to how much you can improvise. All of the equipment needs overhaul—"

"You are not being asked to strip it down and polish the pieces. Merely to have it operating efficiently, within six hours. Six hours, Lieutenant."

The Gunnery Officer spread his slender hands helplessly. "I'll—do my best, sir."

"Good. . . . Now then, Lieutenant Trenton, what about that pump?"

"It'll be serviceable, sir. I can't say more than that."

"Come now"—flicking an emphasizing look at Campbell—"*you're* a small-shipman. You're used to working fast."

Trenton walked closer to the Captain. "The pump will be serviceable in time, sir. But I'm not making any promises about how long it'll hold up."

Wreyford's voice dropped and he waved the papers at him—"You come to me with a list of spares, I make out all the necessary requisitions and rush them through for you. And—according to your own report—every item was delivered. Correct?"

"Correct!"

"Then why are you telling me now that you can't promise efficient running?"

"Because you can't make outworn machinery efficient by filling out forms." Recklessly Harry flung out a hand in a contemptuous sweep. "Or by filing maintenance reports —in triplicate!"

"That's enough!" Wreyford didn't raise his voice, but his hand slapped the wad of papers down against his thigh.

"Sir, I must express—"

"I said that's enough!" The Captain turned away and began to pace slowly. "Do you think I don't know the state of my ship? We need a full overhaul—of course we do. But at this moment we simply can't be spared, and that's all there is to it." He stopped and faced them. "We sail at 0130—and I expect the ship to be fit to face any eventuality. Is that understood?" Trenton gave a surly nod and Campbell murmured grudging acknowledgment.

Wreyford led them into the Chart Room, just off the Bridge. All three came to stand close around him as he unfolded the map on the table under the shaded light.

"*Renown* will steam a course of 055 degrees from base." His finger traced the clean black lines stretching Nor'-Eastward. "The Flotilla will be dispersed to screen her, ranging on parallel courses, here—and here—four miles to port and starboard. . . ."

Glowworm's messdecks were overcrowded to the point at which the seamen barely had space to stow their gear, several ratings were sleeping—illicitly—in the laundry, and serious delays were occurring in watch changes and calls to battle stations and drill; so Fielden had decided that, with the ammo still being loaded and chains of men moving through the main passages, it would be simpler to put the new Midshipman in with Harry Trenton. The Engineer

Officer had cursed lividly, then agreed, and a camp bed was installed.

Jackie loved the cabin from the moment he squeezed through the door. It was tiny, criss-crossed with pipes on roof and bulkhead, but he didn't mind—this cramped and cluttered box, with the thin, worn blankets and the stench of ancient sweat and grease and damp clothing, now was his home, and it was everything he'd always imagined.

He unpacked his toothbrush, sat on his bed and wrote a cheerful letter to Mamma, telling her the little story of disasters and thrills. How he'd lost his cap on the train as he leaned out of the window trying to catch his first glimpse of his ship. How nice the Captain had been; how he'd had to borrow gear from the officers, and how he was fine and she wasn't to worry.

He signed it 'Your loving son, Jacob'—then added, in brackets, 'Midshipman, RN.' That would make her smile. He put it in an envelope, addressed it. Outside the wind was moaning low, like the crooning of a mindless old crone. The ship rolled at her moorings and now and then quivered like a nervous, tethered horse. He was filled with a deep joy. They really were putting out to sea, this very night— sallying forth to brave the U-boats and the Luftwaffe and he, Jackie Rosinsky, 'Midshipman, RN', would be there. . . .

The door of the little cabin smacked open and Trenton shouldered in. He looked strained and disgruntled and had only a curt nod in answer to Jackie's bright grin. Almost violently he began to strip off his tunic and shirt and change back into working rig. Rage preoccupied him. *Bloody Wrey-ford and his fancy filing systems! All I did was state the facts, straight and reasonably, dammit! The man doesn't listen. And oh dear Christ, that awful bullshit about salut-ing—poor old Jim Campbell, the look on his face . . .!*

He glared round the cabin. "Where the hell are my other shoes?"—this really was too much, having to do a ruddy

53

quick-change every time the Old Man wanted to see you. . . .

He bent down, Jackie lifted his feet and he spotted the old pair of shoes—battered, crumpled, and stained—under the camp bed. He sat down on his bunk, facing the boy, and began putting them on, still scowling.

"Anything wrong?" the Midshipman asked shyly, lamely.

"No more than bloody usual!" Harry hadn't meant to snap at the kid. Relenting—"It's the Old Man. Won't let you get a word in. Won't listen."

"The Captain?"

"The civil service mind! Everything according to the bloody rule-book."

A short silence, then Jackie said, "By the way, what do we do about letters?"

Trenton glanced at the envelope in the boy's hand, reached across his own bunk and picked up two letters of his own. In turning, his eyes fastened, sad and lecherous, on the galaxy of semi-nudes pinned to the bulkhead—is there any point in writing to them any more? Haven't had so much as a postcard in months—expect they're all fixed up with Poles or Free bloody French. . . .

"Those creatures," he said solemnly to the world in general, "are called girls. Yes. I distinctly remember. They have a certain intriguing function. Holy Christ, why did I ever join the Navy? Cooped up here month after month with a lot of hairy great mat'lots—my sex life's a wistful memory."

He pulled his gaze from the pin-ups and stretched out a hand for Jackie's letter—"Give it here. Boat comes out just before we sail. I'll drop it in for censoring now, along with these." The boy gave him the letter and he glanced at the address.

"E.1, that's Whitechapel"—the kid was smiling but his voice had a defiant edge and the accent suddenly was distinctly sharper. "Reckon I'm the first Snotty in the 'ole 'istory of the Royal Navy to get 'imself through Dartmouth on a scholarship from the Jewish Free School."

"Well good on you, that's something to be proud of," Harry said at once, with complete sincerity."

"Me Mum runs a second-'and shop."

"I'll bet *she's* proud. Even if you're not."

The boy relaxed, smiled widely and scratched his head— "I can 'ardly believe it, even now, I should be so lucky . . . I expect you can understand, sir—I just can't *wait* to get to sea!" And as though in response, the wind's moan came louder, the ship shuddered.

"Do you get sea-sick?" the Lieutenant asked quietly.

The kid's smile was replaced by a blank, lost look. He put out a hand against the bulkhead. "Ai—who knows? I mean —I never been further than the mouth of the Dart!"

Trenton chuckled. "Well, this is the weather to find out." He rose and lurched out of the cabin. Jackie sat there, a cold flood of alarm welling, gurgling in his stomach.

Glowworm was alive with movement. Her companion-ways and corridors echoed to the clattering feet of hurrying ratings. Every man knew his job and realized the present need for urgency. Nearly all of them were professional sailors—regulars who'd enlisted long before the outbreak of war. They knew their ship and they knew the sea.

The tinny speakers crackled out—"Port and starboard watches, close up! Close up!"

On the darkened main deck the rain was sweeping down from the North in great lunging lashes. Ossie Knowles, hardly recognizable in his voluminous oilskins, was supervising his crew as they whipped the covers off 'Y'-gun. He patted the cold metal barrel—right then, me old beaut, if we meet up with Uncle Adolf's Navy this time, you'n I'll put a few 'ot uns up their 'oles. . . .

'B'-gun: the wind strengthened and now the rain came

55

in huge horizontal gusts. Bunty Baker wiped his eyes and bellowed an order at Tinker Bell. Tink's thoughts smouldered—no bleedin' point in checkin' out the gun, with a faggin' skipper like ours we'll never get the chance to use it. . . .

Down in the steaming heat of the Engine Room Harry Trenton supervised his team, slaving to reassemble the faulty pump. They moved in a perpetual bath of sweat and grime, and the Lieutenant wondered if their skins would ever be really clean and dry again. He glanced over at big Hobson: stripped to the waist, wrestling with a huge monkey-wrench. His body glistened, the great muscles bulged. Hobson paused to wipe the back of a hand across his streaming forehead, and spat, almost contentedly. Harry gave him an encouraging grin. The ERA shook his head slightly—"Old whore!" he murmured.

In the TS Jim Campbell was watching his men finish the reassembly job. Their fingers were deft, their movements assured. Campbell was calmer now. Half-an-hour ago he'd been ready to find fault with everything, eyeing the technicians' every move like a bedridden old woman watching her long-suffering nurse-companion tidy the room.

The business of Wreyford's saluting lecture on the Bridge had humiliated and enraged Campbell more than either the Captain or Trenton could have imagined. To have laboured mightily all day on a hunk of sick hardware, so cumbersome and complex it looked like an unsuccessful early experiment by Marconi, then to be given a bloody talking to, in public, on military courtesy—discipline?—Hell, the Old Man would get better discipline, and maybe even some respect, if he stopped ramming bloody harbours and barges and got on with the war. . . .

Kernohan straightened and nodded. Campbell killed his crouching, mutinous thoughts and lifted a hand mike—"TS to 'Y'-gun. How do you read? Over."

" 'Y'-gun to TS. Loud and clear, sir!" The voice sounded thin and distant. Rotten quality this end, but at least they're receiving it strong. . . .

"Right, Knowles, I want to check the ranging once more —first on your own, then with 'B'-gun. Stand by." His finger juggled with the dials. He was tired, dog tired, and desperately worried—this equipment just wouldn't do, if we get in a scrap . . . well, it could fold up inside five minutes. . . .

Wreyford's cabin was in semi-darkness. Only the shaded metal lamp glowed. He was bent over the desk, writing in a slow, neat hand. After a moment he laid down his pen and picked up the leather-framed photograph of his wife and baby son, and for some reason he loved them more deeply in this moment than he could remember ever before. Always he found writing a letter to Susan a poignant experience, but tonight he was surprised, uneasy, at his depth of feeling. He considered himself neither a foolish nor sentimental man, yet tonight emotion was a sapping pain.

He told himself to be 'sensible', put down the photograph and went back to his letter. A knock on the door: he looked up in slight annoyance as David Fielden entered, followed by a Signalman.

"Latest Met cast, sir."

Unhurriedly the Captain turned his letter over, face down, took the signal and scanned it. "Still building up, David. We may run out of the muck for a while, steaming East."

"But when we turn North we'll head straight back into the thick of it"—Fielden nodded gravely. Wreyford ran a hand through his hair, placed the Met report in the appropriate tray and dismissed the Signalman with a nod.

Fielden saw the sadness and tiredness in the Old Man's face and felt a sudden warmth for him—poor devil, he must be hellish lonely, no-one he can really talk to, not even me.

He knows, precisely, the condition of the ship and the men but he has to take them out just the same, in a half-gale and freezing rain. A ship's captain has only God for company and confidences. . . .

"Can I help with any of this?" he asked.

Wreyford's eyes, which had become momentarily distant and abstracted, cleared swiftly. "Hmm? Oh—no thank you, David. Just writing a letter home."

"When you've finished, why don't you turn in for a bit?"

"Not until I know we're ready—all repairs completed."

Fielden was about to say something more when from deep within the ship, from her innermost entrails, came a low, powerful, steady rumbling—like the deep growls of hungry lions in their stone pens far beneath a Roman arena.

They remained perfectly still, listening, as the sound gradually grew, developing a healthy beat, kicking over at very low revs. Then they felt her moving beneath them, swinging slowly around the mooring buoy. The heart of *Glowworm* was coming alive again, pumping steamy life through her complex system of pipes and turbines.

Fielden grinned. "Well, you know now! Good old Hell-bound Harry!"

The ghost of a smile lifted the lines of Wreyford's wearied face. He swivelled in his chair and reached for the bulkhead phone.

Hobson was standing on the control platform beside the telegraph and dials, amid the heat and the din of the Engine Room, legs wide-straddled, telephone in one slippery hand, the big monkey-wrench in the other. He was coated in a paste of sweat and grime and grease. Strangely, this was a state he vastly enjoyed—the feel of oil on his skin, the way exhaustion took hold of his muscles and bones, steeping them in aching lethargy, and the way his forehead seemed to expand, at times almost to burst. At this moment he was glowing inside and outside—glowing with a pride in his physique, and in his knowledge, which together had conquered the outworn, recalcitrant engines of *Glowworm* and reduced them to this docile, throbbing, even beast that was filling the hot steel room with its hissing breath.

Trenton strode to him in answer to his shout, wiping his hands. Harry's short dark hair was a mass of ringlets, his overalls were drenched and clinging. A horrible sweat-rag encircled his throat and his broad hard chest was bared, pink-polished with the heat. He grinned at Hobson as he took the phone from his hand.

Wreyford's voice came through faintly and he strained to hear the words above the engines. The Lieutenant had no rancour left: he was too tired to give a damn. Besides, in his heart he knew that however much of a bullshitting bastard the Old Man was at times, he was undeniably a fine seaman, and he wouldn't be piling on the pressure now unless he was being pressured himself by Whitey Whitehorn.

"Trenton. . . . Yessir, any time you say." His voice was muffled with exhaustion. He scanned the rows of dancing dials, eyes pricking.

The Captain's voice came from a million miles away—"Would you like us to cast off from the buoy? Take her up to cruising revs?"

"No thank you, sir." Glacing round at the ERA, drawing a finger across his throat. "I'm cutting now, just wanted to kick her over."

"As you wish." A pause, then, "Well done, Harry."

The noise of the engines died quickly, puttering into a long-drawn sigh. Trenton's handsome face split into a small, wry smile. "Pleasure, sir," he said, without a hint of sarcasm.

He replaced the phone and leant back against the bulkhead, eyeing the Petty Girl pinned over the control panel. The doll-pretty face spoke of sweet far-off things—laughter, cocktails, and picnics, and a turn round the floor. And the splendid, impossibly curvaceous, ludicrously long-stemmed body—clad in underclothes that could have been hitched on to those bursting breasts and bulging thighs only by the vaulting imagination of an admirably erotic artist—evoked clasping memories of even more unattainable joys.

Harry Trenton winked wickedly at the Petty Girl and gave a cheerful thumbs-up to Hobson. He felt good. Pure. Fulfilled. Proud of himself, proud of his men—and of this old bitch *Glowworm*.

Wreyford was pacing his cabin, suddenly restless. Fielden was on the phone, speaking to TS. Just inside the door a young Signalman was waiting, pad and pencil ready.

"—fair enough, Jim," Fielden was saying. "Yes, I'll tell the Captain." He replaced the phone. "Campbell says he's done all he can for now."

The Captain grunted, turned to the Signalman—"Bunts, make to *Renown* by aldis: 'Repairs completed. Standing by.' That's all." The Signalman snapped the pad shut, wheeled, and disappeared almost magically. Moments later both officers froze as a low forlorn wail filled the air, rising steadily to a shrill crescendo.

Air raid warning.

Wreyford snatched up his steel helmet and they started for the Bridge.

In the messdecks the seamen grabbed their gear and scurried to their battle positions, cursing and jostling. *Glowworm* echoed to a deep drumming of running feet, and the sirens' discordant wails drowned out the wind.

On the Bridge Wreyford and Fielden, wearing helmets and lifejackets, anxiously scanned the darkness. The Captain pressed his night glasses into his eye-sockets and shivered from the coldness of their rims. He could see nothing, but through the siren howl now they heard the distant drone of an enemy plane. Then over on Hoy one of the big shore batteries opened up. *Thumpa—thumpa—thumpa*—an eerie, jolting sound. All round other guns took up the percussion, shattering the night with their deep-throated barks until every ship was in action.

In TS Campbell was bawling into the microphone, but in the din his words were inaudible. He seemed to be mouthing terrible obscenities to a private devil.

Valentino was cowering in a corner of his galley, whimpering garbled prayers, clammy hands clutching his head. "It is not fair, not fair," over and over again. . . .

Now the whole of Scapa Flow was lit up by a mighty firework display. Curved lances of tracer scored the sky. 'Y'-gun was at maximum elevation, working smoothly. Ossie's eyes were calm and watchful as his crew laboured rhythmically—a well-trained team, expertly hurling a canopy of shells into the sky. He felt proud, confident.

A hundred yards off to port a German flare fizzed blindingly, setting the night ablaze with fierce white light. In the glare he saw a small, hatless figure standing at the rail, gazing up with open mouth, shuddering slightly to the battering of the guns: the Midshipman, Rosinsky. Ossie glided swiftly to his side, pulled him roughly back into cover. He found a spare steel helmet, rammed it on the boy's head and bellowed in his ear—"Gettin' y'self killed is a court martial offence!"

Then, a fast-building roar, and into the searing flare-light a long shape came hurtling, not sixty feet above the black water, straight towards *Glowworm*. Long-range Junkers 88. Ossie screeched at his crew but already they were starting to swing the gun on to the incoming bomber.

On the Bridge Fielden watched the plane looming out of the night and shouted a half-coherent warning. Wreyford

61

wheeled, and then stood, perfectly still, staring blankly at the bomber racing in on his ship. He made no effort to take shelter—not even when the Junkers opened up with its forward-firing cannon, raising fountains of white water all around the bows, then ripping across the foredeck.

Thunder beating at their heads, the hollow clanging and ringing of metal and huge blue flashes. The ship heaving, shuddering beneath them, the air full of fumes and fragments and raw screams.

The shellfire hammered 'A'-gun. One round exploded, with terrible white heat, inside the shield. Two men were killed outright, three others were hurled across the deck and smashed like dolls against plating and machinery. Yet another lay on his back with his legs kicking feebly, his torso a nest of smouldering fire and his face shredded—one huge wound. The raider howled over the masthead and within instants was swallowed up in the sodden darkness.

Still the Captain remained rigid, staring down at the mangled wreck of 'A'-gun—grotesquely silhouetted now in a pool of greedily licking flames. Through the continuing roar of the Fleet's guns he could hear voices yelling for stretchers and water-lines, the harsh cries of the maimed— the whole hideous cacophony of torn limbs and blinded eyes and blazing, beating agony.

Then, as Fielden moved to him, the Captain's whole body began to shake, his teeth chattered in spasms. He clutched at the handrail, struggling to get a grip on himself—but it was uncontrollable. Fielden stood watching in fright and horror, and somehow he could read Wreyford's thoughts, as clearly as if they were being screeched in his ear—of all the targets in this crowded waterway, the enemy singles out this ship, my ship, for his random attack. That's *Glowworm*'s for'ard gun ablaze down there ... and *Glowworm*'s men broken and bloody on the deck—*my* deck, *my* men ... just like that, out of a vast dark sky, thirty seconds of blood and fire. Why? Dear God, *why us*? One more disaster, another blood-red spot on the record—another scar on the ship, and another slur on me. . . .

Fielden pulled himself away, snatched up a phone and called for stretcher parties and the Damage Control squad. When he turned back the Captain hadn't stirred, he was still staring, whey-faced, down at the foredeck shambles, and the tremblings of his body, the tautened muscles of his throat and jaws told of the fight he was having to subdue a strange terror and acute physical revulsion. . . .

Fielden was shocked. He'd never seen his stern, methodical skipper like this, never known him anything but complete master of himself. Yet at the same time, paradoxically, he was reassured—somewhere there was, after all, a human flaw in the Old Man. . . .

He moved closer, spoke in a level firm tone. "Stretchers and Damage Control on the way, sir."

Wreyford didn't stir for a moment, then he took a juddering breath, turned his head and blinked. His voice was hoarse, halting—"Go down there . . . make a quick assessment."

Fielden went down the ladder. Wreyford's eyes swung back to the foredeck. He could still hear the moaning and whimpering of the wounded, and he wanted to weep with them. He straightened and tensed all his muscles, holding his lungs full, pressing his heels down hard. The trembling stopped. He relaxed, turned away, closing his mind to the agony and the obscenity, sealing off by force of will the tender and vulnerable part of him that so suddenly had been exposed, for the first time, to the naked truth of war.

The stretcher-bearers moved carefully through the wreckage with their burdens, supervised by the Doc, a giant Irishman with a flattened nose and a face full of rugger scars. As he looked upon the smashed bodies he muttered low, fierce curses.

Over on Hoy the all-clear sounded. The firing petered out and *Glowworm*'s speakers crackled—"Gun crews stand down! Carry on normal watches!"

Fielden and Rosinsky watched silently as the stretchers were carried down to Sick Bay. Doc paused at the hatchway to speak to the First Lieutenant. His huge shoulders were hunched and fury fevered his small eyes. "Four dead, five wounded—one seriously." Fielden nodded and started back to the Bridge.

The Midshipman watched the stretchers go past. His face was pale yet surprisingly calm. A medic lifted a blanket and he saw a jagged piece of femur protruding from a crimson mash. The injured gunner mewled like an infant. Jackie felt—nothing. He knew he was looking upon the pitiless reality of modern war, seeing it stripped of its spurious, concocted glamour. The paths of glory were strewn with broken, burned, and blinded men like these.

The boy tried to absorb this new knowledge, tried to find a place and a meaning for it within himself. "Four dead"— he told himself that those two simple syllables meant that four living, breathing, reasoning creatures—four personalities, four British citizens, subjects of His Majesty, Arsenal supporters, *Daily Mirror* readers, Watney drinkers, Woodbine smokers, trained professional sailors—had been obliterated in an instant. How puny was humanity, how easily destroyed!

Jacob Rosinsky, Midshipman, officially still on graduation leave from Dartmouth, stood motionless on *Glowworm*'s smoky deck grappling with these thoughts, unable as yet to react emotionally, but already a little older.

Fielden faced Wreyford in his cabin. The Captain was ashen, but composed.

"Can the wounded be moved?"

"I don't know, sir." Lamely.

Wreyford glanced at his watch. "Well, if they can, tell Doc I want them put ashore." His voice sank a little. "The bodies as well."

"Very good, sir." The Number One's face was completely expressionless.

"Can't let anything hold us up," Wreyford said.

"No—no time for ceremonies."

"What's Damage Control have to say?"—swiftly changing the subject.

"Superficial. Welding job on the shield and deck plates." Wreyford seemed almost disappointed.

"Signal *Renown*. Give Whitehorn the facts. Tell him we'll be ready."

"Right."

After Fielden had gone the Captain sat for perhaps a minute at his desk, staring stonily straight ahead. Then he reached for the Log and in his neat hand began to make the entry.

From the signal deck the lamp clacked out, sending its high-speed flashes of thin light stabbing through the dark towards the cruiser. The Signalman crouched under his canvas shelter, tucking himself away from the raw wind. Even so, he was soaked to the skin: spray and rain filled the air like steam. The weather was worsening by the minute. It was going to be a long and gruelling night.

The seamen sat around in their messdecks, waiting— silent, depressed, and shaken. *Glowworm* was stirring restlessly at her moorings and her little creaks and rustlings accentuated their gloom. Daddy Longmore appeared with a big tray of steaming cocoa mugs. His thin body curved like a willow branch as he set the tray down on a table.

65

"Ki up!" He tried to make it cheery. No-one responded. Tinker Bell cradled a scalding mug in his big calloused hands and stared down into the brown liquid, truculent as a child.

Glowworm rolled again, heavier than before. Daddy looked up, listening to the wind—and became as melancholy as the others.

"That about settles it, lads. No kip tonight. With that lot on, 'e'll 'ave us all closed up soon as we're clear o' the boom." He ran a bony hand down his long, pinched face.

Nobby Clark, plump and imperturbable, shuffled a deck of cards and began setting up a patience game. The giant Lump lumbered over and sat opposite him, staring at the cards.

"Want t'play hand, Nob lad?"

Clark groaned good-humouredly. "Aw no, mate—not till you learn somethin' besides snap and bleedin' rummy!"

Some of the others chuckled tiredly—Lump's idea of rummy was rudimentary. The mild mirth broke the mood, suddenly the men were stirring, forcing themselves to brighten up. Lump grinned amiably, not understanding, just pleased that all at once everybody seemed more cheerful.

Keelie Grant strode over to the Jockey, squattin in a corner, reading a magazine, minute and intent. "Hey Jock boy, gi'e us a tune!"

The smallest man on the ship looked up and blinked, hesitant. Everyone knew he was thinking of their four dead shipmates.

"Yeh—go on mate!" echoed Grannie Smith, and several others muttered encouragement. The Jockey fished out his mouth organ, spat into it and began to play softly. Some of the men began to hum the melody with him—a sad, old shanty.

But Tinker was staring at Grant, eyes hissing. "Well bugger me, I dunno. . . . Four poor sods just 'ad their chips,

66

an' four or five more smashed up—an' you start a bloody sing-song!"

Grant studied him calmly. "What d'ye want—a bluidy prayer meetin'? Aw, use yer heid, son. Talk aboot somethin' else, or belt up!"

A cunning note crept into Tinker's voice. "Fair enough, then—let's talk 'bout somethin' else, right. . . . It true what that geezer said in the pub today?"

Daddy, Lump, and Nobby sat very still, watching Grant. The Jockey rose from his corner and ambled to the table, still blowing soft phrases, his eyes flicking between Grant and Bell. The Glaswegian's hewn jaw crept out.

"What *did* he say?" he asked mildly.

"What did 'e say? That Wreyford once put a bloke in the brig for fourteen days—for bein' sea-sick!"

Silence. The Jockey stopped playing but Grant threw him a sharp look and he started up again.

"Aye . . . it's true," Grant said after several seconds, in a deliberate voice. "But it wasna as simple as a'that."

Longmore chipped in—"Course it weren't. There were more to it, see?"

"No, Pop, I don't see," said Tinker. "I don't see at all."

Daddy glowered into the kid's hostile face for a moment, then shook his head forlornly—"No . . . an' I don't s'pose you would if I told ya."

Tinker turned inquiringly to Grant, but he too shook his head—"There's nane sae blind . . . Dad's right, Flower. Just be a waste o' breath."

Bell flushed, he spoke through his teeth—"Reckon, do you? Well mebbe you'll tell me this then—why don't 'e let anyone grow a beard, eh? Like on any other ship? I mean, is 'e round the bleedin' bend, or what?" No-one spoke, he saw cold anger all around. He scowled, reached for his cigarettes, and forced a snorting laugh—"Load-a 'airless wonders! Gaw blimey, wot a ship this is! Wot a faggin' ship!"

Another silence, then the Jockey started to play again— low and soft at first. One by one the others began to hum the melody, or whistle it, and gradually the tempo and volume increased. Somebody laughed, and all at once they were singing lustily—

> *Glow, little Glowworm, glimmer, glimmer!*
> *Don't forget we're rotten swimmers.*
> *We got Dads and we got Muvvers*
> *Try to keep up wiv the others.*
> *Oh little Glowworm, please don't shudder,*
> *Please don't lose your screws or rudder.*
> *Can you get us home and dry?*
> *Try little Glowworm, try!*

They hauled young Eddie Nisbett up on the table and he sang a solo in his pub tenor while they clapped their hands in time.

> *Go little Glowworm! Don't you linger!*
> *Oh, little Glowworm—*

Now everyone came in to make one line a great bellow—
> *FINGER, FINGER!*

Nisbett again—

> *From the Lizard up to Scapa,*
> *Barges, tugs, an' dreadnoughts scarper!*
> *They all know that our every mission's*
> *Bound to end up in collision.*
> *We can always get a tow!*
> *Glow, little Glowworm, glow!*

Once again everybody sang, roaring out in derision of their own folly and misfortunes. Lump with one easy sweep lifted the Jockey on to the table. The little man capered and

68

jigged like a jester, blowing his mouth organ and conducting the swaying mass of singers. Their voices drowned out the ship's creaks and groans and the moan of the wind.

2235 hours
Kiel/6 April 1940

THE WIND sweeping in from the icy wastes of the North Sea struck the *Admiral Hipper* as, with her escort of four destroyers, she left the shelter of the great base and slid very slowly through the dank gloom into the Skaggerak. None of the five ships showed lights and all were observing radio silence. Below decks on each, troops of the landing force huddled miserably in their cramped quarters, feeling their bellies heave and quiver as they began to pitch on the full ocean swell.

Thus began the process, the chain of events that, link by link, hour by hour, was to draw two strangers, two oddly civilized men—Wreyford and Mann—closer to personal confrontation and mortal combat, and *Glowworm* to an epic destiny, in a battle like no other in the history of naval warfare.

BOOK TWO/*The Storm*

THE FULL ocean swell bludgeoned the mighty *Renown*, lifting her bows, as she moved slowly out into midstream, flashing signals through the murk to the rest of the force. In the blackness of the raw night the whole great concourse headed out into the North Sea.

Wreyford, a huge duffelled, hooded figure, conned his ship out of the channel. In the little Chart Room adjoining the Bridge, Fielden was bent over the table, but he wasn't concentrating on his calculations. Part of his mind was still engrossed with the problem, the fascinating enigma, of Graham Wreyford....

It had to be faced: during the air raid the Captain had lost control, his body had shivered and quaked and he'd stood transfixed, useless, staring blankly at his ship's wound. Why? Fielden's long hands tinkered mechanically with the compass—*is* the man a coward, as some say quite openly? Has he in the past, as they allege, taken advantage of all our mishaps and breakdowns to avoid combat?

Fielden felt ashamed, disloyal—impossible to judge him, no real, hard evidence. But this outing may well provide the proof....

He straightened and paced out on to the wing. He would wait upon events and try not to think about it any more. For the moment all that mattered was to see that the *Worm* kept up with the others. He looked out of the side screen, shading his eyes to penetrate the darkness. Then he tilted his wrist to catch a little stray light on the tiny, illuminated numbers of his watch.

71

HIS WATCH was a large and intricate piece of equipment, and Admiral Mann liked the feel of its steady heartbeat against his own pulse—he wore it always on the inside of his left wrist. A masterpiece of Swiss craftsmanship: watches were a favourite subject of his. He checked the time once more, then handed the Luftwaffe's signal back to von Scholtz.

"So—they're still in Scapa Flow, eh?" Disappointment tinging his voice. He heaved himself out of the padded conning chair and moved quietly to the wing. Von Scholtz paced with him.

The Admiral was in a stern, thoughtful mood. "They can still come out, mind you. I hope they do. Raeder has kept us locked in port too long. It's getting too much like the last war. We *need* a fight!"

"But first we have to get those troops ashore. That is our primary task, sir. If we can make the landings without interference from the enemy that in itself will be a great victory." Von Scholtz's well-bred tones were reflective, without the conventional enthusiasm. Mann stopped and regarded him gravely.

"You do not make victories by proclaiming them, Max. It is not enough to sneak through the darkness and the mists, running for shelter again—and then crying 'Victory!' simply because we were not challenged."

Von Scholtz shifted his weight uncomfortably. He respected Mann, and so greatly wished to please him, that this mild rebuke struck deep. He told himself he was lucky to be serving under such a commander. Mann was universally esteemed, even the new Party members tempered their arrogance when they came up against him. He was, after all, a gentleman of the old school—and a brilliant seaman.

"There is so much to make up for," the Admiral said, staring intently into the blackness ahead. "Out there lies Jutland. Almost exactly twenty-four years ago, in these waters, the man this ship is named after—Admiral von Hipper—fired the first rounds in the greatest sea battle of this century."

Von Scholtz studied him closely, nodded. "But that *was* a German victory! We engaged vastly superior forces and we inflicted twice as many casualties as we suffered."

"True. And yet . . . after that our High Seas Fleet left the Bight only once again—and then came running home at the first sign of a challenge. Ironic—there can be no denying it, Max: Jutland left the British undisputed masters of the seas. And they still are. That is why we must hope they come out from Scapa now, and give us our chance to change all that."

Von Scholtz said nothing more. He watched the Admiral's face, the hard grey eyes drilling into the distant dark, and sensed the thoughts in his mind. Far beyond the spray-jewelled glass Mann was seeing the British squadron, willing them out of their lair, pulling them over the western horizon.

0600 hours
HMS Glowworm/North Sea/7 April 1940

THE WESTERN HORIZON was still cloaked in darkness and cloud but to the East *Renown* and the other ships of the van were limned starkly, pitching silhouettes against a broad band of raw half-light. The rain had stopped and out ahead the overcast was beginning to break up. The wind had slackened just a little—but still the sea ran high and fast.

Knowles, coming on watch, emerged on deck and paused to inspect the sky, sniff the icy air. More like January weather than April's. Ugly fronts to the North, an odd yellow tinge to the dawn. Sea-years of experience told him that not far off a savage storm was thrashing the ocean. He pulled his foul-weather gear closer around him and headed aft, moving with easy sureness on the rolling, heaving deck, leaning his body against the wailing wall of the wind.

Ahead he saw a small figure lurching and weaving, clutching wildly at stanchions and rail. He recognized Rosinsky, the new Snotty. Rubber pins, a toddler. Probably sick as a pie-maker's bitch an' all. . . . He came up behind the boy, took hold of his shoulders and steered him into the shelter of 'X'-gun. He swivelled him round—and stared in surprise. The kid was laughing. His breath chugged out, forming fat puffs in the chill air. His yellow mop was thrashing, his cheeks glowed pink and his eyes were alight.

They had to keep their faces close together and shout above the dull, commingled roar of sea, wind, and engines— "Where you trying to get to?"

"Nowhere partic'lar—just practising!"

'Well you wanna go careful, start with. Specially down aft 'ere." The Snotty nodded, eager. "Use your 'ands well as your feet, see? Never take more'n a coupla paces without a grip on somethin'. C'mon—I'll show you how."

Ossie set off along the tilting deck, moving unhurriedly, expertly. The boy followed, copying the Petty Officer's every move, grinning like a kid on a fairground cakewalk. Ossie looked over his shoulder, saw the lad reach a davit and grab for it with both hands just as a huge wave broke over the side.

" 'Ang on!"—bawling through the blast of spray. The diminutive figure in the ill-fitting borrowed oilskins vanished completely in the hissing cataract of white water—Gawd Almighty, 'as 'e gone? The wave swirled past. Rosinsky was still there, blowing out water, coughing, but laughing still. He gave Ossie a cocky thumbs-up sign.

The sky grew brighter and there were scattered breaks in the clouds. The wind blew steadily at Force 7 but the sea smoothed out a shade as the squadron steamed on Eastward, the destroyers in handsome echelon, protecting the suave battle cruiser.

In *Glowworm*'s wardroom Doc, Campbell, Rosinsky, and the Wireless Officer, Kelsey, were at breakfast. Young Jackie, cheeks flushed and eyes glittering, was tucking into a huge plate of porridge. The hot, gluey oats warmed him up after the icy drenching on deck. Doc was stolidly munching toast and narrowly watching Campbell. The Gunnery Officer's face was bloodless and moist. He half-raised a forkful of egg, decided he couldn't swallow it, and pushed his plate away. He got up from the table, legs unsteady.

Doc rose, followed him to the door and caught his arm—"I could give you something that might help, you know."

"No need," Campbell said expressionlessly. "I'll be all right."

"Don't be a damn fool, man! Ye know how the Captain is about sea-sickness."

"Yes. I know how the Captain is about sea-sickness. Thanks." And he walked out woodenly, bumping into Anderson, the Second Officer.

Anderson rubbed a bruised shoulder—"What's up with him?" Doc shrugged, said nothing, but his mind was crackling—that bloody man, he won't accept help, a friendly gesture. . . . Feels he doesn't belong here, shuts himself off from the rest of us, plain bloody-minded!

Wreyford came up from his small sea cabin on to the Bridge, feeling the better for a few hours of untroubled sleep. Fielden was in the Chart Room, working out a course. Rosinsky was standing by the port screen. He came smartly to attention and saluted.

"Mornin', sir."

"Good morning. You're up early," the Captain said pleasantly.

The Midshipman grinned. "Matterafact, sir, I haven't been to bed."

Wreyford's eyes narrowed and his voice dropped a tone. "Why not?"

"Didn't want to miss anything, sir." He faced his Captain, pinkly innocent.

Wreyford spoke sharply now. "I told you to get a good night's rest, didn't I?" The boy's grin buckled, he nodded quickly. "At sea, in time of war, sometimes we have to stay closed up at action stations for forty-eight hours on end— or more. Everyone must take every minute of sleep he can get. Is that clear?"

"Yes, sir," Jackie said earnestly, "I see that ... but honestly, if I 'ad turned in, I couldn't've slept. Too excited, y'see, sir." And he smiled again, disarmingly.

Wreyford stared at him, oddly disconcerted, aware of Fielden watching from the Chart Room hatchway. "Well ... in future, obey my orders."

"Ay ay, sir!"

The Captain grunted, turned to Fielden. "Number One" —a more businesslike tone—"the wind's dropping. Reduce to half-speed. I'll speak to ship's company, right away."

Chief Petty Officer Bill Truman raised his head and peered up at the scudding clouds. He was sure he heard, through the wind and the ship sounds, a faint distant drone.... For perhaps a minute he stood in the shelter of the hatchway, tilting his head one way then the other. His keen eyes searched the ragged patches of clear sky, but he saw nothing. And then the squawk-boxes hissed and rasped, he couldn't hear the drone any more. . . .

"This is the Captain speaking." Throughout the ship men paused, edged close to the speakers. "Within the next few days—hours, perhaps—the Germans are expected to invade Norway and Denmark." Everywhere a stirring of reaction. "The job we have to do is vital, and the enemy will do his utmost to prevent us succeeding."

Six thousand feet above the sea and some four miles North-East of the British squadron, a German Kondor was droning over the mottled cloud on a routine reconnaissance patrol. The second pilot, scanning with binoculars through a break in the clouds, spotted a tiny white feather of wake and a glint of metal.

"Ship, eight o'clock—no *two* ships!"

The Captain immediately swung the huge plane round, easing back his throttles—almost silencing the motors. Now he too could just see the ships, narrow grey slivers cutting through the hazy ocean.

"Destroyers," he said.

"*English* destroyers!"

The Captain called over his shoulder—"Willi, Willi, up here quick!" The radio operator scrambled forward and stood between the two pilots, notebook and pencil poised. The Captain held the plane in a slow, descending turn, keeping his distance, inspecting other nearby gaps in the overcast. Suddenly he stiffened, and straightened out the plane. "Look—over there!"

The second pilot and the radioman switched their attention to the new sighting. "Cruiser! *Heavy* cruiser."

"Check our position," the Captain ordered. "And get this off fast, Willi. Fully coded." He consulted his watch. "Zero-seven-twenty-two hours, sighted British naval force. Battle

77

cruiser with destroyer screen. Course zero-six-zero, estimated speed sixteen knots."

"It certainly looks as though the real war is beginning at
last," Wreyford was saying. "We may be a small ship, but
with luck we'll have a big part to play. It's high time our
luck changed. I know I can rely on all of you to do your
jobs. And when we get back I promise you, you'll all get a
proper leave—if I have to signal the First Lord!"

Throughout *Glowworm*, a ragged, derisive cheer. . . . The
Captain permitted himself a thin smile as he put down the
microphone. "You know, I think I'll turn in again for a bit."

Fielden and Kelsey—who'd come on to the Bridge to
check the broadcasting equipment for the Captain, were
surprised and pleased. "Grab all you can while you can,
sir," Kelsey said.

"Jolly good idea," Rosinsky added perkily. Wreyford
peered at him.

"I may not sleep, but at least I'll give my feet a rest. If I
were you, Snotty, I'd do the same. We're going to run into
really rough weather before long."

The boy came to attention—"That an order, sir?"

"An order." And the Captain strode into his sea cabin,
still smiling.

"How long will 'e stay in there, then?" the kid asked
morosely.

"If nothing turns up . . . three, four hours," Fielden told
him.

"Just so long as I know." A wry grin. "Don't want t'get
back before 'im, do I, sir?"

All that morning Whitehorn's force steamed on East-
wards through a heavy swell, under a pewter sky. At noon
the flag-ship flashed a signal to the Flotilla, and the echelons
of destroyers wheeled in unison to port—on to a Northerly

78

heading. And now the sky ahead grew swiftly darker: an unbroken ridge of storm clouds, black as anthracite, was advancing out of the Arctic to meet them. The wind began to lunge in shrieking frenzy, the temperature dropped five or six degrees in as many minutes and the waves heaved and exploded into driving sheets of spume.

Early in the afternoon Wreyford relieved Fielden, but the Number One knew it wasn't worth trying to sleep: the storm's ferocity was still mounting and in half-an-hour or so the Captain was sure to order 'all closed up'—every officer and man at his battle station. So he sat in his cramped, groaning cabin and contemplated his shelves of books—Oscar Wilde, T. S. Eliot, a row of Dickens, Thomas Mann, Walt Whitman, and an incongruous, tattered Robert Smith Surtees.

He smoked a cigarette and after a minute or two unlocked a drawer of his small desk and drew out a thick, black ledger. His personal journal. Written secretly, joyously—on wild days like this when the ship writhed and bucked beneath him; on hot, quiet evenings in port. . . . He turned the pages. His close writing covered the coarse paper in a black web: accounts of his solitary forays into bazaars and back streets of Suez, Aden, Alex, and Algeciras; dreary spells in Hull, Harwich, and Scapa; patrols in the shimmering heat of the Red Sea and in the cold grey Atlantic—all interspersed with intimate personal thoughts, hopes, fears; reflections on the war news, books he read, occasional films he saw, people he talked with.

For many weeks now two subjects had dominated his writings—the war and Garry Wreyford. He'd striven to clarify his own attitude to war, to the killings and maiming in which, sooner or later, inevitably he would be involved, and to the probability of his own death in action. By seeking to define the enemy's nature and intentions he'd reached a firm conclusion and found moral strength.

79

"There is a creeping evil menacing all Europe," a key passage declared. "It is the sad old dream of domination, the dream of minor minds who can fulfil themselves only in static doctrine, and narrow nationalism, sustained by frenzied hate. Hitler's Germany is a juggernaut, brutal and inexorable, threatening to stamp out Mankind's brave, slow striving for some form of moral and political grace—humanity's age-old, hopeless yet magnificent seeking for perfection.

"The Nazis plan to rule over nations of bound and blinded automata. A world without soul, peoples deprived of spirit and all individuality. This monstrous thing must be stopped, with blood—it can *only* be stopped with blood. So I must be prepared to shed a river of blood, my own and others', without a moment's doubt or guilt."

Re-reading now, he smiled tiredly at his own pomposity—wonder what Wreyford would think? How does *he* feel? It was the one subject they'd never discussed. He didn't want to re-read what he'd written on the Captain—his attitude changed every hour and the portrait was blurred, incomplete. Perhaps in ten years' time he'd look over it again and see the man more clearly.

He took up his pen and began to record the events of the last thirty-six hours, describing in detail the air attack and Wreyford's disturbing reaction—or *in*action. "The Captain," he wrote, trying to be objective, "was pale and shaking for several minutes and gave the impression of being in a severe state of shock. This was the first opportunity I have had to observe his behaviour while under fire."

As he finished the entry the ship slammed into a rampant comber and reared up on her stern, shuddering. Several books toppled from the shelves, some of them narrowly missing Fielden's head. He clutched the desk for support and it occurred to him, powerfully as never before, that this was an absurd way for a civilized man to live—boxed up in a damp and airless steel compartment that creaked and groaned, rose and fell, shook and rolled, day and night for months on end until his every muscle, bone, and joint ached from the constant shocks and strains and the land animal's mind screamed for the stillness, solidity, and space of its natural domain; clamoured to be free of the massive forces of the fluid world, that alien portion of the Earth that had been moving ceaselessly, through a million moods and wicked whims, since the very dawn of time.

1400 hours
Admiral Hipper/North Sea/7 April 1940

TIME seemed frozen, Ernst thought the afternoon would never end—they would go on sailing for Eternity in this boundless greyness, through this awesome, hammering ocean, with the cold, the dampness, and the nausea holding them in numb and helpless misery. Land-fighters out of their element, hopelessly lost, debilitated. Still, Colonel Zeltmann was right: in this weather they were better off up here on deck than in their cramped and stuffy accommodation below, where one sea-sick trooper could 'infect' a score of his neighbours.

The 1200 shock troops, with all their fighting gear and wearing cumbersome lifejackets, had been herded on to the main deck. Some were trying to sleep, under greatcoats and waterproof capes. A few were half-heartedly playing cards on blankets spread across their knees. Some lay inert, or draped over the rail—grey, shivering bundles. The chill rain stung pinched faces, soaked through uniforms.

Ernst's squad—Stummer, Metchik, and Schiller—were crouched against a 'midships bulkhead directly under one of the 37 mm gun positions. Stummer was in a kind of coma—clammy-faced, limp, his eyes glazed and straining.

81

Metchik squatted nearby, avidly studying a 'health' magazine, with a husky, near-naked blonde as cover girl. His narrow face shone in the rain as he lost himself in a fantasy world of splendid female bodies, all flaxen hair and blue eyes—the pure Aryan prescription for beauty and sex, pumped by half-a-dozen men into the male libidos of a nation. Ironically, it was a world in which Metchik himself, with his sallow, runty body, could never be accepted.

Schiller glanced at the magazine—"For God's sake, Metchik, why do you torment yourself?"

Metchik stared at him blankly, then laughed harshly. "What do you mean? I'm having a fine time!" Turning a page. "And it's costing me nothing."

Schiller suppressed a shiver and blew on his mittens. "We must be heading North. Where do you think they're taking us?"

"Iceland, perhaps," Metchik said brightly. "For a winter sports holiday."

"I can't stand snow," Schiller growled. "I'm from Bavaria, but I hate snow. Swimming—that's what I like. I'm a very good swimmer."

"Yes, well if you ask politely, maybe the Admiral will stop for a while and let Schiller take a dip."

Schiller forced a weary grin, then—"Neuhofer will know where we're going. That's why he's with the Colonel. Getting briefed."

Metchik put down his magazine, suddenly serious and excited. "It can be only one place—Norway. Full-scale invasion. It'll be over in a few days—faster than Poland!"

Petty Officer Hart, burly and good-humoured, came along the deck, body swaying in easy balance to the rolling, heaving deck. He stopped, looking down at the inert Stummer. "The invincible Wehrmacht!" he proclaimed with kindly gruffness. Metchik and Schiller eyed him guardedly. "How long has he been like this, Corporal?"

Metchik sneered at the grey, comatose trooper. "Ever since we got off the truck and he saw the ship."

Hart shook his head slowly, reached under his heavy storm-jacket and produced a small, flat bottle. "Sit him up, Corporal. We'll see what a mouthful of Schnapps will do for him, eh?"

Metchik and Schiller gripped Stummer's shoulders and hauled him into a sitting position. He moaned softly. Hart stooped and put the bottle to his lips. "Come on, soldier—get some of this down."

Stummer was vaguely conscious of a strange, heavy figure looming over him. This stranger was trying to break into the trance of misery to which he'd managed to adjust and in which—if he kept very still, and hugged the nausea—he knew he could survive. Feebly he tried to push the bottle away but the stranger was firmly persistent, so he swallowed some of the stinging spirit. He spluttered and gasped, his eyes watered again—and then he felt the warmth running down inside him, like a hot flue-brush.

Hart straightened, corked the bottle, and put it back in his pocket. "He'd be better off back there," he said, nodding aft.

"We're out of the wind here," Metchik said in a surly tone. "He'll be all right."

Hart hesitated, looking at all three of them, then he reached in his pocket again. "Here." He tossed the bottle to Metchik, who caught it deftly, then moved away with his swaying gait. Schiller and Metchik stared after him then regarded each other, startled. Until now they'd been so sure the Navy had nothing but contempt for the Wehrmacht.

Metchik took a long swig, coughed it down, then wiped his mouth and offered the bottle to Schiller. But the youngster scowled, shook his head quickly.

"No."

"It'll warm you, man."

Schiller snarled in sudden, surprising fury—"I don't need it!" He snatched up his cards, turned away. Metchik grunted, took another swig and began to turn the pages of the magazine. He studied the white female forms and felt warm and good inside—just like after the blowing of the Rudna bridge. . . .

He chuckled to himself, remembering the twelve leaden minutes he'd waited that night, with his hand on the plunger —hanging on and on for the moment of maximum destruction; until the bridge thundered under the cavalry's hooves and you could hear the horses wheezing, and beside him Sergeant Neuhofer whispered in hoarse, pleading panic again and again, "Now, now. . .!"

1740 hours
HMS Glowworm/North Sea/7 April 1940

"NOW—'ere it comes!" Daddy Longmore, mournfully surveying the lowering sky and the rising sea, knew they were plunging directly into the savage heart of a freak storm. "*Now*—runnin' North, right back into the shit."

Knowles, following him up on deck, turned up the collar of his skins and headed for his watch on 'Y'-gun. *Glowworm* was burying her bows, juddering like a runaway cart over a hard-frozen ploughed field. Every stay and halliard was straining, and the ice-laden blast half-blinded Ossie, lanced through his clothing and felt for his bones. In the gloomy, sodden dusk the sea was a foaming cauldron, throwing up enormous smoking waves. And in the dark troughs white veins stood out in fury.

In the Asdic Room the apparatus gave off a faint *ping*, a meagre bleat of contact, a tiny regular noise, like the dripping of a tap. "U-boat!" breathed Bill Truman. Somewhere deep beneath the troubled surface, under the storm, slipping silently through still dark water: a long, black cylinder of destruction—a predator. The mortal foe this ship had been created to destroy. . . .

He grabbed the phone—"Asdic Control Room to Bridge . . . Contact! Contact bearing green four-five!" He got a curt acknowledgment, reported the estimated range—almost maximum. Then he wiped his brow with the back of a hand and took a swig of tea from a chipped pint mug. The tea was cold and it hung sweetly, stickily to his tongue and the roof of his mouth—come on in, you bastard! Come in closer and we'll bloody do you! Crush you like a beetle!

The Bridge was leaking light, profound shadows and a piercing cold gathered in the corners. Jackie Rosinsky was bent over the chart-table, laying off distance and bearing, plotting the estimated position of the U-boat. He hardly noticed the growing gloom and sharpening chill. His whole mind, almost his whole being, was consumed by the technical problem in hand. He'd done it all before, many times —as an exercise, as part of an examination. Wreyford stood near, observing with silent satisfaction the way this youngster controlled his excitement and worked with a resolute efficiency. Fielden came hurrying on to the Bridge, fastening his duffel. He'd been dozing in his warm cabin and his fingers were clumsy, fumbling at the wooden toggles of his coat. He came to the chart-table, mentally shaking himself —"What's the range?"

"Long way off," the Captain said. "At least ten thousand yards."

Fielden peered out into the wild dusk. "Be dark in a few minutes. *Pitch* dark." Wreyford looked at him narrowly. An odd remark—is there something behind it? Is he offering me a way out, an excuse to shirk the job?

He walked to the hatch and spoke in a firm voice to the Officer of the Watch, Anderson—"We'll run ahead and investigate. Signal the flagship. Steer one-two-five. Full ahead."

Glowworm dipped her starboard rail as she swung on to the new heading and her engines thrummed to full power. Her bows splintered into the huge waves and she bucked and shook violently. The wind had matured into a gale now, a screaming wanton thing that threw the sea in roaring cataracts over the fo'c'sle head.

Eddie Nisbett clawed his way to the stern racks and set the depth charges to 'live'—ready for firing. His frozen hands had no feeling but they worked deftly, blindly from experience. Incredibly he felt almost cheerful, vividly alive. Through the welter of noise and lashing white water he heard himself singing—

> *"Oh I do like to be beside the seaside,*
> *Oh I do like to be beside the sea. . . ."*

Jim Campbell gripped his leather chair as the TS tilted again, more sickeningly than before. Everything—weather, faulty apparatus, the bull-minded skipper, and this tired toy of a ship—was conspiring to disgrace and perhaps destroy him. Soon his head would burst open like a rotten bladder, his churning bowels would split. . . .

Kernohan watched him narrowly. It was obvious that Campbell was having trouble focusing his eyes on the dials —by Christ, if he pukes in here I'll report him to the Old Man, s'elp me . . . !

Far below decks the golden-skinned Petty Girl swung seductively on her single drawing-pin. Trenton eyed her plaintively as he clung to a stanchion and bawled into the phone—"No trouble so far, sir, but I'd like to reduce the revs before *much* longer." Glancing at the tremulous gauges. "Oh—still got the contact? That case, we haven't much option, have we? Right, sir. Full Ahead it is, then. . . ."

He put down the phone and gave the pin-up an extra

flick with his calloused finger—swing low sweet harlot, and keep your panties dry, huh . . . ?

Rosinsky wasn't frightened by the condition of the sea; he didn't have that secret recurrent dread of great waves plucking him from safety and pounding him, pulling him under heaving, choking tons of water, that so many sailors know all of their lives. As he looked out from the Bridge into the raging dusk he felt only a profound awe. He was overwhelmed by the immensity, the incalculable power of the storm that gripped them.

All around, all the way to the greying horizon, he could see the ranks of all the sea-hills marching, all ribbed like marble with foam along the flanks, and snowy crests all tumbling, smoking in the wind. The gale's high keen was everywhere—a long, thin, insane screaming. All the rawness of Nature was there about him in the gloom. He was seeing what the elements could do in full fury—out here where they were still primitive, their surge unbroken all the way from the ice-cap—unobstructed by coastlines, mountains, houses, the solid things of the world of Man. Out here, in what was still *their* world. . . .

He wasn't afraid, yet now the ship's violent movements were beginning to affect him : a cold stirring of queasiness in his intestines. . . . He put a hand to his brow, felt icy perspiration—oh, Gaw, I'm goin' to be sick and make a proper twerp of m'self! Frantically he began to form panicky plans—make some excuse, get off the Bridge, don't let the Captain see. Go to the bog and get it all up. . . .

Fielden saw the Midshipman's damp, ashen face and knew the boy was fighting a losing battle. Sea-sickness was a struggle with your conscience fought on two fronts—in the mind, and in the body. A man against different parts of his own self. But Wreyford didn't see it that way, he had an adamant contempt for any man who 'gave in'. If Rosinsky was sick here the Captain would be furious. But the kid

87

couldn't leave the Bridge so long as this storm lasted—
no-one could.

So far Wreyford hadn't noticed the Midshipman's discomfort. He was staring ahead out of the Kent clear-vision
screen, into the passionate night. The phone gave off a tiny
bleep and Anderson picked it up—"Bridge." The phone
crackled, buzzed, and whined as if a thousand insects were
battling to the death inside the black plastic, but he made
out Truman's words. He turned to the Captain—"Contact
lost, sir."

Wreyford nodded, unmoved—"Not surprised, in this.
We'll reduce to half-speed, let the others catch up." He
glanced at Fielden. "That should please Hellbound Harry!"

The First Lieutenant smiled weakly, edging forward to
screen the wilting Snotty. Anderson went back to the
phones—"Bridge to Engine Room. . . . Half speed ahead!"
Very faintly he heard Trenton's acknowledgment. "Pretty
hopeless now," he said, indicating the phone as he replaced
it.

"Yes, we'll go over to the secondary system, I think,"
said Wreyford. "And we'll have an extra messenger up
here."

"Right, sir."

Anderson called the Coxswain, and had to bellow—"All
posts will go over to secondaries. Relief messenger to report
to the Bridge immediately!"

Fielden sneaked a look at Rosinsky sagged against the
side of the Bridge, gasping. Any moment now . . . the Captain was still intent upon the Kent screen and Anderson,
who must have realized the situation, moved up to stand
close behind him. Fielden moved swiftly. He crossed to the
boy, grabbed his neck, swung him round and—praying that
Wreyford wouldn't turn—propelled him into the Chart
Room.

It was blessedly dark in the Chart Room. Jackie grasped

the table and was shaken by a racking spasm. The heaves of vomit filled his mouth and his nostrils again and again until his stomach was empty and he was spitting a thin, acid fluid. Leaning against the table, weak as an infant, never had he been so miserable—*my life, just look at me, in me bor-rowed baggy clothes, sweaty and shivering and stinking of sick. .And I'm supposed to be an officer . . . !*

Oi veh!—*what am I saying? I 'aven't used a Yiddish phrase in years . . . not since Papa died. Poor papa: the permanent, professional refugee, arriving from Poland—a boy not much older than I am now—carrying only a few family trinkets, his Torah, and carrying all his Jewish sor-row and pain . . . I don't reckon 'e lived a day when 'e felt at 'ome in England—even after fifteen years 'e was still a stranger, an exile from Nowhere, mourning the life 'e'd never 'ad, the kinsfolk who were just names. Always a Jew, always lost, always 'Papa' and never 'Dad'—and me always 'Boychick'. Now me—I feel British first, an Englishman who 'appens to be Jewish. Jackie, not Jacob. I don't live in the shadow of the Wailing Wall. And even for the Jews in the camps and ghettos in Germany, an' Poland, no matter 'ow I try I can't feel any special, family grief, nor any personal kind of hatred for the Gerries—only anger and disgust, like every other Britisher. There's the difference, the breaking away. And 'e gave me this new life—but I wonder would 'e understand . . .?*

Fielden glanced round as the Midshipman moved un-steadily back on to the Bridge, and gestured for him to get back to his post—luckily the Captain hadn't noticed his absence. But Rosinsky hesitated, made an anxious, answer-ing gesture—pointing back at the Chart Room floor.

Fielden glared fiercely at Rosinsky and gestured again—sharply. Meekly the boy glided back to his post on the wing, taking slow deep breaths. And still Wreyford didn't look round. . . .

Alone at the stern, Eddie Nisbett was hauling himself along the racks of depth-charges, trying to set them back on 'safe'. But several were jammed in the fused position. He had a line around his waist and he was moving one step at a time, from handgrip to handgrip.

No singing this time—he struggled against the weight of the hissing water, coughing out salty mouthfuls, cursing to himself. It was like trying to work in a stormy, freezing surf, battling to stay on your feet and make delicate adjustments while the breakers battered at you and you were sucked this way and that by the ebb and flow with only a bit of rope to stop you being swept away to a rotten death.

Another exploding wall of water covered the racks for several seconds. When it had passed he saw two of the dustbins hanging loose, shuddering. He struggled over to them and tried to push them back into their cradles, but he didn't have the strength. . . .

Nobby Clark bowed his head into a driving gout of hail and spray and fought his way for'ard, foot by foot. The barbed wind tore at his skins, plugged his nostrils. He reached the lee of the 'midships machine-gun post and ducked in as a huge wave came crashing down. Keelie Grant and young Dicky Bird were huddled there—glistening, shivering black bundles. When the spray had been whipped away Keelie summoned a travesty of a grin and bawled, "What's this then, Flower—takin' the dog for a walk?"

"Wanted on the Bridge, bugg'rit!" Nobby yelled back.

Keelie tapped his headset—"Phones are playin' up again. 'Spect they want an extra messenger up there."

Nobby grimaced. "That'll be it, then." He made to move out again, peered up into the sodden darkness. "Rain in the air, doncha think?"

Keelie gave him another clenched grin—"Och, a wee April shower, mibbe. . . ."

Nobby lurched on, hunched against the blasts of hail and spray. Far ahead now faint flashes of lightning ripped the sky and in one of them he glimpsed something lying on the deck, flapping feebly like a stranded seal. He hauled himself nearer and in the next flash identified it as a Carley float; it had worked loose from its lashings and was slewing about. Dangerous: someone could trip over it, and be washed over the side. He would have to secure it.

The lashings were tangled and his fingers were stiff and clumsy as clothes-pegs. Frustration boiled up in him. He straightened, swung a savage kick at the bucking float—and for an instant lost his balance. Before he could steady himself a giant wave swept down the deck, burst upon him, squeezing and scouring. He felt his feet leave the plates and his body toppling backwards. As the torrent somersaulted him over the rail his lungs exploded in a wailing scream.

Keelie heard the shredded cry and glimpsed the oil-skinned figure flailing in the foam, hurtling past him, going down into the racing, raging blackness—aw no!—aw guid Christ, it's Nob, he's gone! Fuggin' hell, the poor bastard, he'll freeze an' choke all alone in the dark—I'd sooner be chucked into a bluidy furnace, so I would . . . !

Beside him Bird began to shudder and sob. Keelie cuffed him with the back of his hand then reached across him, groping for the secondary phone.

1815 hours
HMS Renown/North Sea/7 April 1940

THE SECONDARY PHONE system on the flag-ship hadn't been resorted to as yet—the big battle cruiser was steadier, more insulated against the storm, and normal communications were operating efficiently enough. When *Glowworm*'s relayed lamp signal was received on the Bridge the Captain got through to Admiral Whitehorn in his cabin.

"Man overboard—in this weather?" The Admiral was gruff. "He can't last, the water's freezing."

"Just the same, sir, Wreyford's asking permission to turn and search."

"Sheer damn nonsense!" His patience snapped—bloody *Glowworm*, in trouble again, what's Wreyford up to this time? The Fleet could not be delayed now, nor its strength depleted, over the loss of one man. A search in this howling darkness was utterly hopeless. And yet Whitehorn knew that if he denied the request it would affect the morale of *Glowworm*'s crew—which by all accounts was low enough already. . . .

"Dammit, if Wreyford wants to make the gesture, I can hardly refuse him. Let him try. But I want him back on station *in one hour*. Give him a rendezvous."

The Admiral put down the phone and fed himself a fierce pinch of snuff, sniffing it up his nostrils like a fiery old dragon—bloody *Glowworm*! Garry Wreyford better not play games with me this trip or I'll have his ballocks! He's got one hour!

1852 hours
HMS *Glowworm*/North Sea/7 April 1940

"ONE HOUR—in God's name, no man could survive ten minutes in this sea! Odds are he was dead as a Druid before we got the helm over. You know that fine!"—Doc's massive frame filled the doorway of Fielden's cabin like a belligerent bull straining in his pen.

Fielden continued to rummage in the drawers, in search of his night-glasses. His hands groped through disorderly assortments of shirts, socks, underclothing, notebooks, writing paper, and wads of old letters and newspapers. He spoke quietly, without looking up from his task—" 'The miserable hath no other medicine, but only hope.' Didn't they teach you that in medical school?"

"You an' yer blasted quotations! Every mother's son on t'is stinkin' tub is miserable as a titless sow. An' how the hell can we be anyt'in' else when we keep on *bluidy well turnin' back*?"

Fielden's fingers touched the leather case containing the glasses. He drew it out, closed the drawer and faced Doc. "It may seem hopeless—all right. But the Captain wants to try."

"The Captain wants any excuse he can find to turn this ship around—an' avoid a fight!"

Fielden jerked straight. His fingers clenched on the glasses case. "That's a helluva thing to say."

"It's a helluva thing to happen!" Doc snapped, coming right into the cabin and slamming the door. "Now look, David, *you* know there's no point in this search, no point at all. *I* know it—an' he bluidy well knows it! Face it man, face it!—every time we come out with the Flotilla, sooner or later the *Worm* turns. We're never t'ere when the chips are down. Jesus, I could understand it once, even twice— but *every time*! Dammit, David, you don't have to be a consultant psychiatrist to see what it's doin' to the men. How can Wreyford expect them to have any fightin' spirit when he turns tail the moment there's a whiff of action?"

Still Fielden tried to find excuses. "It isn't the Captain's fault. We've had all kinds of bad luck. The men know that."

"The men know a ship's as good as her skipper. An' there's an ugly word for a commander who persistently avoids battle!"

Anger flared in Fielden—a guilty anger, for Doc was only voicing his own secret suspicions. It was obscene to hear them expressed so brutally—like reading aloud his own private journal, with its intimate observations, uneasy thoughts, and all the heresies between the lines, to the entire ship's company assembled on the Quarter-deck. . . .

He pushed past Doc, wrenched the door wide and blundered from the cabin. As he made his way back to the Bridge his memory projected a clear and discomfiting image: Wreyford's face after the bomb hit on 'A'-gun—a slack mask of horror and helplessness. The face of a person revolted, immobilized, by the sight of war's havoc. . . .

Glowworm's powerful searchlights, trained low, swept the waves, making the foam of the crests glow in ghostly malice. At their various posts throughout the ship the lookouts, muffled in heavy, sodden clothing, strained their eyes, hopelessly scanning the turbulent night sea. After the first ten minutes none could muster the wildest hope for their missing shipmate. Yet in their hearts most of the men were glad that the Captain had turned back. It was a gesture, empty, indefensible perhaps—but somehow seemly.

In TS Campbell was fighting a mind-melting giddiness. He was only vaguely aware of the search, and what had happened—all he knew was that he was trapped here, trapped in a ship he loathed and which loathed him, and he knew he'd never escape, never. He felt a new wave of nausea swirl through him. He got to his feet and, gripping chairs and tables, still hopelessly trying to disguise his misery, lurched for the door. Kernohan watched him leave with evil glee—it's beaten the bastard, 'e's goin' outside to puke 'is little ring up . . . !

Campbell emerged on deck, the heavy door slammed behind him and he was alone with the yowling wind, the stinging hail, and the flurries of icy spray. He staggered for'ard, gripped a stanchion, doubled over, and vomited from the soured depths of his belly. It was as if the life were draining out of him. After three or four minutes he was so

94

emptied of strength it was all he could do to pull himself upright and open his eyes. He sobbed in freezing air, lurched into a sheltered niche, and fumbled a phial from an inside pocket. He swallowed two pills. A minute more and he knew the worst was over. He turned and with small faltering steps went back into the TS.

Kernohan watched him return, winked at his mates. "Good job it's rainin' out there. It'll wash away 'is sins." Campbell overheard, but pretended he hadn't.

Some twenty minutes later an enormous roller, a racing mountain of water, loomed out of the night and struck *Glowworm*. Every plate and rivet shuddered under the momentous impact. The ship seemed to stop short, like a vehicle hitting a brick wall, then she leaned over, dipping her port rail, deep, and everywhere men went sprawling, slithering.

In the wheelhouse the young coxswain, Bobby Boyce, was thrown jarringly against the bulkhead. He cursed, massaged a bruised shoulder, lunged back, and grappled with the spinning wheel. He steadied her then looked at the gyro-compass, to bring her back on heading. His gaunt face—already lined and cured by a sea career that had begun at the age of fourteen—creased in dismay and he snatched up the tube. "Wheelhouse to Bridge!" A muffled, breathy voice acknowledged. Anderson. Boyce tried to make his report in a calm, clear tone—"Sir, the gyro-compass has toppled."

Wreyford stared ahead through the clear-vision panel, wooden-faced—gyro toppled. Misfortune upon misfortune—a terrible sense of inevitability misted his mind, seeped into his muscles. He recognized the development of a grimly familiar pattern. A chain of small disasters. . . . Steering accurately by magnetic compass in these conditions would be next to impossible.

He shook off the paralysing sense of helplessness and at once felt a rare flurry of fury—he wanted to batter his fists against the rain-streaming glass, to yell oaths against the sea, this lame dog of a ship, and the blind, relentless elements. Against his own grotesque luck.

He became aware of Anderson beside him, waiting. "Very well, Dick. I'll speak to him." He went to the speaking tube. His voice was controlled, unemotional as ever—"Are you all right, Cox'n?"

"Yessir, but the Mag's playing up, an' all."

"We're pretty far North, that's why. Do the best you can. Steady as you go."

As he hung up Fielden came to him—"Almost time to set course for the rendezvous, sir."

"Going to be damned tricky finding *Renown* again with no gyro."

"Yes, unless the storm clears."

"Hmm—not much chance of that." Wreyford seemed matter-of-fact, unworried. Fielden regarded him grimly. The Captain read his disquiet, frowned—"Well, if we *don't* find 'em, no-one can blame us. We *had* to turn and search, whatever the odds. This ship's company is ninety per cent professional seamen—regulars. Most of them have been with me three, four years. And Clark was one of the best." Now his face and tone hardened. "Poor devil—rotten to go out like that. Just because a line parted. A line that should have been checked and renewed. David—that man is dead because someone on this ship didn't do his job properly!"

Fielden was astounded—my God, the man really believes that, he's passing the buck again! Doc's right, he's snatching at any excuse, he's incapable of examining his own actions for sub-conscious motivations. . . .

But he spoke gently—"Even a new line could have snapped in a storm like this."

Wreyford didn't seem to hear. The old stony look reestablished itself and he glanced at his watch—"All right, let's check our course for the rendezvous."

Fielden followed him into the Chart Room and switched on the low, shaded lamp. The green-tinted globe threw an intimate glow over the chart and its complex dead-reckoning plot. As Fielden took up the protractor the Captain stiffened, gave a soft growl and began sniffing the air, like a finicky old woman. Then he looked down at the floor, and in the green glow his face seemed to grow narrower.

"Who did that?" A voice of ice. "*Who was sick in here, Number One?*" Fielden didn't reply—he'd forgotten all about Rosinsky's misfortune. The Captain strode back on to the Bridge and nailed the ratings with a flinty stare.

"Which of you made that mess in there?" His voice cut through the storm, the words clear and separate as pistol shots. "Come on, speak up!" No-one stirred. Then the Midshipman stepped out of the shadows at the side, tiny and forlorn in his baggy clothes, and faced the Captain.

"It was me, sir. Sorry."

Wreyford wheeled on him in furious incredulity. "You? *Are you sea-sick?*"

"I was, sir," the boy said with easy candour. "But I'm all right now, honest. You don't 'ave to worry, sir—it won't 'appen again. I was going to clear it up—"

For a long moment Wreyford stared at him, searching for any trace of impudence. There was none. He grunted, spoke in a measured, adamant tone. "A man who gets sick is no use on a destroyer. Why didn't you tell me you were liable to sea-sickness?"

"Well, 'cause I didn't know, did I, sir? I mean, 'ow could I, till I got to sea? But it's OK now—reckon I got it all out o' me system at one go, if you see what I mean." And he smiled like a cherub.

Fielden noticed the ratings smothering grins of delight. This was beautiful: the lad's patent honesty and innocence were disarming Wreyford completely. . . . And now came the ultimate ingenuousness—"I'd like to say, sir, I'm very grateful to you for noticing. I mean, considering 'ow many more important things you've got on your mind just now." The Captain could only stare, helpless, and grunt again, ignoring the suppressed laughter of the ratings.

Then abruptly: the shrill whistle of the speaking tube. Anderson took it. "Bridge. . . . Yes, yes right." He turned to Wreyford. "Sir—depth-charges breaking loose on the after-deck!"

For an instant the Captain's eyes clouded, his shoulders slumped—next in the chain of mishaps. . . . Then he straightened, spoke crisply—"Messenger!" Daddy stepped forward, snapped to attention. "Ah, Longmore . . . Get down to 'Y'-gun. Tell Petty Officer Knowles to form a work party, see what he can do."

"Ay ay, sir."

Daddy clattered off down the ladder. Wreyford turned back to the Midshipman. "Mr Rosinsky, get along to Damage Control. Warn them to stand by with tools and tackle. Knowles may need some help. Keep me informed."

Delighted, the boy saluted and was gone.

Daddy made his way aft, not attempting to hurry—making use of all his long experience of the sea, waiting his chance to make each small advance, hanging on tightly and bracing himself as each wave thundered along the deck. A crackle of lightning momentarily lit up the stern decks and he saw Eddie Nisbett and two others, roped together, struggling to secure the loose depth-charges, but several had come completely adrift and were rolling about the after-deck, cumbersome barrels, weighing enough to crush anyone who got in their way. . . .

He moved on and had almost reached 'Y'-gun when a wave smacked *Glowworm*'s flank and the ship rolled sharply. Unperturbed, he went with the motion, sidewise down the slope, and put his hand out for the rail to check himself.

But there was no rail. Only a tangle of loose wires—one of those loose charges must have smashed through, carrying away the upright.... As he went over the side in a flailing cartwheel he let out a hoarse cry.

Huddled behind 'Y'-gun's shield with his crew, Ossie heard a faint-wind-torn wail—"What the 'ell was that?" All of them listened, and Ossie stuck his head out, peered around—and spotted the broken section of rail. "Gimme a line!"

He stripped off his lifejacket and oilskins. Somebody passed him a coiled line and swiftly he looped one end round his waist. He rammed the waterproof flashlight in his belt and crawled out on to the open deck. His crew paid out the line as he inched forward towards the gap in the rail. Once or twice the breaking waves swept him along and he slithered wildly, clawing at the plates. In one lightning flash, when the whole after-deck emerged from murky blackness into an instant of blue-white clarity, he saw the loose depth-charges rolling about and knew how the rail had been smashed. He prayed none of them would come trundling his way.

He reached the gap, lay flat and trained the flashlight downwards. By some fluke Daddy had been caught up in the trailing web of broken wires. He was hanging there, semi-conscious, one leg twisted—obviously broken. Each time the ship rolled to port he disappeared beneath the racing black water, and when she rolled to starboard he was lifted up and slammed cruelly against the hull—a human rag gripped by the sea's mighty and merciless rhythm, simultaneously being drowned and pounded to a pulp.

Ossie shoved the flashlight away, tore some of the broken wires aside and edged forward until his shoulders and chest were over the edge. A roaring wave snatched at him, covering him in icy, tearing darkness for endless seconds, but he clung to the tangled wires and the taut line held him fast. When he could breathe again he reached down and managed to grasp Daddy's limp right arm. He pulled with all his strength and wriggled backwards—c'mon mate, I got you! Gaw, make an effort cancher? Wake up, try and 'elp me! Get that leg loose, kick the wires away with your other foot. . . .

Somehow the dazed man understood what was happening and tried to play his part, kicking feebly. Ossie hauled with all his considerable strength, until he had Daddy's head almost at deck level. But the injured leg remained ensnared. And now Ossie himself was stuck—he couldn't move any further, couldn't get himself fully back on the deck unless he let go of Daddy.

Another freezing deluge exploded over them. Ossie's muscles throbbed and trembled as the cold squeezed the strength out of them. The lifeline was taut, cutting into his waist as his men hauled hard. But still he couldn't budge— I can't do it on me own, Jesus Christ come an' 'elp me, somebody . . . !

Rosinsky was picking his way aft from Damage Control, slipping and sliding, hanging on as the torrents tore at him, heading for 'Y'-gun to find out whether Petty Officer Knowles needed help. Through the swirling hail and spray he saw the smashed rail and the two men struggling there. He worked carefully closer, from handhold to handhold, then went down flat on the deck, grasped Ossie's line and hauled himself out to the gap.

Ossie felt the extra weight on the line and twisted his head round. His labouring heart thudded even harder and he bellowed through the tumult—"Put a loop round yer waist! Wait till she lifts!" The Snotty nodded, tugged at the line, and waited. The gun crew saw what was needed, paid out a little slack. Sluggishly the *Glowworm* rose on a roller. "Now!" Ossie screamed.

The boy got up on his knees and quickly passed a loop around himself. The line went taut again. Just in time he threw himself flat as once more the deck tilted and plunged down, and all three of them were completely immersed.

As the water drained away Rosinsky worked his way out along the line to the edge. "Can you get 'is leg free?"—Ossie was spluttering desperately. The boy yanked on the line again, got some slack, reached over, and grasped the wires which held Daddy's injured leg. It took him a full minute to bring them down over the broken shin and the dangling, twisted foot.

"Right—heave away!" Together they strained, faces contorted, and managed to raise him a little. As they prepared for another heave they heard a low rumble behind them and twisted round. One of the loose dustbins was lumbering slowly towards them.

They watched, rigid, as the heavy metal drum gained momentum, racing at them. It wasn't more than ten feet away when another wave swept down the deck. Rushing, freezing blackness. When they raised their heads again they saw that the charge had gone through the rail two yards further aft. . . .

They rallied their strength. One more heave brought Daddy's trunk up over the edge and Ossie got a loop under his arms. Out in the blackness astern: a long-drawn roar. Then a great cloud of spray. The dustbins exploding, a hundred feet down, hurling a hunk of water into the wild air.

Lump and two other ratings from Damage Control reached 'Y'-gun just as Ossie's crew felt the urgent tugs on the line and began hauling in. But now they had three men on the other end. Lump saw their plight, dumped his tool box, wrapped his huge fists around the rope and pulled with

101

smooth ease, pausing each time *Glowworm* rolled and shipped water. Two minutes later Daddy's bedraggled form was tenderly lifted into the shelter of 'Y'-gun.

Rosinsky and Ossie crawled in, drenched and trembling. Daddy was moaning softly. Lump cradled the little man's head and looked down at him with infinitely gentle eyes— "Leg's all funny, must be broke."

"That's the bloody least of it," Ossie gasped through chattering teeth. " 'E's swallowed 'alf the bleedin' ocean, an' 'e's frozen to the marrow. We gotta get 'im down to Doc."

At once two of the gun crew took the line and looped themselves to Daddy. The others helped them get started on the difficult and dangerous trip. As soon as they moved him again, Daddy gave a weak yelp and passed out.

"And somebody best report to the Bridge," Ossie said. A third rating straightened and set off. Lump found more blankets and threw one to Ossie, then moved to the Midshipman, who was huddled under the shield, shivering. He draped the blanket round the boy's narrow frame.

Ossie reached into a recess under the breech and fished out an oilskin package. The Snotty watched blankly. Ossie winked at him—"Me emergency box. Dry pair o' socks, shoes ... tin o' bully, biscuits, fags and"—triumphantly— "a pint o' rum!" He lifted out the bottle, but his hands were shaking so much he couldn't open it.

"Give it 'ere," said Lump. He uncorked the bottle, handed it back. Ossie held it out to the boy—"After you ... sir."

Jackie blinked. He'd never tasted rum, nor for that matter any raw spirit. But he couldn't imagine a better time to start. He grinned, grasped the bottle in both hands, and took a manful swig. The liquor burned a fiery trail down his throat and tears sprang to his eyes. He stifled a cough.

"Now tha'd best get outa them wet things," said Lump.

"I can get out of them, all right. Problem is, what do I

get into?"

Ossie chuckled, swallowed a mouthful of rum—"I'll 'ave a word with the Jockey."

Half-an-hour later Rosinsky reappeared on the Bridge. Wreyford and Fielden stared incredulously. The clothes the boy was wearing now were even more ill-fitting than the last lot. The trousers were at least five inches too long, forming bulky concertinas at the ankles. The duffel was like a smock, and the hem reached down well below his knees.

The Captain found his voice. "Good Lord, Rosinsky, couldn't you have borrowed from someone nearer your own size?"

"Sir, *nobody's* near my size. Except somebody they call the Jockey—but we couldn't get 'old of him. . . ."

Wreyford shook his head slowly. "Come with me." He nodded to the Number One to take over and led the way to his sea-cabin. There he opened a locker, took out a very smart-looking seajacket and handed it to the Midshipman.

Without a word the boy undid his lifejacket, shook off the dwarfing duffel and slipped on the jacket. Except for the sleeves it fitted him well enough—as a three-quarter length coat. . . . He turned back the cuffs, glanced at himself in the wall mirror then shook his head quickly—"I can't take this, sir—I mean, it's new! Thanks just the same."

He started to take it off. Wreyford made his voice gruff—"I'm not having you standing on my Bridge looking like a damned scarecrow. Keep it on."

"Oh—well, that case sir—it's very good of you. I'll take good care of it, I promise." He smoothed the jacket down. It felt marvellous.

Wreyford coughed quietly. "I'm told you helped Knowles rescue Longmore?"

"Not exactly, sir. I just 'appened along at the right moment. Petty Officer Knowles 'ad it all under control—I just gave him a hand back to 'Y'-gun." Inspecting himself in the mirror he suddenly grinned. "Oh my, the girl friend should see me in this! It'd really knock her eye out!"

Wreyford regarded him gravely. "What's her name?"

Rosinsky turned to face him, surprised, flushing slightly. "Lily Goldman. . . . She works in a munitions factory, but she's studying art. Evening classes. She's going to be a dress designer—when this lot's over, y'know."

"Is she a good artist?"

"Terrific! Well, I mean, not that I understand 'alf she does, like. But Lil says you 'ave to paint what you feel, not what you see."

"You might tell her to try both."

The boy stared—" 'Ow'd you mean, sir?"

"Well, she ought to feel deeply about something she sees, and then paint it."

"Ah!—now *that's* worth remembering. Tell you what, sir—when we get back I'll bring 'er to see you. Then you could tell 'er yourself. She'd pay more 'eed if it came from you."

The Captain smiled—"I wouldn't bank on that. Young women as a rule aren't too keen on taking advice from—er, the older generation."

"Don't you believe it, sir, you don't know Lil! She'll like you, I know she will!" A pause, then more seriously, "I shall marry 'er soon as I can. No sense in 'anging it out, is there? I mean, if you're sure?"

"None at all."

"You married, sir?"

"Yes"—Wreyford was amazed at himself. . . .

"You see—nothing like it, is there?"

"Well," Wreyford said presently, "we should be getting back now."

"Ay ay, sir." Pulling on the lifejacket. "And I'd just like to say, sir, what an honour and privilege it is to serve under a Captain like you. I consider m'self lucky, sir, dead lucky!" He saluted smartly, picked up the discarded duffel and went out.

Wreyford stood very still, alone in the sea-cabin, for the best part of a minute before he followed.

As he stepped back on to the Bridge a rating emerged from the Chart Room carrying a bucket and mop. Wreyford strode past him, switched on the green-tinted light and stood frowning down at the chart.

0630 hours
Admiral Hipper/North Sea/8 April 1940

THE CHART showed nothing new on the British force—not a single report since the Konder's sighting nearly twenty hours ago. Not surprising: the freak storm which had broken soon after that had blinded the U-boats and grounded the planes. But Mann, working from the enemy's last known position, knew that *Renown*'s squadron could be entering this area now. Almost certainly they were heading for Narvik Fjord. The coming dawn might well reveal them converging from the West, or even lying to the North, barring his way.

Across the chart table von Scholtz and Stenz faced him. Stenz lifted a clipboard, glanced through the latest weather-cast—"No chance of a break."

"No, not in the next twelve hours," the Admiral agreed.

"I would like to send two of the destroyers scouting ahead, sir," von Scholtz said.

"Very good, Captain." It was the right thing, the only thing to do. If, in the first daylight, the scouting destroyers sighted the enemy then *Hipper* and the others would take evasive action and try to slip past in the poor visibility—

105

God in Heaven, what I would give not to have to run! So
much to make up for, and here is a chance to fight—but not
with twelve hundred troops on board. No, not until the
landings have been made. . . .

Von Scholtz was on the phone to the Signals Officer—
"Make to *Bernd von Arnim* and *Paul Jakobi* . . . Proceed
full ahead."

Colonel Zeltmann, muffled in his leather greatcoat, paced
the darkened deck at his stiff, jerky gait. The hail had
stopped but the wind howled on, driving gusts of spray in
his face. He liked the cold-burning sting of the spray: it
made him feel strong, indestructible. . . .

Most of his men now were below, either at breakfast—
those who still had appetites—or trying to snatch a few
hours' sleep in their cramped hammocks. The few still on
deck were in a bad way, some hanging over the rail, others
sprawled inert like corpses.

The Colonel looked at them and was infuriated. His men,
his stormtroopers, reduced to gasping shivering wrecks.
What use would they be when they reached their destina-
tion? Half of them couldn't stand. Unreasonably, he saw it
as the Navy's doing. He'd felt the Admiral's dislike since
the moment he'd come on board. Mann was typical of the
Navy's senior officers, 'a gentleman of the old school'—
there's no room for them in the armed forces of the Third
Reich! Where did such aristocrats get Germany before? In
the last war? Between the wars? They were content to live
off Jewish gold while the rest of the nation starved and the
Mark fell day by day. . . . Well, that's all over, now Germany
is governed by Germans! A new élite! Men who are purging
the nation of its rottenness. . . .

Nearing a for'ard gun position the Colonel was heartened
to see Sergeant Neuhofer on his feet, talking gravely to the
men of his special demolition squad—no doubt going over
the details of their specific mission. Ernst held a flashlight

106

trained on a map spread on the deck and he was smoking one of his stubby cigars. Zeltman stepped into a patch of shadow and stood watching the little group.

Metchik, squatting opposite Neuhofer, had opened a strong steel box and as he listened he was checking his fuses and explosives, fingering them lovingly. Schiller was crouched beside him, scowling ill-temperedly at the map. Stummer sat propped against the bulkhead, his face grey and blank, shivering violently. Zeltmann edged closer.

"—and our task is to blast this pill-box." Neuhofer was stabbing his cheroot at the map. "Then the others can rush those main gates and take the power station, before the enemy can destroy the machinery. We may have to blast the gates, too."

"With this little lot, Sergeant, we could blow up the whole town!" said Metchik happily.

"No doubt, Corporal. But the idea is to capture it intact. And that pill-box is the key."

Schiller lifted his head, blinked into the flashlight. "You really think the Norwegians will fight?"

"For a few hours, here and there." Ernst shrugged. "They'll try blowing a few bridges, scuttling ships."

"Like in Poland," said Metchik, a small nostalgic smile stretching his thin lips.

"I don't get it," Schiller said. "Why do we want to invade a God-forsaken country like that? Ninety per cent ice, snow, and bloody mountains. . . ."

Ernst's voice rose—"A soldier doesn't ask that sort of question! We have our orders, we will carry them out. And from now on you'll keep that whining mouth of yours closed or you'll find my fist in it!"

Schiller jerked straight, barked like a nervous pup—"Yes, Sergeant!" Metchik smiled and went on checking his equipment.

Ernst turned to the shivering Stummer and let go a raw

107

shout. "And you, Stummer—man, pull yourself together!"

Stummer recoiled, taking long breaths and struggling to focus his eyes—"I'll be all right, Sergeant, once we're ashore. Soon as my feet are on solid ground again, you'll see. . . ." Ernst sneered and turned away, just in time to see Colonel Zeltmann coming towards him. He snatched the cigar from his mouth—"On your feet!"

They scrambled up, Stummer swaying groggily.

"Everything all right, Sergeant?"

"Yes sir, all correct."

The Colonel glanced at the damp-faced Stummer. "Very good, carry on." Ernst saluted with parade ground precision and Zeltmann acknowledged briefly as he strode away, the wet leather of his coat making soft creaks—a good man Neuhofer. Solid, unimaginative, disciplined. And there are others like him—many of them. . . . If only this damned weather would lift. . . .

As Zeltmann's square shoulders disappeared Ernst looked at Stummer again then growled at Schiller—"Take this monkey for a walk, and if he doesn't brighten up—kick him over the side!" Schiller, resentful at having to move out from the shelter, grunted sullenly, grabbed Stummer's arm and hauled him off.

Ernst glanced at the sky off to starboard—dawn wasn't far off. He went to the rail. The wind smacked his face, forcing him to screw up his eyes, and the great ship was rolling and pitching heavily. After a moment he swallowed thickly, took the cigar from his mouth, looked at it critically and threw it over the side. He cursed softly and viciously: no use denying it, for the first time he was beginning to feel it himself. . . .

Bleakly he gripped the rail, suppressed a shiver and began to count slowly to one hundred, staring Eastward into the endless grey.

Dawn
HMS Glowworm/North Sea/8 April 1940

ENDLESS GREY sky and sea, unbroken, empty—scanning with the glasses in the early gloaming Wreyford's tired eyes saw only the desolation of marching crests and swirling sleet. No *Renown,* no sister destroyer.

He lowered the glasses and Fielden saw his face was devoid of expression. "Well, that's that, David. We've lost contact with the rest of the squadron."

"The Admiral will have something to say, sir. *One hour* he gave us!"—trying to keep the bitterness out of his voice.

"What the Hell *can* he say? If he will bring us out with the ship in this condition."

Oh dear Christ, that same old story again. . . . "The wind's dropping, sir, and the visibility's better. The storm may be blowing itself out. All we have to do is steam on, take a zig-zag, and with any luck we'll soon pick them up."

Wreyford pursed his lips, surveyed the overcast sky. "This is only a lull. We're well inside the Arctic Circle now. It could blow up again any time."

Fielden no longer could contain his anger and contempt. "Then what *do* we do, sir—put about and go home?"

Wreyford tried to ignore the accusing hiss of that final phrase. Without looking at the Number One he spoke in his usual calm, clipped tone. "Listen, David, we've no way of fixing our position, but we're certainly no more than sixty miles from the Norwegian coast. We can't go much closer, on our own." He tapped the damage report. "Certainly not with all this."

He offered the report to Fielden. "I've seen it," the Number One snapped, with barest civility.

Wreyford was silent for a time, scratching the back of his right thigh, then—"We'll give it fifteen minutes more. It'll be fully light then. If we don't sight the Fleet we'll put about and return to base. Work out a course, will you?"

Fielden didn't move. "We can't do that, sir!"

The Captain turned and regarded him with a mild frown. "What do you suggest? After a night like that, they may be miles off course themselves. And we certainly can't break radio silence, that could jeopardize the whole operation. Work out a course, please."

Fielden hesitated a moment, then wheeled and stomped into the Chart Room. He picked up a protractor and a pencil and immediately broke the pencil point on the chart. He said "Shit!" loudly and vehemently.

Wreyford heard the expletive. So did Anderson, Rosinsky, and the ratings on the Bridge. The Captain gestured to Anderson then moved in to the Chart Room, drawing the heavy weather curtain behind him.

He came to stand beside Fielden. "It's the old jinx again, David." Wearily. "*Glowworm*'s special jinx."

"Is it, sir?"—deadly accusation in the tone, in the way his penknife hacked at the pencil. (He must have known there were dozens, ready sharpened, in the chart table drawer. . . .)

"Now look here," said Wreyford stiffly. "You don't think I like having to turn back, do you? For Heaven's sake . . . !

"I don't know, sir. I honestly don't know!"

Wreyford moved round the table, stony-faced now in the green glow—"I think you'd better explain that remark."

Fielden stopped slashing at the pencil and stuck his head into the splash of light—"All right, dammit, I will! Why is it that something always happens to *Glowworm*? Why is it always this ship that drops out before the shooting starts? Is it the ship—or is it you?"

"My God, David! What are you saying?"

But nothing could check Fielden now—"You call it bad

110

luck, a jinx. Well all right, maybe—up till now. . . . But this
time? Was it bad luck that made us turn round in the middle
of the night on a useless search for a man overboard?"

"We had to look for him! We had to *try*—I told you—"
Wreyford was glaring now, the strange light of panic in his
eyes.

"It was hopeless! Hopeless—and you bloody well knew
it!"

"Are you suggesting I planned it all?" Voice shaking.
"Do you think I *pushed* that man overboard? Toppled the
gyro? Let those depth-charges loose . . . ?"

Wreyford was so patently shocked that Fielden's anger
collapsed, leaving only a crushing weight of sadness and
uncertainty. He bowed his head and several seconds passed
before he spoke again, in low faltering sighs—"No, no. . . .
I'm—I'm sorry. Maybe you're right. Maybe it is *Glowworm*
that doesn't want to go. . . . But you expect that from her.
And you accept it, you give in to her too easily. Oh Hell,
let's drop it!"

He raised his head and for a time they stood silent,
regarding each other in the little heaving room and Fielden
saw the despair and confusion he'd sown in Wreyford's
heart. The Captain was facing it now, facing something
he'd never allowed himself even to consider before.

"Captain, sir—ship on the port bow!"—from outside
Rosinsky's young voice rang clear and assured, breaking the
tension. Wreyford, with a little twist of his cap to straighten
it, strode back on to the Bridge and Fielden followed. He
fumbled with the glasses case, acutely aware of the others'
eyes upon him.

"Red two-five, sir!" the Midshipman sang out.

The Captain trained the glasses on the faint horizon off
the port bow. A tiny dark smudge sharpened into focus—
mast and superstructure. Beside him Anderson and Fielden
were focusing up.

111

"Destroyer," Wreyford pronounced calmly. "Can you make her out?"

The ratings on the Bridge were stirring, smiling in relief, sure they'd at last made contact with the squadron. But the Captain and the Number One continued to scrutinize the distant vessel, oddly grave.

"*Two* destroyers!" Anderson said suddenly—and in almost the same moment Wreyford discerned a second smudge, smaller and fainter, to the right of the first. Both were heading East, across *Glowworm*'s course.

"Yes," Wreyford said softly. "Two, destroyers . . . but—" He broke off, slowly lowering his glasses.

"But they're not ours!"—Fielden finished for him. A moment of silence, then Wreyford spoke curtly—"Challenge them!"

The duty Signalman moved to the port wing and the lamp clacked busily in his mittened hands. Wreyford scratched at the back of his right thigh. Everyone else was still.

At this moment Valentino came on to the Bridge carrying a tray of cocoa mugs. Instantly he sensed tension, danger. He stood rigid, eyes flicking from face to face—once more silently cursing the vile fate that had snatched him from his home, from the haven of familiar things, and dragged him out of the sunshine across alien seas into the bitter cold. A prisoner of these strangers whose war this was, and who somehow had involved him, a helpless civilian, in its grimmest hardships and gravest perils. . . .

"Port ten. Full ahead." Anderson swiftly relayed the Captain's order. Now Wreyford could see the leading ship flashing in reply to *Glowworm*'s challenge.

"Swedish," he read aloud.

"Ten to one it's a cover, sir!" Fielden declared with sudden urgency, turning a demanding gaze on the Captain. Wreyford's face was grey and taut. He opened his mouth to speak, then changed his mind and once more trained his glasses on the distant ships. As the outlines sharpened on the lenses he saw two flashes, puffs of smoke. And a moment later all of them heard the shells screaming through the air.

"Stand by to engage!"—the order broke from Wreyford, a reflex reaction, firm and clear. It created an immediate flurry of activity on the Bridge. Each man had his specific task, his role in the routine that had been drilled into him. Only Valentino remained still—staring out into the greyness with his soft brown eyes. . . .

Within instants, while the enemy shells were still on their way, *Glowworm* began to resound with alarm bells and everywhere her crew sprang into action. And as she swung on to her new interception course, increasing revs, the shells crashed down thirty yards off the starboard beam, raising white pillars. The ship lifted in the water, as if shying away from the onslaught. A second salvo already was shrieking overhead.

In the Sick Bay far below the waterline Daddy Longmore tried to raise himself in his cot. His mind was groggy with drugs but a deep dread gripped him as he heard the second lot of bricks fall close to the ship and felt her lift again. He was alone down here in this little room, and probably forgotten. It was something that had haunted him like a recurrent nightmare ever since his first sailing days—the dread of being caught below in a stricken ship. *Somehow he must get up top.* . . .

He started to heave himself out of the cot. His smashed leg, encased in plaster, held him like a massive ball and chain. He tried to lift it with both hands: terrible shocks shot through him. He flopped back on the mattress and lay gasping, staring at the dripping, vibrating plates close overhead, listening to a third flight of bricks howl down on the ship.

The bells jangled on and on, and in TS Campbell's operators fed their equipment the information just received from the Bridge: bearing, estimated range, course, and speed of the target. Other essential data—wind speed and direction, drift, own speed—already had been set on the appropriate instruments. The equipment automatically did the calculating and provided sighting and laying data which was passed to the gun crews. All the machinery seemed to be working smoothly and Campbell, eyes aching, head spinning, prayed it wouldn't fold up as he bellowed his orders through the scream of the falling shells and the clamour of the bells.

Out on the after-deck Ossie had his crack crew poised— the loaders ready to pass fresh rounds from the ammo hoist to the breech, the gunlayer keeping his pointer precisely on top of the automatic director's indicator on the dial. They ducked only momentarily as the enemy missiles tore into the water close off the port bow and hissing clouds of spray thrashed over them.

Ossie Knowles cursed, and Jim Campbell cursed, as the ship lay over to starboard, dunking her freeboard. Daddy Longmore cursed as he was thrown against the side of his cot. And on the Bridge Fielden heard himself snarl profanities as the spray rattled the for'ard screen.

Wreyford stood very straight, hands clenched, ivory-knuckled, on the glasses held in front of his chest, mouth open and eyes needle-bright. Fielden glared at him—what the Hell's he waiting for? The bastards are getting our range, the next salvo may blow us out of the water!

He lurched over to the Captain, gripped his arm—"Sir, for God's sake!"

Wreyford shuddered once, took a deep breath—"Open fire!" His voice a hoarse whisper that only Fielden heard. Immediately he cleared his throat and repeated in his normal tone—"Open fire!"

Ossie's 'Y'-gun opened up first, then 'B'-gun crashed into action with Bunty Baker in command and Tinker Bell grinning in excitement as he laboured in the loading section. 'A' and 'X' were only seconds later. *Glowworm* seemed to be on fire as she cut through the waves with all four 4·7s blazing out in a rhythmic and polished performance. A fourth enemy salvo smashed into the water scant yards astern, but still she remained unscathed.

Rosinsky had found glasses, trained them on the distant adversaries. He saw a tremendous flash on the nearest ship, and then billowing smoke.

"A hit, sir!" he screeched. Wreyford and Fielden whipped up their glasses and saw a fire glowing amidships in the leading vessel. And even as they watched both enemy ships ceased firing and abruptly turned away. Fielden couldn't believe it—they were breaking off the action!

On the stern of the nearest ship the Nazi flag was plainly visible. More shells from *Glowworm* raised tall plumes close around both Germans as, displaying superior speed, they raced North and were swallowed up in the haze.

Wreyford lowered his glasses, suddenly much calmer, frowning. "Cease fire!" he ordered.

When the guns had fallen silent Fielden came to him, flushed, a gleam in his gaze—"One of them's severely damaged, sir. She'll slow up. We can catch her!"

"No." The syllable dropped like a leaden weight, and crushed Fielden's enthusiasm.

"But—we can't let them get away—"

Wreyford exploded, startlingly—"I said no! Dammit, David, don't push me!"

Now everyone on the Bridge was watching them intently. Fielden held the Captain's gaze for several seconds, then wheeled and started to walk away.

"Number One!" Fielden turned back slowly. "Officer's call!"

Fielden's jaw sagged—"Officers' call? Here, sir?"
"Here and now!"
Fielden, in a complete daze, moved to comply.

'Y'-gun's crew stood amid the heavy cordite fumes still oozing from the breech, straining their eyes to see the enemy. But they'd vanished. Ossie spat contentedly. "Dead 'midships—shit hot, lads! Sent 'em packin' that did!"

The sleet had stopped but now came more sharp gusts of hail, thick as stair-rods. It was fully light and the wind was rising again, scooping the tops off the rearing rollers. The ship's officers were assembling on the Bridge. Fielden was fairly certain that no English captain had called such a conference, with the enemy so close, since Elizabethan times. A ludicrous decision, an unforgivable waste of time.... Campbell was last to arrive—pale and woozy. He saluted. Wreyford acknowledged and said crisply, "Tuck that thumb in, Lieutenant. You're not hitch-hiking."

The others stared, incredulous, and Fielden had to bow his head to hide his despair and frustration—dear God, at a time like this ... ! Trenton exchanged a glance with Anderson then raised his eyes to the scudding hail clouds in silent supplication, and Doc glowered fiercely.

Wreyford turned his back on all of them and stared out after the vanished foe. He compressed his lips, took air in through his nose. He gripped his right thigh so hard it hurt, but it was no good—the tremor lay too deep, and he was afraid they would see it quivering....

"We have to make a choice here, gentlemen. We have a problem to discuss, and then a decision to make. A vital decision." He spoke reflectively, as though totally unaware of their suspicion and hostility.

"First, I think, a few facts.... Most of the men haven't slept in more than thirty-eight hours. The weather shows no

116

sign of breaking—it's getting worse again, if anything. So shadowing is out of the question. Too big a gamble in this sea, and this poor visibility." He paused: some grudging grunts of agreement. "And we all know the condition of the ship. . . ."

He turned to them and surveyed their faces, waiting, as though expecting someone to challenge him. But no-one spoke. "Very well. Now we must ask ourselves, gentlemen— why did the enemy break off? There were *two* of them, they could see we're on our own. Yet after a short engagement, at long range, they suddenly break off and withdraw. . . . Lieutenant Trenton—why do you suppose they did that?"

Harry—still in sweat-soaked working overalls, uniform jacket thrown about his shoulders—cleared his throat and stared out past Wreyford towards the hazy horizon. His eyes grew small and very bright and he spoke with low excitement. "Only one possible reason. There's something over there. And they're trying to draw us on to it. . . . Something big. Maybe a whole German battle squadron."

A long hush, everyone still and deeply solemn. Wreyford nodded slowly—"Precisely. So we have four possible courses of action. One—we break radio silence, now, and warn *Renown* and the others that *something* is out."

Campbell shook himself out of his groggy daze—"But, sir, the enemy will intercept our signal," he rasped thickly. Wreyford dealt him a piercing look, for the first time noticing his unsteadiness and pallor.

"Quite—and take evasive action. I don't think we'd gain anything. All right, second—we carry on for Narvik, in the hope that we meet up with the rest of the squadron somewhere on the way and can warn them by visual signal."

"But that could take hours!" Trenton burst out. "And while we were searching the enemy could get clear away!"

Wreyford met his wild gaze—"Correct." A pause. "It might be quicker to turn around and run for base."

A shocked, unbelieving silence. Fielden twisted his mouth into a bitter smile, turned away with a deliberate jerk and stared out of the side screen.

Wreyford didn't seem to notice the Number One's contemptuous posture—"Three hours steaming would take us well clear of these waters, then I think we could risk a coded signal. Even if the enemy intercepted it, he wouldn't necessarily connect it with us."

Fielden wheeled back, eyes blazing, fists bunched, all patience and prudence spent—"And what would you say in that signal, Captain? What information have we got? A quick glimpse of two enemy destroyers, that's all you can report. My God, for all we know there could be a convoy of troopers over there—a whole invasion fleet! It's our duty to find out! Now!"

Wreyford fixed him with a cold look, slightly out of focus. "What are you suggesting, Number One? That we go after them? One destroyer against—Heaven knows what?"

"Yes, sir! Exactly that! I believe we have to accept the odds—and I think most of the others would agree." Recklessly now. "But we can't take a bloody vote. You're in command."

"I'm aware of that!" Wreyford snapped, shaken, glancing round at the others. "But I called this conference because I wanted to hear your views first."

"There's no time to discuss it, sir. Those enemy destroyers are getting away while we stand here"—Fielden forced calmness into his tone, stepped up close to the Captain. "In God's name, let's get after them, find out just what's over there. And do as much damage as possible—before we're sunk!"

A stirring, all faces set, gravely purposeful. Wreyford heard his voice, faltering—"You realize ... there could be other destroyers ... we may never get through the screen—"

And now the little Midshipman stepped forward, chin

high, eyes steady—"Still we've *got* to 'ave a go, sir! I mean, that's what you're trying to say, isn't it? And I'm with you, sir—all the way!" He said it without a trace of guile or histrionics.

Wreyford looked down at him, wrenched, speechless—oh dear Lord, the innocence of it, the incredible *innocence*. He doesn't know, he doesn't begin to understand—he's a babe, he shouldn't be here God help him. . . .

He looked down at the slight figure in the ridiculous clothes, at the eager unfinished face, and his expression changed. The boy's simplicity and directness—"We've *got* to 'ave a go!"—made it inevitable. Wreyford realized the decision had been made for him. He moved to the microphone, picked it up and clicked it a couple of times. Still working.

"Attention please. This is the Captain."

Throughout the ship the men were instantly still, looking up at the speaker boxes. Lump, mopping up flood water in the for'ard Messdeck, blinked around him, wishing he had some mates with him—he was vaguely uneasy here on his own. . . .

On 'B'-gun Bunty Baker was long-faced, fighting down black apprehension: beside him young Tinker made a chest and grinned in bravado.

Keelie Grant rested his stubbled chin on the butt of his machine-gun and tilted his head to catch the skipper's voice, reaching him only faintly on the gusts of wind.

"We are going after those ships—going in to attack an enemy force. As yet we do not know the strength of that force. Our task will be to assess that strength, to identify their lead ship and get off a signal which will warn the Fleet.

"To do this, we'll have to fight our way through their destroyer screen. We've already damaged one of them with first-class shooting."

Ossie looked round the faces of his gun-crew, cocked his

119

head and winked jauntily. Some grinned, but one or two were very young and they looked bewildered. Quietly he reached a hand into the recess under the shield, checking that his emergency ditty box was there.

"We can give the other enemy ships some of the same medicine. I know every one of you will do his best."

Bill Truman, in Asdic, swivelled his chair to and fro very gently as he listened, lips pursed—'England expects' is it? Shit, here we go, sprinting to our bloody graves. . . .

Daddy lay very still on his Sick Bay cot, feeling terribly small—shrivelled. His wild eyes tried to drill through the ceiling. . . .

In the Engine Room Hobson and the other ERAs huddled close to the speaker, struggling to hear above the din of the straining engines. . . .

Valentino, long, lovat face streaming sweat, cowered alone in his galley. . . .

The Jockey squatted, gnome-like, in the after magazine and kept his eyes away from the hundreds of live shells stacked on either side of him ready to be loaded into the hoist. . . .

"This is not by any means the first time we've started out with units of the Fleet and finished up on our own. But today things are different. Today *Glowworm* has a chance to show the rest of the Flotilla what she can do when she has the enemy all to herself. I know you won't let me down."

The speakers went dead. For a timeless moment no man moved or spoke and the ship was silent save for her own beating heart. And then the spell was broken, the men stirred, and began final preparations for the coming action.

In the for'ard messdeck flats Lump fumbled in a pocket and fished out a damp, dog-eared postcard—the one he'd been writing to his Mum, a thousand years ago. He frowned at it, then let it flutter down into the dirty floodwater at his feet.

And down in the Sick Bay Daddy licked dry lips, called again for help. No response. He gripped the edges of the cot and, teeth clenched against the jolting pain, managed to pull himself over the side and flop on to the deck. He started crawling towards the hatch and the ladder that led upwards.

In the Engine Room big Hobson swigged mightily from a churn of cold water and poured what was left over his head. Then he moved to his controls, checking gauges—passing the Petty Girl pin-up without so much as a glance.

Ossie, standing by at 'Y'-gun, heard a high whistle. He motioned to the gunlayer, then made his way for'ard. Bunty was waiting in the shelter of the torpedo tubes below 'X'-gun, roughly halfway between their two posts. Somehow he'd contrived to light two cigarettes and he fed one to Ossie.

"Reckon we're gonna find out now, all right," he said.

"Find out what, mate?"

" 'Bout the Skipper, that's wot."

"Yeh, reckon," said Ossie after a moment. He stared out across the endless acres of tortured, freezing sea, through the slanting flurries of hail, to the vague line of the horizon. "Wonder what it is, over there?"

"Whatever it is, it's bigger'n us. We got no chance. All on our tod." Matter-of-factly.

"No chance," Ossie repeated, as if it were part of a ceremonial dirge.

Bunty stuck out his hand—"Just wanted to say g'luck."

Ossie clasped—"Luck, mate."

Bunty headed back for 'B'-gun. Ossie stayed and stared out at the sea again for perhaps a minute; finishing his cigarette, trying to remember this was April and resisting the pull of home, visions of Ruby, the irony of the daffodils.

BOOK THREE/*The Battle*

0735 hours
HMS Glowworm/North Sea/8 April 1940

HIS MAJESTY'S destroyer *Glowworm* was a tiny speck in the vast and stormy wastes of the Arctic Ocean. Such was her loneliness, so enormous seemed her isolation, it was hard to believe that any other vessel could pass within a thousand miles of her—that her destined course could carry her across the path of anything but a drifting iceberg. She pounded on at full power, bludgeoning through the immense humps of water, at times almost vanishing from view. Nor'-Eastward, in pursuit of her quarry, over the horizon to confront the unknown; taking the bait, allowing herself to be led on to destruction.

Wreyford stood in the exact centre of the Bridge. Fielden hovered nearby.

"I want the Cox'n to stay at the helm," the Captain said.

"Yes sir, he's still there."

"Good. . . . Rosinsky, you will attach yourself to Damage Control again."

"Very good, sir." The Midshipman's eyes by now were bleary and his voice was slurred with tiredness, but he saluted and moved off smartly.

Now that they were committed the Captain seemed as calm and confident as if they were on a routine exercise. He moved up to the clear-vision panel and studied the wild water ahead—"Firing torpedoes in this is going to be sticky." Fielden nodded gravely, glasses at his eyes again, peering through the writhing gusts of hail all the way to the blurred, leaden band that marked the merging place of sea and sky. No sign of the enemy as yet. He was filled with an impatience that surprised him. He lowered the glasses and felt a strange

123

aching, as on occasions long ago, in the heavy heat of tropic ports, when he'd suppressed an urge to dive into a pool. . . .

"We're sure to be hopelessly out-gunned," he said presently. "Supposing it proves impossible to launch our fish—or they just won't run in these conditions?"

"Then," Wreyford said, "I shall attempt to ram their lead ship."

Yes, of course, the only answer, it's as simple as that—'Rammer' Wreyford. . . . No coal barge or harbour wall this time! He's planning to fight *Glowworm* through the enemy's destroyer screen and, if she stays afloat, try to drive her bows into the guts of the German flagship—be she cruiser, carrier, or pocket-battleship.

They would, of course, come under fire from the big guns of the main massive long before she was within range of *Glowworm*'s puny 4·7s, and on the final run in they would have to take a point-blank pounding. Suicide. In modern naval warfare there was a law as imperative as gravity: 'God is on the side of the force with the biggest guns.'

Whether they succeeded or failed, one thing was certain: *Glowworm* was about to become the property of Lord Neptune, the well-known shipowner. Still, Fielden was satisfied that it was the only honourable thing they could do, the only purpose they had left: " locate—identify—engage—destroy!", that was the rule.

In a kind of wonderment, he searched the Captain's drawn face: no trace of doubt or reluctance now. At long last this man had crossed his private Rubicon, there could be no going back this time—all that concerned him now was how best to handle his ship in order to inflict the maximum hurt upon the enemy before they went down.

"You agree with my plan, David?"

"Yes. So long as we get off a signal the instant we've identified their lead ship and estimated their total strength." Then, softly—" 'No captain can do very wrong if he places his ship alongside that of an enemy.' "

Nelson's words evoked a small, grateful smile, then Wreyford looked out into the greyness again and spoke only for Fielden's ears—" 'Do the thing you fear to do, and the death of fear is absolutely certain.' Who said that?"

"Emerson, I think."

"Hmm . . . rather good for an American."

Doc and his medical team were busy converting the Ward Room into an emergency dressing station and operating theatre. The big dining board became the operating table and blood transfusion equipment, sterilizers, and instruments were arranged on the bar.

Daddy Longmore, teeth gritted against swooning weakness, was levering himself up the ladder, step by step, dragging his plastered leg. From time to time he paused to gather his strength and call for help, but no-one heard him—everyone else was at action stations and the passages and companionways in this part of the ship were deserted.

Up in the for'ard messdecks Lump straightened from his labours, smiling warmly, as Rosinsky came clattering down from Damage Control. The last of the floodwater had been pumped away and mopped up and two other ratings had turned up to help pack the equipment.

"Leave that," the Midshipman said briskly. "We're shorthanded on the firefighting squads. This way." And he led them off down the passage.

Bill Truman's voice, coming over the tube, had behind it the sinister *ping* of an Asdic echo. "Sub contact, o-three-o, red. Two thousand yards. Over."

"Red o-three-o, two thousand yards," Fielden repeated. "Out." Turning to Wreyford—"Contact, sir!"

The Captain thought for a moment. "We can ignore that, I think. A U-boat can't harm us in this weather. And we're after much bigger game." Again completely cool. Fielden was filled with a quiet, wondering assurance.

"Campbell's sea-sick—did you see?" Wreyford asked presently.

"Yes, but he'll do his job. He scored a hit on that Jerry, didn't he?"

Wreyford nodded. "You think I've been too hard on him?"

"Yes, frankly."

The Captain sighed reflectively and his eyes became glassy, staring back across the months—"Remember that troop transport in the Med, David? Packed like a slaver. Seven thousand men . . . seven thousand."

"I remember," Fielden said. Then very firmly: "But not the way you do."

"We could have saved her! Those E-boats must have passed just ahead of us."

"Maybe. But you're forgetting: there was no moon. A pitch black night—"

But Wreyford went on as if he hadn't heard—"Our for'ard look-out should have seen them—if he'd been alert, carrying out his duties. Instead of lying there, vomiting his heart up. . . . Over two thousand lives lost, because one man was sick!" His voice and colour had risen.

"Sir, a lot of men get sea-sick, but they can still do their jobs," Fielden said quietly. "And Jim Campbell will do his, I'm sure."

Wreyford looked at him sharply and the pain left his face. He spoke without passion—"Yes . . . yes, I believe he will. They *all* will. Now." And then, to Fielden's astonishment, he solemnly recited a poem—

> " '*From too much love of living,*
> *From hope and fear set free,*
> *We thank with brief thanksgiving*
> *Whatever gods may be*

> *That no man lives for ever;*
> *That dead men rise up never;*
> *That even the weariest river*
> *Winds somewhere safe to sea.'* "

"Swinburne?"

"I don't know," Wreyford confessed. "It's a verse my father sometimes quoted. He was a sad man, a pessimist, resigned to man's inhumanity to man, yet always trying to love his neighbours." Then, startlingly, he smashed both hands down on the little ledge before him, making the phones rattle. "Dammit, David, he was the gentlest person I've ever known! He couldn't stand the sight of blood, the mere thought of human suffering. My God, how he loathed violence of any kind! 'Turn the other cheek—no man is without some good in him—God alone has the right to take a life'—he had a kind word for the most brutal criminal."

He paused and his voice became weary. "He was a fool, David. A gentle, loving fool. But quite irresistible—too much of his thinking rubbed off on his children. Lord knows no man ever meant so well, but it was a rotten training for the sort of world we have now. If he'd lived, I'd never have joined the Service. I think I did it in a sort of defiance, after he was gone. Because I resented the lingering grief . . . and because he'd stifled, *hurt* me with his gentleness. Can you understand that?"

"Yes, I think so."

"Then you know why I'm a misfit here. A peacetime officer, caught up in a war."

Fielden felt a stab of remorse. "No sane man likes war, Garry"—the familiarity slipped out.

"Then this Earth must be governed by madmen!" Wreyford's head sank—"You were right, you know. I'm a rotten coward."

"I didn't say that!"—alarmed, deeply ashamed now.

127

"I saw it in your eyes, David. Don't be upset.... Oh God, one day I'd like to meet the men who brought us here! I'd like to ask them a few questions!" Fielden was embarrassed, his mind in cascade. Wreyford regarded him ruefully and then touched his arm—"Don't look so worried, David, I'll be all right. Making the decision was the worst part. Now that's over, I'll do the best I can."

There followed a long, very intimate silence. They turned back to the screen and scanned with their glasses again. Two minutes later the curtain of hail suddenly thinned ... parted. Off to port, less than two miles distant, an enemy destroyer was switchbacking through the racing hills of sea towards them.

Wreyford lowered his glasses, closed his eyes, took a full breath.

"Port fifteen! Engage!"

Glowworm swung to intercept the German—the *Paul Jakobi*—and both ships opened fire almost simultaneously. Within twenty seconds Campbell's automatic shooting had scored a hit on the enemy's stern. But almost immediately *Glowworm* staggered in the water under an immense impact.

TS took a direct hit. The blast swept into the little room and Campbell felt himself picked up in a massive hand of heat and thrown to the deck. The air was fouled by choking, stinging fumes that made his lungs heave in desperate surges. His eyes were streaming, smarting till he thought they would melt. The squalls of the wounded assaulted his ears, curdled his brain. Blindly he hauled himself to his feet, wiped at his eyes—and saw that the room was flooding. Oily water was creeping up the bulkheads, swirling among the twisted, thrashing bodies of his men. He realized his clothes were in shreds and his face was bloody from a cut on his forehead, but he felt no pain.

He fought dizziness and panic and surveyed the chaos: tangles of smashed equipment, broken leads, charred, scarred instrument panels. The water was rising steadily, already lapping around his thighs. He sloshed to his transmitter and rasped into the mike, praying to God it was still functioning—"Local firing! Over to local firing! Acknowledge! Acknowledge!" With the director knocked out the 4·7s were left mindless—somehow he must make sure the gun captains knew they were on their own. . . .

He waited, leaning on the splintered desk, fighting for air until the water was creeping coldly around his waist. Then as he raised the mike again, across the wrecked room he saw Kernohan struggling towards him, spluttering and whimpering, fighting to keep his bloodied face above the water. Campbell waded over, reached for him. He felt a hand claw at his ripped clothing and he put an arm round the man, lifted him, held him. Kernohan's right eye had gone, all that side of his head was raw flesh and exposed bone. The other eye fixed on Campbell—agonized, huge with shock.

"All right, I've got you, I've got you."

He fought his way back to the mike and tried again to contact the gun captains, holding Kernohan close, like a little hurt child. One by one, faintly through the din of continuing battle, he heard the posts acknowledging.

" 'A'-gun on local, 'A'-gun on local!"

The water was up around his lower chest now and Kernohan clung tighter, began to wail. Campbell shook him, and in a strange fury yelled in his face—"Shut up, you stupid bastard!"

" 'B'-gun firing on local!"

" 'X'-gun—right, on local, sir!"

" 'Y'-gun. Okay, sir, firing on local!" Knowles—remote, yet still workmanlike. . . .

And then the lights failed.

Clasping Kernohan in both arms he groped through the wreckage and the swirling black water to the hatch. Eager hands helped him out on to the deck, the icy air thrust into his lungs and he felt the dead weight of the wounded man lifted from him. He lurched across the deck, brushing off ministering hands, and rested his head against a shattered small-boat. And there he vomited helplessly.

"Sir!" Fielden was pointing ahead, his voice high and urgent. Wreyford turned swiftly. A second destroyer was emerging from the belt of hail to starboard. Her guns flashed, white pillars grew eighty yards ahead. The trap was closing. . . .

"Make smoke," Wreyford ordered, entirely composed. "Starboard twenty."

Glowworm veered to starboard and from her after-funnel a lengthening cape of thick smoke streamed and settled heavily upon her white wake: a solid, black wall. All around now the water sprouted white plumes as the cross-fire from the two attackers reached for her. The British gun-crews kept up a steady answering fire—'A' and 'B'-guns swinging round to meet the new attacker, 'X' and 'Y' keeping their sights on the *Paul Jakobi*.

The casualties from TS were carried into the converted Ward Room. Doc worked on them in a controlled frenzy, his big, furry-backed hands expertly staunching blood, straightening twisted bones and injecting drugs, while from his lips came a low, furious hum of Gaelic profanities.

Wreyford remained coolly purposeful. Somehow he must get past the enemy destroyers without exposing himself too much to their fire. For this, he knew, was only the beginning, a foretaste. *Glowworm* was going to need all her strength for the confrontation with the leader of the German force— assuredly not far away now; lying off to the East, withheld in the hailstorm's gloom.

130

Campbell staggered on to the Bridge, clay-faced, holding a red-soaked handkerchief to his injured brow.

"Sir, TS is knocked out. All guns are operating on local."

Wreyford appeared unperturbed—"I see. You all right?"

Campbell nodded dazedly. Wreyford immediately returned his attention to the second destroyer, now almost dead ahead—identified by Anderson as the *Bernd von Arnim*. He was charging at her, almost head on—gambling on being able to hurt her, knock her out of the fight or at least slow her up, while the other German was blinded by the smokescreen. They were closing rapidly, rearing and dipping all-out across the rugged white-capped peaks, and very soon he saw that his boldness was throwing the enemy gunners off target.

The flurries of hail were lighter and fewer now and visibility was improving by the minute. 'A' and 'B'-guns were finding the range, kicking up snowy columns close around the enemy ship, at times almost obscuring her.

For an endless ninety seconds the antagonists raced at each other, on collision courses, pouring their shells—and then through the tall spikes of spray surrounding the German those on *Glowworm*'s Bridge saw two tremendous flashes, in quick succession. Within moments huge tongues of flame enveloped the enemy's foredeck. She leaned over, turned away, slowing up, and her firing became ragged and wild.

In turning the German presented her full length as target to the British gunners. Wreyford held his course for another sixty seconds and saw a third hit gouge an ugly hole in the hull just aft of the Bridge and on the waterline. The *Bernd von Arnim* would do no more fighting or chasing this day.

He was tempted to go after her, to close in for the kill.

131

One well-placed torpedo would finish her, he knew, and at long last the ill-fated *Glowworm* would claim victory honours. But he also knew that at any moment now the *Paul Jakobi* might come slicing through the smokescreen behind him. . . .

"Stop making smoke. Starboard—hard over!"

Glowworm heeled over and put about—doubling back into her own smokescreen. And as the firing ceased, through the batterings of wind and sea and the throb of engines a new sound arose, a sound that had not been heard on this ship in many a long, dreary day.

The men were cheering. Lustily.

Fielden glanced at the Captain and saw his eyes were moist and glowing. But his expression was one of painful sadness.

Wreyford ran his ship along inside the smokescreen for a full three minutes—until the smoke grew thin and tattered. The *Paul Jakobi* did not come through.

"All right, let's take a quick look. Port twenty!"

They cut into the smoke at an acute angle and just before they emerged on the other side he began a turn to starboard —so that they would be in clear view of the enemy for only a matter of seconds before snaking back into cover. The smoke thinned out, the light grew, then they broke into the open—and there was the *Jakobi*, not more than a thousand yards off the port quarter. She was running on an opposing course, parallel to the smokescreen, at half speed, and high on her Bridge structure a signal lamp was blinking out a message—aimed at something far to the South-East, out of *Glowworm*'s view.

A brief, fierce exchange of fire, but before either ship could find the range *Glowworm* had plunged back into the protective blackness. As she came into the clear on the inside again the Captain spoke gravely to Fielden—"He was signalling his main force."

"Yes sir, asking for help, no doubt. That destroyer skipper isn't going to come through the smoke on his own."

"No. He's not going to risk letting us get between him and the lead ship."

"Sir, if we can tie him up, and make enough nuisance of ourselves—maybe we can lure the big ship through!"

Wreyford was strangely serene now. "I was thinking the same thing. If we were to make a series of quick forays, in and out of the screen—"

"Keep hammering his destroyers, and the Fleet commander's going to lose patience!"

Wreyford paced a moment, nodded ponderously—"Very well. See that the gun captains understand what we're up to, will you?" As Fielden went to the speaking tubes the Captain beckoned to Campbell. "Lieutenant, we're going to save our torpedoes for the big one. But check your sights and communications right away, please. It's going to be damned difficult in this sea, so I want you to fire them, personally."

The grey and tattered Campbell pulled himself upright and saluted—very correctly. As he lurched off, still unsteady, Wreyford moved to the side and stood rubbing the back of his right thigh, staring fixedly at the smokescreen—seeing far beyond it, in his mind's eye, the huge dark silhouette of the German capital ship.

0800 hours
Admiral Hipper/North Sea/8 April 1940

THE GERMAN CAPITAL SHIP was steaming North through the murk, bows dead into the near-gale, punching massively through the heaving humps. On her Quarter-deck a muffled-up rating was ringing out the hour on the ship's bell. The wind snatched at the chimes, giving them a weird, ghostly quality.

In the warm shelter of the big Bridge, Admiral Mann was seated in his padded conning chair reading a signal just received from the *Paul Jakobi*—"Engaging G-class British destroyer, 64·05° North, 06·18° East. *Bernd von Arnim* in support has taken several hits, fire on board and losing power. Enemy slightly damaged but making raids through smoke-screen in effort to draw us through. Request assistance."

Mann rose and strode to the chart table. Von Scholtz, Stenz, and several other officers grouped around him. Colonel Zeltmann, his pale blue eyes pink-rimmed from the wind, stood on one side, listening intently. Stenz pinpointed the position of the action on the chart: some 17 miles North-West of *Hipper*'s present position. Mann tapped his fingers on the table in a light tattoo of meditation, then smacked his palm down on the chart—"The enemy ship must be from *Renown*'s squadron. Scouting ahead—the others cannot be far behind." His eyes grew small and excitement fibred up his voice. "We will turn and seek contact!"

The others exchanged uncomfortable glances, then Von Scholtz ventured softly—"Before we have landed the troops, sir?"

"We have no choice now, Captain. If the British are this close they could take us by surprise—attack us while we are in restricted waters, or actually putting the men ashore. I will not take that risk." Von Scholtz nodded at once, accepting the logic. Mann returned to his conning chair, the other officers went back to their posts, and Stenz got busy on the chart, working out the course alteration.

Zeltmann stood in stiff, gimletty silence. He had sensed Mann's excitement, his eagerness for a fight, and felt the responsive stirring among the younger officers—damn the Navy, selfish glory-chasers! Off on their private war without a thought for their mission, the overall operation—nor for my men, and what they'd have to go through in a sea battle. . . . They're disobeying orders signed by the Führer

134

himself—it amounts to treachery! If they get involved with this English force, and as a result fail to land my troops exactly as planned, by God I'll see Mann disgraced, dismissed!

As the great ship turned on to her new course those troops on the main deck who were not too sick to care saw the long barrels of her guns increase their elevation and swing round to point Westward—and they sensed danger, a departure from the plans. Leaving their card games and their magazines they flocked to the rails. A babble of talk, a storm of conjecture—at least this development made a break from boredom. . . .

Stummer was too weak, and Schiller too cold and miserable, to move from their blanketed nook, but Metchik joined Ernst and peered into the hazy distance.

"What is it? Why are we turning?" the Corporal asked.

"How should I know?" Ernst grumped; and Metchik noticed his pallor and the way he was breathing in small, fast jerks through the mouth.

"How is Stummer?" the Sergeant asked abruptly.

"Better, I think."

Ernst grunted and scowled at the sea. Metchik moved very close and rasped into his ear—"Stummer is scared, you know that? *That's* why he's sick. It isn't the weather. Man, he's scared stiff!"

Ernst turned his head and grated contemptuously—"Like you were in Poland most of the time?" Metchik stepped back, eyes blazing, mouth clamped. "I'll tell you something, Metchik," Ernst went on. "You spend too much time trying to be smart. You let those two sit around and talk about their *feelings*, so that you can sneer and make yourself out superior. This group's going soft and it's your fault, damn it!"

Metchik glared, spread his arms—"That's not fair, Sergeant, blaming it all on me! I tell you that Stummer's a real

135

misery—the brainless bastard. And young Schiller—he's always bragging, criticizing. . . ."

"You're more experienced than either of them. You're the Corporal, aren't you? Get tougher with them, man! I'm warning you: if I hear any more of this talk about *feelings*, somebody's going to feel the toe of my boot!"

Metchik dropped his gaze and glowered furiously at the damp and dirty deck. Petty Officer Hart sauntered up and stood behind them. Ernst glanced round at him—"Why has the ship turned? Are we near our landing area?"

Hart shook his head and spat expertly over the Sergeant's shoulder. "No. We've turned *away* from the land."

Metchik and Ernst stared Westward again, thoroughly uneasy now. Hart began to roll himself a cigarette. And after a few minutes the rim of the sea seemed to grow darker—to become firmer, until there was a distinct line etched between the water and the overcast sky. Ernst pointed to it—"What's that black stuff?"

Hart's weathered face suddenly was like a block of oak. "Smoke." He moved off quickly, leaving them staring, wordless. And then, as their eyes fastened again on the long band of black, stretched like a ribbon of mourning across the faint, far horizon, the wind fell away momentarily and they heard the sullen rumble of the guns.

0815 hours
HMS Glowworm/North Sea/8 April 1940

THE GUNS opened up as once more *Glowworm* came curving out of the smoke and within thirty seconds Fradgeley's crew were roaring triumphantly, claiming a hit on the German's forepeak. The *Paul Jakobi*, racing southward now, full out and keeping her distance, was quick to reply. Her bricks straddled the British ship but only spray hit her, and once more *Glowworm* retired into sanctuary without further damage.

By now the smokescreen was becoming tattered, teased out by the high, gusting wind. Wreyford ordered more smoke to be made and they laid a second woolly wall inside the first. Perhaps moved by an obvious association of ideas, the Captain went to his sea-cabin and reappeared on the Bridge holding an old briar pipe. He thrust it into his mouth, looked about him and called almost jauntily—"Anyone spare me a little tobacco?"

One of the ratings, Dunlop, brought him a pouch and matches. As he filled the briar Fielden watched with a dazed, sardonic smile. Wreyford struck a match, gave him one of his rare grins and said between puffs—"I know ... haven't smoked this in years. Always thought of it as a weakness. But I just got the urge."

Again the Number One marvelled at the change in the Captain since the officers' conference. But he couldn't help wondering whether Wreyford's new calmness and confidence would hold up when the time came to face the flag-ship.

0835 hours
Admiral Hipper/North Sea/8 April 1940

THE FLAG-SHIP pounded on at full power, closer to the smokescreen. The *Paul Jakobi* was in plain view now, a fire blazing on her foredeck. The destroyer's signal lamp blinked out again and Mann frowned fiercely, incredulously, as he read the transcription.

"Still only one enemy ship?"

"Apparently, sir," the Signals Officer said. "But as you say, there must be others near at hand behind that screen."

"We have to find out. At once!"

Zeltmann stepped forward—"Herr Admiral, I have twelve

hundred men on board this ship. Any further delay and they will not make their landing on schedule."

Mann fixed him with a cool stare. "It would be rash to proceed without my destroyers, Colonel Zeltmann. And if there *is* an enemy squadron over there, it would be sheer madness to let them get on our stern and bottle us up in the Fjord." He swivelled the conning chair to the left, turning his back on the SS officer, and trained his glasses on the black barrier of smoke. "We must find out, immediately, exactly what we're up against. Order *Paul Jakobi* to make a quick penetration."

The Signals Officer hastened away and moments later *Hipper*'s lamp was flashing the Admiral's order to the German destroyer.

0841 hours
North Sea/8 April 1940

THE GERMAN DESTROYER smashed through the smokescreen and by grim chance emerged only four cable-lengths astern of *Glowworm*. Both ships opened fire in the same instant, and neither could miss. *Glowworm* got the worst of it this time: her hull was holed in several places and as she veered to starboard to bring all four guns to bear a hit near the bows started a fierce deck fire. One of 'A'-gun's crew was killed and two more were wounded by shell splinters. The roasting heat drove the survivors from their posts, and stacked ammunition began to explode.

The *Jakobi* dived back into the smoke, trailing broken rigging. *Glowworm* came round 180 degrees, the billowing smoke from her burning fo'c'sle obscuring the port half of the forward Bridge screen.

"Get some lines on there! Don't let the fire spread! Report extent of damage below decks!"—Anderson was yelling into the emergency tube. Fielden stood with Wreyford at the clear side of the screen. The Captain was pale but composed—it wasn't like the last time he'd looked down on a burning foredeck. . . .

"You know why he came through?"

"I think so, sir. The big ship's come up and ordered him to pinpoint us."

Wreyford nodded very slowly, then—"Damn it, let's make sure. Hard a-starboard! Hard over!" Fielden, startled, re-layed the order then put out a hand to steady himself as *Glowworm*, streaming flames and smoke from her fo'c'sle, made a tight 90 degree turn and once more charged towards the smokescreen.

Daddy clawed his way on up the steep companionway. He knew the ship had been gravely damaged—the impact of the last hit had thrown him off the ladder, sent him crashing painfully to the deck. He fought down panic, hauled himself up again. Only two more decks to go, but his muscles were numbed and bruised, his plastered leg was a massive millstone—Oh Christ, dear Christ, help me, don't leave me here, help me up top. . . .

Everyone on the Bridge strained their eyes as *Glowworm* began to emerge once more on the enemy's side of the smokescreen. Through the last hazy wisps they spotted the *Jakobi*, limping off to the North, and then Fielden's arm shot out and he uttered a shaky cry. He was pointing to the South-East: steaming solidly towards them out of the greyness—massive, majestic, seemingly impregnable—came the enemy's big ship.

Wreyford trained his glasses. "Heavy cruiser—10,000 tons!" He spoke rapidly and clearly, the absurd pipe still clenched between his teeth. "My Godfathers, it's the *Admiral Hipper*! Signal *Renown*—and Admiralty!"

Fielden snatched up the tube—"Bridge to Wireless Room! Bridge to Wireless Room!"

"She's carrying troops—it's a landing, all right!" Wreyford called. Then through the powerful glasses he saw *Hipper*'s huge eight-inch guns traverse smoothly until they were trained precisely on him. The first salvo flashed and fumed and the sound reached ahead of the shells—a clap of thunder that rattled the perspex screen and sent everyone on the Bridge reeling.

0843 hours
North Sea/8 April 1940

REELING under the deafening blast of the cruiser's heavy armament the troops on the main deck fell back from the rails, hands over their ringing ears, and cringed in whatever shelter they could find. Some cried out, others snarled curses, but their voices were squashed by the second salvo—a noise like the planet splitting. . . .

Ernst found himself flat on the trembling deck next to Schiller. The youngster was quaking, his fingernails scraped at the steel plates and he had his eyes screwed up, his mouth agape. Ernst felt a deep disgust. He wanted to punch the boy, kick him.

He pushed himself up on his arms and looked about him. Stummer was curled up in a ball, his head under his blanket. Metchik squatted nearby, palms pressing on his ears, looking up at the smoke from the for'ard gun turrets whipping past close overhead—a sickly grin distorting his narrow face.

A third thunderclap: once more Ernst felt the deck jolt and judder under him. His gullet twitched, his eyes throbbed. He went down flat again, cushioning his head on a forearm.

140

And as the ringing ache left his ears, from high above and far off he heard the weird whining of the big shells drilling through the sodden air, and then distant explosions.

0845 hours
North Sea/8 April 1940

EXPLOSIONS rocked *Glowworm*, lifted her high in the water and filled the air with searching metal. One shell struck amidships almost directly above the Bridge, carrying away a section of the foremast, the aerials, and rigging. The blast blew Anderson and a rating, Dunlop, over the side—they simply vanished. Two others were hurled against bulkheads, knocked unconscious, and Fielden lay clutching his left side.

Another shell struck the forepeak, for'ard of the deck blaze where Rosinsky's firefighters were battling. Living men were cut apart by the shrapnel. Two more went overboard, probably dead before they hit the water. The wounded lay crumpled, twisted like rags, or came staggering or crawling out of the fumes, wailing for help.

Hipper's first salvo had fallen close ahead, smothering the destroyer with tearing clouds of spray. Wreyford had taken her round to starboard on maximum rudder, racing back for the smokescreen while the Wireless Officer, Kelsey, began to tap out the vital signal.

Glowworm couldn't return the enemy's fire : the German was still well out of range for the 4·7s. The second salvo had struck wide to starboard and for a moment it looked as if Wreyford would con her back behind the smoke without more punishment. But then the third salvo had screamed down. . . .

Rosinsky's right shoulder was a mass of pain, paralysing all the muscles and sinews of the arm and crushing the air out of his lungs. He was sprawled on his face against the

141

mangled rail close under the starboard side of the Bridge and for a long time he couldn't move. When he struggled to his knees he found blood was pouring down his chin.

Big hands gripped him under the arms and raised him to his feet. Lump had lost his helmet, his hair and eyebrows were singed and he had an ugly burn glaze on his left cheek. He peered down into the boy's gory face—"Nowt to worry on, sir. Lip's coot, 's'all." With his good arm Rosinsky reached into a pocket, found a crumpled handkerchief, applied it to his split mouth: within moments it was saturated. He eased out of Lump's grasp, lurched for'ard, skirting the deck fire—he must assess the damage wrought by the hit at the bows, and report to the Captain. . . .

Daddy heaved himself up the last few rungs on to the main deck and lay gasping. Dead ahead, mere yards away: the Ward Room entrance. He could see Doc and his medics working on the wounded. He gathered his strength and crawled to the door, calling feebly. One of the orderlies heard him, turned, and came quickly towards him. Daddy stretched out a hand, mustered a smile—"Blimey mate, your lot left me below, all on me own. I wouldn't've stood a dog's chance."

The orderly held his hand, bent over him. And then they heard another salvo whistling down. The sound grew steadily, to a piercing pitch, and both men froze, breath congealed, staring into each other's eyes. . . .

Glowworm's battered bows were only fifty yards from the refuge of the smokescreen when in quick succession, the shells smashed into her—one, two, three.

THREE soft, comfortable plops, as the precious lumps sank into the mug of strong, steaming tea. Captain Charles Alan Dunsmore, Duty Officer, Admiralty Operations, lifted the old tablespoon, wiped it with the end of his tie, stirred slowly and told himself he was fortunate to have a weight-conscious wife who used saccharine and gave him her sugar ration.

He raised the brimming mug carefully and sipped. The hot, sweet brew set up a pleasant inner glow. He sat back in his padded chair, warming his hands. The big room was cold and draughty—the solitary gas fire was operating at low pressure again. He stamped his feet on the old, bare boards.

A sharp rapping on the door: it opened and his Wren assistant hurried to his desk. "Sir—just received from *Glow-worm*."

Dunsmore put down the mug, jerked out of the chair, took the signal from her and as he started to read strode briskly to the big operations map which covered the inner wall. His voice came loud and jerky—"Great Scot—she's engaging the *Admiral Hipper*!" Swiftly he marked the position on the map. "Off Trondheim. How the Hell did she get *there*?"

For seconds he stared at the tiny, solitary marker-pin, then he wheeled—"Top priority—to Admiral Whitehorn and Chief of Operations!" The Wren worked pencil and pad. "Give them this position—approximate only." Consulting the signal again. "*Hipper* has destroyer escort, including *Paul Jakobi* and *Bernd von*—" Stopping abruptly, looking up, frowning. "Where's the rest of this?"

The Wren's eyes were steady and solemn—"That's all there is, sir. It wasn't completed."

143

Captain Dunsmore looked at the unfinished signal again and his voice grew tight—"I see . . . very well, carry on."

The Wren took the latitude and longitude from the map. Her pad snapped closed and she hurried from the room. The Captain stared in helpless anguish at the little coloured pin—a blood-bright dot amid the ice-blue wastes which, he knew in his heart, marked the grave of HMS *Glowworm*.

0903 hours
North Sea/Off Trondheim/8 April 1940

HMS GLOWWORM was a shambles. She was wallowing in the storm-lashed sea close inside her smokescreen, with her engines barely alive and flames and steam pouring from her several wounds. The gunfire had stopped and the wind seemed to shriek the louder.

One shell of *Hipper*'s last salvo had plummeted down through the foredeck and exploded in the for'ard section of the Engine Room, slaughtering most of the stokers and ERAs and fracturing the main steam line. A second had passed through the Ward Room and burst just beyond, wiping out Doc with his entire team and all the wounded they were treating in a mighty blast of yellow and orange flame. The third hit had demolished the Wireless Room, killing Kelsey, then penetrated the main deck and started extensive fires at lower levels.

Amid the hissing, scalding steam in his stricken Engine Room, Hellbound Harry Trenton lay under a ganglion of ruptured pipes and plates, both his legs smashed to pulp. Wally Hobson crawled to him, heaved the wreckage aside and tried to drag him to the ladder. Trenton was conscious but Wally saw that with every beat of his heart the arterial blood was pumping out of him.

Harry snarled, clawed at Hobson's arm—"No, dammit!

Listen, the main steam line's gone! Tell the Old Man he hasn't got long—we'll start losing power any time!"

Wally nodded, still struggling to move the dying officer. Again Trenton pushed his hands away—"Wait man, *listen*! You'll have to go over to the emergency throttles—and give Rammer all we've got, while the pressure lasts!"

The big ERA looked down into the glazed, straining face and rasped—"Yessir, I'll see to it." The steam was getting hotter, thicker, burning up the air, blurring his vision.

"Right then, get along there, *sit* on the bloody throttles boy! Keep 'em wide open! Understand?" Wally nodded again, gasping and swaying now.

"Go on then, get on with it!"—he coughed out the words and then slumped back, mouth wide, his whole body quivering. Wally hesitated only a moment then staggered to the ladder.

As he passed the buckled control panel, through the choking steam cloud he saw the Petty Girl pin-up rippling weirdly. The paper was curling, shrivelling in the tremendous heat, distorting the elongated legs and the absurd doll's face, melting the shapely breasts and slender body into a ghastly blob.

Down in the little wheelhouse the young Cox'n Boyce came to, and groggily disentangled himself from a heap of debris in the corner where he'd been hurled by the blast. Close over his head jagged pieces of deck plating hung down like ravenous jaws, breathing evil fumes.

As he got to his feet he felt a wave of giddiness, but no pain. He had a throbbing bump on the crown of his head and he saw that his left arm was hanging like a piece of rope, dripping blood. The wheel was spinning one way and then the other—hopelessly, aimlessly. He tried to steady it with his right hand but it kicked powerfully, out of his grasp. He gripped his left wrist, lifted the limp, bloody hand and

145

dropped it on a spoke, then snatched a hold with his right and leant his full weight.

The big wheel wrenched him, tried to throw him to the deck. And now the pain came, shooting through his shoulder and his chest, up into his head, jolting the top of his skull. A cry was torn from him and he almost swooned, but he held on, took the strain and halted the spin, then centralized the rudder.

Experience told him the steering gear was still intact. But he could feel *Glowworm* losing power, beginning to flounder in the grip of wind and sea forces, and he wondered how long she could stay afloat. . . .

Rosinsky climbed stiffly to the battered Bridge, holding the handkerchief to his smashed lip. The Captain was speaking loudly into an emergency tube—"All right, Hobson, give me full ahead, for as long as you can!"

Fielden had got to his feet. He stood with his back against the bulkhead, minus his helmet, his left hand pressed to his side below the lifejacket. Blood was trickling through his fingers and in a weird spidery pattern down his cheek from a web of cuts above the right eye. His face was wet putty, his mouth loose, twitching.

Wreyford turned from the tube and saw the Midshipman. The boy was grimy, gory, and his eyes were large and glassy.

"You're wounded."

Rosinsky tried to square his shoulders but a wave of pain made him reel. He gulped air. His voice was oddly distant—muffled by the handkerchief, thickened by the swollen lip. "Bit of a knock, that's all, sir."

"Very well, make your report."

"The fire on the foredeck's still under control, sir." Struggling to think and enunciate clearly. "But there are others below—I dunno how many, we can't even get at 'em . . ."

His small body shook in a brief spasm. " 'A'-gun's out for good, sir—all dead, I reckon. And 'B'-gun's shield is jammed."

Wreyford took the big pipe from his pocket and rattled it against his teeth. He moved closer to the Midshipman, his feet crunching on broken perspex, and surveyed him carefully. Then he spoke with surprising gentleness— "You've made a mess of my jacket, son."

Rosinsky squinted down his blood-smeared chest and his eyes came into focus—"Oh Lor'! Sorry, sir—when we get back I'll 'ave it cleaned, honest."

"I'll hold you to that, Snots." An odd hoarseness in the Captain's voice now. "Right—back to your post."

Rosinsky changed hands on the sodden handkerchief, saluted, and left the Bridge, his step steadier. Wreyford watched him start down the ladder then strode over to Fielden.

Campbell, back from checking the torpedo tubes, had loosened the Number One's lifejacket, cut away the clothing and was about to apply a field dressing to the mushy wound. Fielden's voice was a feeble monotone—"You're wasting time, the big one'll come through that screen now, any minute!"

A tiny fleck of red appeared at the corner of his mouth. A grim look flashed between Wreyford and Campbell: the lung was pierced. . . . Then the Captain rammed the unlit pipe back into his pocket, turned away. Hiding his pain, he strode to the starred and blackened for'ard screen.

Campbell gently applied the crude dressing then led Fielden to the starboard end of the Bridge, made him sit down with his back against the plates and wrapped him in a blanket—"Don't try to move, David. We'll get you proper attention, soon as we can."

Now Wreyford could feel *Glowworm* throbbing under his feet, beginning to move again, punching through the loom-

ing waves and slowly gathering speed. He trained his glasses
on the smokescreen but everything was blurred and misty.
He turned his face to the side, blinked his eyes clear, focused
up again and scanned slowly, meticulously, searching for the
first, vague shadow forming in the thinning smoke—the
enemy knows we're crippled, he *must* come through now to
finish us off. . . . Dear God, not another destroyer—let it be
the *Hipper*.

0910 hours
Admiral Hipper/8 April 1940

THE HIPPER was running at half speed past the drifting,
burning *Bernd von Arnim*—towards the place where the
British destroyer had vanished into the smokescreen. Mann
stared ahead, frowning. "At least four hits, but she's still
afloat—still able to fight, perhaps." He thought a moment
then shook his head. "This is taking too long. We must
go through and finish her. Full ahead!" Von Scholtz, stone-
faced, acknowledged the Admiral's order and moved off to
join his officers.

Colonel Zeltmann stood just inside the entrance hatch,
wolf-faced, promising himself that if just one trooper were
wounded, or the timetable changed by more than five
minutes, the Admiral would answer for it in some tall
chamber in Berlin. . . . He stalked from the Bridge to join
his men.

Reaching the main deck, he could feel the great cruiser
gaining speed, surging forward again at full power—why, in
God's name, why? Obviously the English destroyer has got
off a signal long ago, warning the rest of the force, so the
longer we linger here, the greater the danger. But Mann
must preserve the Navy's honour—that Englishman has
damaged two of our destroyers, so he *must be sunk*, regard-

less of the cost.... Once more the Navy betrays the Wehrmacht, betrays the Fatherland!

Most of the troopers had drifted back to the rail. The Colonel strode to Sergeant Neuhofer and stood silently beside him, staring at the great, grimy smear of smoke. He considered ordering the men below, but thought better of it—that would only unnerve them. Unable to see what was going on, they would feel trapped....

"Sergeant, get the men back into cover."

"Sir!"—Ernst moved along the crowded rail, bawling the order, hauling and shoving some of them. "Back—and keep your heads down! Come on, *move*, damn you!"

By the time the last of them had found corners to crouch in, and the Colonel had ordered Ernst himself to take cover, the ship was within five hundred yards of the smokescreen.

0914–1000 hours
North Sea/8 April 1940

THE SMOKESCREEN was thinning out rapidly now. The gusting, swirling wind dragged it over the racing waves, tore gaps in the upper layers. And through one of these gaps a lookout, sticking to his post high on *Glowworm*'s rigging despite the crackling tongues of flame reaching for him from the deck, spotted *Hipper*'s towering masthead cutting into the barrier less than five cables astern, and yelped a warning to the Bridge.

Glowworm was running North now, about one cable inside the smoke. Amazingly, she still had almost full power—but Wreyford knew it couldn't last. Every second must be made to count. Fate had ruled that the enemy cruiser was going to come through at very close range. He must select, swiftly and with utmost cunning, their closing paths, so as to give Campbell the best possible chance with his torpedoes.

149

"Starboard—hard over! Stand by to fire torpedoes! Portside first!"

Campbell, clothing in grimy shreds and white face set in dire resolution, started for the torpedo on the partially wrecked port wing. "Good luck, Jim," Wreyford said quietly as he passed. Campbell glanced at him, nodded, and picked his way through the debris. He found the sight still intact—and was startled at the surge of excitement he felt.

Over by the starboard bulkhead Fielden tried to push himself on to his feet—I have to see, I must *see*. . . . But his body wouldn't obey. His muscles were jelly and the slightest exertion made him giddy and breathless. He twisted slightly and studied Wreyford's profile. The Captain was intently watching the smokescreen. His face was composed—almost, it seemed, at peace. Emerson's line sang in Fielden's mind—'Do the thing you fear to do, and the death of fear is inevitable . . .'

Valentino lurched, choking and shaking like a man in fever, from a hatchway on to the wind-whipped deck. Smoke and heat had driven him from the wreckage of the galley-pantry where he'd been huddled for more than an hour. His wild eyes stared for'ard at the dull-roaring flames then lifted to the shattered aerials and rigging.

On his way up he'd passed the remains of the Ward Room: a smouldering charnel house. The fumes of burning paint, cordite, and the stench of roasted human flesh clung to him like a slimy, suffocating caul. He had ceased to reason, he was impelled now only by a crazed need to get away from the sights, sounds, and smells of this appalling event—to break out of this burning, disintegrating prison, to be free of the terror and the torture even if it meant leaping to oblivion in the freezing sea.

He began to grope his way aft, away from the fo'c'sle fire, keeping close to the superstructure—like a blind man feeling his way along a blank and unfamiliar wall. He drew near 'Y'-gun and halted, body hunching in revulsion, as he saw two wounded men huddled in blood-blotched blankets under the shield, shuddering in shock, like lost children in a bus shelter. Ossie Knowles was bent over them, feeding them sips from his rum bottle. He had a quick nip himself and then as he straightened he noticed Valentino.

"What's up, Rudi?" With forced cheerfulness. "You hurt?"

The steward didn't answer. He stayed slumped against the superstructure, boggling about him with his huge eyes. The ship was turning tightly, dipping her freeboard. Stinging spray drenched all of them but Valentino didn't stir. Ossie stuffed his emergency box back into its recess and moved closer to him.

"Ain't you supposed to be below?" Still no response. Ossie gripped his shoulder, shook him. "Look, you can 'elp take those lads along to Doc, then stay an' give an 'and in Sick Bay, eh?"

A flicker of expression came back into the slack brown face—"Doc . . . ? Doc is gone—they are all gone." Little more than a whisper.

"What—you sure?"

Valentino closed his eyes, moved his head in small quick nods. Ossie groaned a curse, a glimpse of the bear-like Irishman flashing across his mind—'Olcers, Knowles! Olcers is what ye'll have me boy, sure as little pigs grow tails! The drink's burnin' up yer liver. Bluidy olcers, big as fried eggs . . .'

He turned and for a moment gazed desolately at the raging fire for'ard, then he jerked a thumb at the gun and the two surviving members of his crew—"You can give an 'and on 'ere, then. I need another loader." Valentino cowered back, shaking his head. Ossie gripped him again, roughly—"C'mon, Malt! You'll be a bloody sight better off

151

with a job to do. Take my word for it."

Valentino went limp and allowed himself to be led to the gun.

Glowworm came about, plunging and rearing boisterously. She was a sorry, incredible sight—trailing tangles of shattered rigging, lines, deck gear, and assorted wreckage. Her bows were a grotesque tangle—black-gaping like a dead mouth, gulping tons of white water each time she pitched—and everything between them and 'B'-gun's raised platform was engulfed in flames and smoke. Big, ragged holes scarred the length of her hull; lifeboats, rafts, and floats hung broken and askew and her for'ard funnel had more holes than a nightwatchman's bucket. Yet miraculously she was still making more than twenty knots, slicing Sou'-East, approaching the smokescreen at an angle of roughly forty-five degrees.

Campbell manipulated the port torpedo sight. As the ship jarred into a roller, then rose and tilted over the next trough, his stomach heaved and his head spun. He dry-retched helplessly. When he opened his eyes again Wreyford was beside him, staring intently at the smokescreen.

"Any moment now," the Captain said, almost blithely. "I'll hold this heading as long as I can. All right?"

"Fine, sir," Campbell croaked. Wreyford shot him a searching glance but said nothing more. Campbell leant out and looked aft. Keelie Grant was on the port torpedo tubes. He sat on a small, raised platform, exposed to wind and spray, ready to operate the firing switches. Below him, on the open deck, at times waist-deep in rushing white water, Eddie Nisbett manned the electric controls which trained the tubes.

Campbell checked his communications once more—"Bridge to portside tubes, how do you read?"

Grant had the headset. He looked up at the Bridge and gave a cheery thumbs-up sign—"Loud'n clear, sir!"

"Right, stand by." He straightened, wiped his aching, watering eyes. Moments later Wreyford jerked forward, pointed. A huge grey shape loomed through the thinning smokescreen, about half-a-mile off.

"Target bearing red four-o-degrees, range eight hundred yards! Engage, engage!" The Captain's voice rang out and a rating, standing by on the speaking tubes, instantly repeated the order. Campbell swung the sight, lined up and began calling off the settings to Grant.

The crews of the two guns still in action, 'X' and 'Y', frantically swivelled their pieces on to the huge target. On 'B'-gun, just below the Bridge, Bunty Baker's men and two of the Damage Control party were still slaving to free the shield, jammed by a chunk of the shattered for'ard winch, wedged underneath. Tinker Bell was howling curses, ripping his fingernails as he levered and jabbed with a crowbar.

Wreyford could see the heavy cruiser's for'ard guns coming round and down to bear upon him, and in those few seconds, before both ships opened fire, he felt the full, terrible magnitude of what he was doing. Yet at the same time he knew, without the smallest doubt now, that it was inescapable.

He seemed to be two people: one detached, cool, and clear-minded, the other tense and heavy with sadness—I know what I must do, exactly, and it's as if I were watching myself. My men are going to die, I'm doing this to them, they know it and I know it—and yet it isn't wholly real, a part of me is dissociated.... This is the moment I have always feared, sought so hard to avoid. But the moment is here, unavoidable. I am facing it—and suddenly there is no more fear, only this anxiety to do it well, not to waste all we have already spent; and this regret, this deep grief that war has brought us to this extremity....

He tore his gaze from the enemy ship and glanced quickly

all around him—at the flames, the wreckage, the firefighters and gun crews toiling amid the chaos fore and aft; at Campbell, weak with cold and sickness, bent over the sight beside him; at the others, still at their posts on the Bridge. And at Fielden, propped up in the far corner, everything about him still as a carving except the bright, anxious, flicking eyes. . . .

Even in the poor grey light everything seemed sharper etched. David's face, Campbell's, and those of the ratings—their colouring, the very texture of their skins—were vivid and poignantly familiar. This whole little world of which he was ruler—this tired, battered, despised ship and her long-suffering inhabitants—in this moment was magnified and overwhelmingly dear to him.

And then—all thought was squashed in the crazed, crashing symphony of combat. *Glowworm* staggered and heeled over as all around her the sea erupted in giant white geysers.

Mann's officers scrambled for handholds as one of *Glowworm*'s small shells struck the lower Bridge. Slivers of perspex flew perilously close by the Admiral's head. He didn't flinch. He stood at the sidescreen, still and grave, then turned and looked down at the main deck.

A young gunner, Ritter, manning a secondary post, was slumped over the shield, quite obviously dead. Everywhere the soldiers were down flat, some covering their heads with their equipment. Shrapnel and fragments of metal from the hit had rained down and wounded several of them. Between the crashings of the guns Mann heard shrill screams. He walked back on to the Bridge, beckoned to Stenz—"There are casualties down there. Inform the Medical Officer."

A man close to Schiller was writhing, shrieking, fumbling with a gaping wound in his thigh. Schiller felt some of the spurting blood splash his cheek. He scrambled up and started to run, blindly, stumbling over prostrate men, panic drumming in him. Ernst yelled in rage, launched himself after the boy and brought him down with a hard tackle. Their chests slammed the plates an instant before another British shell struck the 'midships turret. It made no impression on the tough steel but it filled the air with singing shrapnel and more cries went up. Schiller kicked and squirmed. Ernst rolled him on to his side and belted him on the jaw. The kid subsided, limp, in a trembling trance. Ernst glared into his grey, glistening face and cursed him slowly, methodically.

Valentino, taking the place of the wounded loader, had become part of the rhythm of Ossie's depleted crew. He toiled in a daze, his terror stilled by the steady, repetitive process. Deaf to the din of battle, blind to the fire and iron raining down around him and immune to the reek and heat, the Maltese was hypnotized by the smooth action of the hydraulic tubes and valves—the gun's powerful, flexing muscles, receiving and absorbing the tremendous shock of each explosion.

Ossie, virtuoso of the 4·7, knew at least one of his bricks had smashed into the *Hipper*'s superstructure. But he was having difficulty now in sighting: the spray thrown up by the enemy salvos was obscuring the target.

Then: a cataclysmic blast, just aft of the Bridge, and a wave of heat that sent the men reeling, clutching for support, completely thrown out of their stride. When the smoke cleared they saw that 'X'-gun, for'ard of them, was a smashed, blackened ruin. The gun captain, Grannie Smith, and four other survivors, all wounded, came crawling out of the smoking wreckage, two of them mindlessly, like crushed beetles, dragging themselves in circles.

Ossie's gunlayer started for'ard to help but Ossie flung an arm across his chest—"No! Keep firing!" The layer stared blankly. Ossie shoved him back to his post. The others

155

picked themselves up and another brick slid into 'Y'-gun's reeking breech.

Smith and another man reached them and crawled behind the shield. Grannie's legs were raw flesh and his face and hair were burned. His companion's right foot was almost severed, hanging by a strip of skin and sinew. All that Ossie could do was to reach under the shield and hand Smith his emergency ditty-box.

In a dim cubby-hole several decks down, Hobson was holding the emergency throttles wide open. Near-naked, his skin streaked with dirt and blood, his lungs heaving in more steam than air, with the massive muscles of his arms and shoulders bulging and quivering he was the lone Atlas holding up the small disintegrating world of *Glowworm*. But not for much longer: the pressure was dropping, the power was ebbing away steadily—he could feel her dying under his hands. . . .

Baker and his crew were still struggling to dislodge the chunk of mangled winch-drum jamming 'B'-gun. Tinker hurled away his crowbar, clawed at the metal with his bare hands and tried to curse it loose, to blast it away with the force of his own fury. A few yards away the foredeck fire, fanned by a gust, flared up again momentarily and most of the men fell back, shielding their faces. But Tinker stuck to his task, ignoring the licking flames and the sparks showering on his bent back, and the ammunition-ready boxes stacked only a yard from him.

Bunty, lying helpless behind the shield with his broken shoulder, watched the fire anxiously until the flames died down again. Then through the glare he saw Rosinsky with Lump and three or four others from Damage Control advancing on the blaze, pouring water into the heart of it, hauling their heavy hose-lines behind them like huge unwieldy tails. The Midshipman was waving an arm, shouting directions, but his voice was lost in the tumult.

Bunty felt rage rise in him. He pushed himself up on his good elbow, bawled at his exhausted crew—"Get back there, you useless bastards! Frigger—find us some tools! We'll cut through the bloody shield!"

Campbell waited for the columns of spray to settle and got *Hipper* in his sight again. The range was reasonable, the angle was good—if only the sea were calmer. Bile rose in his throat, the image blurred. He coughed harshly, heaved in cold air. The image sharpened again.

Wreyford was still beside him, biting on the unlit pipe. Campbell had to shout his final directions into the mike— "Coming up . . . Stand by—FIRE!"

On the portside firing platform Keelie Grant's numbed hand pulled the lever. The four big torpedoes, set to fire simultaneously, were launched from the long tubes into the raging sea by their small explosive charges. They hit the steep rising scend of a wave with mighty smacks, tossing up broad fans of spray. Somehow one of them caught the rearing crest—and bounced. The nose came up and it seemed to rise vertically, like a rocket, and hang there . . .

"Bluidy Christ!"—Keelie threw himself from the platform, crashed to his side on the deck. Nisbett was already flat against the side of the tubes.

Keelie twisted round, saw the huge fish suspended in the air, sliding very slowly astern—and was sure it was going to topple backwards on to the deck. Time measured in millionths of a second: until lazily, agonizingly, the missile tilted over and plummeted nose first into a yawning trough.

And went straight down.

Keelie sat up, flexing a bruised arm, and Nisbett warily raised his head. They saw the three remaining torpedoes creaming out through the monstrous humps of water, towards the enemy cruiser.

157

Mann riveted his glasses on the three faint, broken lines hem-stitching through the racing grey mounds, stretching out towards a point ahead of his bows—"Hard a'starboard!"

Precious seconds before the great ship began to swing—slowly, so slowly. Thrown off target by the sudden change of heading, *Hipper*'s guns fell momentarily silent and a talk-less tension gripped all those on the Bridge.

The torpedo tracks reached closer, drilling through the turbulence. And then suddenly there were only two of them: one must have been caught by a breaker—tipped over so that its gyro-controls toppled. Either it had swerved off out of control, or dived straight to the bottom.

The cruiser was coming round smoothly now. Thirty seconds more and it was clear to Mann that the remaining torpedoes would pass harmlessly to port.

The suddenness and boldness of the torpedo attack had surprised him—the damned audacity of it. . . . One little ship, maimed, dismembered, burning. Doomed, but defiant still—I cannot allow this to continue, we must *finish* her, at once. . . .

He dropped his glasses—"Hard over. We'll come right round, and run at her head-on!"

Wreyford dropped his head a moment in disappointment, then straightened—"Port, hard over!" He watched Campbell, ivory-faced, disconnect the communications leads, cross to the other side of the Bridge, and prepare to fire the starboard torpedoes.

Fielden sat in his corner, a hunched ghost, staring vacantly at the Lieutenant's legs, his hand pressing his wounded side. Wreyford walked over to him. The bleeding seemed to have stopped but his breathing was shallow and his eyes, lifting to meet the Captain's, were clouded, defocused. His jaws were stubbled and Wreyford noted with surprise that around the mouth and chin his beard was pure white, giving the lower part of his face the appealing look old dogs have.

Glowworm was slowing now, Wreyford could feel her pulse weakening—and David is dying with her ... David, the only man I can call my true friend, the one I can really talk to—and who had the nerve and the honesty to talk back to me. ...

He looked down into the slender aristocratic face, now so strangely older, and wanted very badly to say something sincere, comforting. But no words formed. So he touched Fielden's shoulder and gave him a small smile.

Both ships were firing again: it sounded as if only one of *Glowworm*'s guns was still in action. Wreyford glanced at his watch, turned and marched into the Chart Room—the ship's plot no longer mattered, but the Log must be kept up. ...

Fielden watched him go. Turning his head was an effort. His senses were numbed but his mind was clear, moving in a sad, affectionate, rueful theme—this sweet, grave, monotonous man, Garry Wreyford, with his senseless, infuriating scrupulosity, suddenly is holding history in his hands and I don't believe he even knows it. ... According to the Royal Naval College, Osborne, 'a good, average officer,' but in fact a rarity—son of a pacifist, and himself deeply compassionate, totally unfitted for making war—my God what is he *doing* here?

Damned stupid—what are any of us doing here? Who among us is fitted for this savagery?

He felt like a man pleasantly drunk, verging on the maudlin, full of a wry humility—none fitted less than I, a gentleman addicted to the countryside, to the crackle of a log fire in an old iron basket and the occasional hiss of a syphon ... a dabbler in writing, basically indolent, given to pompous quotations, amateur psychology, and melancholy meditations—Lord, why am I here?

Because my name is Fielden—there have been Fieldens

159

in the Navy since the days of Drake, a family full of cocked hats and sea-chests. . . . I was born into the Service—boxed in and lagged up by tradition. . . . I wanted to farm, I never wanted anything else. Perhaps if I'd had a brother, if I hadn't been an only child, there might have been a chance— I'd have married Lucille and by now I'd have my dairy herd. . . .

But an only child, who's a sailor's child, is a lonely child— and so I stayed alone, and surrendered to the tradition, surrendered myself to the sea . . . and to this bloody day. . . .

And here the Fieldens end. I felt sure it would come one day, it seemed obligatory, the only fitting end to the tradition; but not so soon—who could have foreseen this morning's events? No one. I am not the only one asking himself 'why am I here?' We are all the prisoners of an evil time, condemned to pay for Mankind's failures.

And Garry Wreyford, having accepted the verdict, is as well-equipped as any man to lead us to our graves. . . .

Keelie Grant had made his way across to the starboard firing platform. He clambered into position, plugged in his headset and answered Campbell's test-call while Nisbett swivelled the long tubes through their full arc. As *Glowworm* straightened on to her new Nor'-Westerly heading the tips of the tubes, protruding over the side, at times disappeared beneath the rearing racing water and the men were drenched by splatterings of spray.

Then Keelie saw *Hipper* again, closer now, just under half-a-mile away. She was converging, full out, at an angle of about forty-five degrees, but swinging to port to close at almost right-angles, thereby presenting the smallest possible target. Her great guns were pounding and once more *Glowworm* began to take impossible punishment. Shell after shell plunged into the destroyer. Hunks of plate and shrapnel clattered on her decks, hissed into the water, and new fires sprang up all along her. Keelie knew she had only minutes left.

And then Campbell's voice crackled in his ears, calling the settings. He bawled them out to Nisbett and they began to line up the tubes.

In the after magazine four men were toiling fiercely, keeping the shells flowing up the lift to the one remaining gun. They were blind to the battle, shut away in their small steel box, but explosion after explosion staggered them, sent them bumping into one another, mouthing oaths, and they could feel the ship shuddering, reeling under each blow. Of the four, the most energetic was the smallest—the Jockey. Gasping, soaked with sweat and grinning with fright, he worked in a snatching, fumbling frenzy.

They didn't hear the explosion, it was too close. The shell burst on the same level, two compartments away. The flush-tight hatchway was blasted inwards. A rating standing a yard from Jockey was caught by the thick slab of metal and smashed to a pulp against the bulkhead. The Jockey felt himself picked up, dashed against the inner wall. The lights went out but the room was filled with a flickering glow.

As he disentangled himself from the confusion of bodies the heat lashed at him. Beyond the shattered hatchway the passageway was a seething inferno. The others picked themselves up, shielding their faces. The flames were licking towards them, burning up the air. In a matter of seconds the stacked ammunition would go up. . . .

"Out! We gorra run through it!"—he grabbed the man nearest to him, Keegan, and shook him frantically. Keegan stared at the flames, lurched towards the door—then recoiled with a strangled cry.

The Jockey screeched at Keegan and the third man—"It's our only chance!" He pulled at his clothing, trying to cover his hands and face, then he closed his eyes, shivered once convulsively, bowed his head, flung himself at the hatchway and vanished into the flames. Keegan uttered a moan, threw his arms over his head and launched himself after him.

The third man was Ted Pearson, aged twenty. Left alone, he pressed back against the inner bulkhead, sobbing in terror. The heat grew more intense, his lungs were bursting, he could feel his hair begin to smoulder and his skin frizzle taut. He threw up his arms, lurched towards the wall of flame but the searing blast of it drove him back. Twice more he tried, but it was like throwing himself against a screen of spikes.

Now there were flickers of flame, flowing like liquid on the floor all around him. He flattened himself against the bulkhead and released a raw despairing wail. Then he threw himself face downwards across the rows of shells, arms spread wide. Body shuddering, eyes screwed up tight, he waited for the annihilating blast. . . .

The Jockey burst on to the deck not far from 'Y'-gun. Ossie and his crew froze as the nightmare figure careered past, the remnants of clothing, even his hair, ablaze. He blundered into some wreckage, went down and rolled, like a small bundle of burning rags, into the scuppers. A wave broke over him, putting out the flames. He lay blackened, his small body twitching.

Then came Keegan, a second blazing brand. He stumbled straight to the rail, screaming harshly all the way, and threw himself headlong into the sea.

Ossie bawled his men out of their shocked trance and started across the littered, buckled deck to the Jockey. But he had taken only three paces when the ship lifted in the water and there was an immense, roaring flash. He was thrown back against the gunshield. And there he watched a huge split open diagonally just for'ard of the gun. Tongues of flame thrust up and were fanned by the wind.

The after magazine had gone up.

Wreyford craned far out over the starboard Bridge wing, surveying the ruin. Everything aft of the Bridge now was swathed in smoke and flame but he glimpsed the two ratings manning the starboard tubes, and 'Y'-gun's crew still at their posts, shielding their faces from alternating gusts of fire and spray.

Beside him, Campbell sagged to one side and was violently ill. Wreyford straightened, looked at him, said nothing, Campbell gulped air, wiped his mouth and went back to work on the sight—"Coming up, stand by!"

"Ay ay, sir!"—Keelie gripped the firing lever. The crackling flames from the ruptured deck and the leaping fans of spray completely obscured his view of the enemy, but he could *feel* the cruiser's nearness. The Lieutenant, up on Bridge, must have her clamped in the sight. He yelled down at Nisbett—"We'll do the bugger this time, bet yer bluidy life!"

Neither of them had an instant's warning. The shell hit the deck six yards behind them. Keelie was decapitated. His body was slammed forward over the controls, big hands dangling, swinging. Nisbett was hurled through the air, slammed against a bulkhead. He lay senseless, blood pouring from a broken nose and shattered mouth. Campbell tore off the headset, leaned out and peered aft—"Oh, Christ, oh, Christ!" he said, over and over. Then he pulled his gaze back and saw the dim, enlarging outline of the *Hipper* bearing down for the kill. He blundered to the ladder, started down for the tubes.

Wreyford didn't see him go. He was at the for'ard screen, looking down on the blazing foredeck, watching Rosinsky and his Damage Control party pouring water into the heart of the fo'c'sle fire. A wonder that their lines were still working—and it seemed to him that they had the flames under control now, preventing them from spreading aft to the Bridge structure.

Fielden stared at Campbell's abandoned headset, swinging on its lead two yards from his face. He realized what had happened: the men on the tubes were knocked out and the Lieutenant had gone down to try to fire the torpedoes himself—blind. . . . He tried three times before he succeeded in hauling himself to his feet. As his body straightened the pain moved through his chest like a slicing blade. He stifled a cry and, leaning a shoulder against the bulwark, edged along to the sight.

He reached for the headset. His hand shook, his fingers were like mutton, but he fumbled it on. As he jerked out the words he could taste blood in his mouth, feel it oozing down his chin—"Bridge to tubes—do you read me, Guns?"

Seconds passed, then Campbell responded—faint as a voice from another planet. He couldn't make out the words but that didn't matter—*as long as he can hear me. . . .*

He coughed, spluttering, spewing blood. The pain in his chest almost doubled him up, his eyes dimmed and his knees tried to fold. But he gripped the sight, clung on. He could see *Hipper* racing in, almost head on now, not more than five hundred yards away. He manipulated the sight and began to stammer out the settings.

Through his glasses Mann saw *Glowworm* now as little more than a smear of smoke and flame intermittently veiled by spouts of spray from *Hipper*'s shells. But still she held to her course and as she porpoised heavily over a mighty wave he glimpsed a lone figure at the torpedo tubes.

"God in Heaven—he's going to try again!"

Campbell had had to heave Grant's headless body off the platform. His hands and clothes were soaked with blood. The tubes appeared to be only slightly damaged and when he donned the headset he could hear Fielden's voice. But when he tried to line up the tubes to the new settings he found the electric motors were useless. He began to align them by hand, working the control wheels and levers frantically. His arms and legs were weak and his movements were awkward, unco-ordinated. His feet slithered in the pool of Grant's blood. A terrible nausea heaved in him. He heard himself cursing shrilly.

Slowly the big tubes swung on to the prescribed bearing. Praying that the enemy hadn't altered course in the meantime, he got back on to the platform, grasped the firing levers. The left side of his face and those parts of his body exposed by his torn clothing were being roasted by waves of heat from the flames licking up through the split deck a few yards aft. His eyes began to stream, he could see nothing but scudding spray and billows of smoke. He plugged in the headset and bawled—"Tubes to Bridge, tubes to Bridge. . . ."

Back came Fielden's thick, labouring voice—"Fire, fire, fire . . . !" But in the same moment the ship rolled to starboard and the tips of the tubes were buried in a hill of water. Campbell was inclined to risk firing anyway, but thought better of it—the angle was too steep, the gyros might be toppled. He waited, listening to his heart mark out the long seconds and Fielden's slurred, desperate intoning—"Fire, fire . . . !"

Glowworm heaved herself on to an even keel, the tubes rose clear. Campbell threw the lever. The four long cylinders flopped into the sea. When the splashes subsided he saw they were running true, scoring clean wakes along a wide trough.

Von Scholtz and Mann had seen the torpedoes go in. The range was down to only four hundred yards. It wasn't going to be so easy to dodge them this time, but the Admiral sounded crisp and confident—"Port, hard over!"

Just as *Hipper* began to wheel her guns scored another hit on *Glowworm*, aft of the Bridge structure, high up. Then the firing tapered off again as the controllers adjusted to the changing angle and range.

Ernst Neuhofer left Metchik with the inert Stummer and the trembling Schiller and crawled to the rail. The sight he beheld was awesome, he would remember it forever: the wrecked and burning British destroyer still boring in, so frighteningly near now he felt that if she blew up—as he was sure she would, at any moment—the blast would rip the cruiser apart and shower her decks with blazing debris. And reaching out through the tumbling water, straight as spears, vanishing where the waves reared and reappearing in the furrows, came the four torpedo tracks.

Ernst wanted to creep away—to cower on the other side, hide his head and hold on to a life raft. But the oncoming torpedoes hypnotized him. He could feel *Hipper* turning sharply, but it seemed impossible that she could avoid all four. He felt helpless—he was a fighting man, but this was something he couldn't fight. He had an insane urge to grab a machine-gun and blaze away at these weird white enemies that were charging in on him. . . .

Wreyford clambered to his feet, pushed aside the rating who was trying to help him. The latest hit, high overhead, had thrown him across the Bridge into a heap by the Chart Room hatchway. He'd lost his helmet, but so far as he could tell he wasn't wounded. He lurched over to the port wing where Fielden was draped over the sight, his clouded eyes fixed on the four faint torpedo tracks.

Wreyford found he still had his glasses slung from his neck. He whipped them up and saw almost immediately that three of the fish were going to pass astern of the tight-turning target. Everything rested on the fourth.

Fielden swayed, bumped into his shoulder. The Number

One's breathing came now in grunts and gurgling coughs. Wreyford held him and kept watching the fourth torpedo, their last hope—until it too passed out of sight under the enemy's stern plate.

It had missed by a few yards.

Fielden slumped and Wreyford lowered him gently to the deck. The blanket lay near by, soggy and rumpled. Wreyford reached for it, then changed his mind. He slipped out of his lifejacket, took off his duffel and wrapped it round Fielden. Then he took off his jacket and folded it to make a pillow.

Mann released pent air from his lungs—" 'Midships!" Then beside him the normally phlegmatic Von Scholtz was fiery-faced, waving a bunched fist.

"Fire! Fire! *Sink* her!"—he almost screamed it.

Hipper began to come out of her turn and once more her guns crashed out. Now the range was almost point blank, but still the dying destroyer ploughed on and from somewhere amid the moving island of flames and smoke one of her guns continued to pump defiance.

Mann couldn't understand how she remained afloat—and still moving. He'd lost count of the hits she'd taken, she should have gone down, or blown up, long ago. . . . He felt, more than saw, the stiff figure of Colonel Zeltmann reappear at the top of the ladder. He moved closer to the sidescreen and raised his glasses again—to avoid looking at him.

Fielden's lips moved and Wreyford bent over him closely. Blood was oozing steadily from his mouth, thick and dark. His eyes now were strangely large and soft, like a woman's.

"One move left, Garry." Wreyford could barely catch the gurgled syllables. "You'll do it—you and *Glowworm*." Wreyford only nodded: his own voice wouldn't come at all.

167

"You'll do it...." Fielden felt his vision dimming away. He closed his eyes. Behind the lids bright, warm images flickered—he was walking up a steep cobbled street in a country town, a street banked like a staircase, with tiny flower-proud gardens, tiny cottages, tiny shops and cafes.... White walls, black beams, the sunlight blowing past in bright gusts. A busy town, life bubbling about him, yet he walked alone. Always, always alone—each of us enters this world alone, and leaves it alone. 'I never found the companion that was so companionable as solitude,' says Thoreau—and he's right. I am by nature an observer of life, a traveller and a spectator—but the world has tricked me, made me feel an involvement, a duty, and thereby forced me to participate in a most savage event....

Now he had left the town, he was crossing a high meadow, not walking any more—riding, I'm riding the bay hunter. Towards the trees. Beeches, oaks—sometimes I'm afraid of trees, the way they thrust up so straight and dwarfing, with such awful strength in their limbs and sly twists to their trunks. Looming silently over me, more monstrous when they're still than when swaying or lashing in a wind....

But beyond the trees: old sandy bricks and pitted beams, a leaning chimney, long low rooms with latticed windows that bulge like thyroid eyes and floors that slope and creak —all a million miles from the sea. Home. The small Tudor manor cold and empty and, like an old man, so beautiful in its dilapidation—oh, God, who will live here now? I'm the last Fielden. Always alone, I leave no-one, nothing, not even a grave. Only the trees! What madness led me to choose the sea, a bare cold plain? Let me see the trees, the great, green trees, I must see the trees again....

His head slumped forward. Wreyford touched the tangled hair, then slowly stroked both hands down the slender stubbled face. His fingers lifted blood from the

168

chin. He stared at the blood, and sorrow and outrage were a blinding, beating pain—this death was to him a wholly physical thing, like an amputation.

He stood there, more alone than ever he had been. A dishevelled, doomed man, with bloody hands, hatless and in his shirtsleeves, the Arctic wind plucking at his hair and clothing. The storm beating about him, and inside of him. The battle sounds growing again and sparks from the fore-deck fire spitting in his face.

He looked about him: this jinxed ship, the *Worm*—the joke ship, dunce of the flotilla, with all her mishaps and breakdowns—now behaving magnificently, mortally wounded but stubbornly, astoundingly refusing to die. . . . His senses were wide open to all the moment's epic sights. Once more he looked down at the inferno of the foredeck, at the jammed 'B'-gun and the men still battling to free it. He looked up at the tangle of broken mast, rigging, and aerials—and wondered again if enough of his signal had reached *Renown* or Admiralty before Kelsey and the Wire-less Room were destroyed, or if *Glowworm's* martyrdom was completely futile. . . .

He walked back to the port screen and looked aft, at all the ruin—at the wreckage of TS and the Ward Room; at the dead and dying left sprawled where they'd fallen and at the flames shooting up through the long ragged split in the deck. . . . On all sides: sundered bulkheads, splintered rafts and twisted metal and the grey-white ocean reaching up hungrily, snapping at them.

Everywhere, death. Naked death there on the open deck, secret death in the boiling bowels of the ship—men were being roasted alive down there, their bodies splitting open, their fat and their blood vaporizing. And here on the Bridge: the closest death—David lying at his feet. He stared down at him and after a while became aware of some-one standing behind him. He turned to find Chief Petty

169

Officer Truman, his left arm soaked red, his hewn face streaked with soot and grime.

"Captain, sir, I've just been below. ERA Hobson's been trying to reach you. He's still on the emergency throttles. It's proper grim down there, sir—the fires are spreading, you can't hardly breath and the heat's something awful. But he won't leave."

"I see . . . how's the steam pressure?"

"Dropping fast now, sir. Hobson said to tell you, we won't have power more'n a few minutes."

Wreyford nodded solemnly—"Thank you, Chief." He lifted his head and saw, through the smoke, the *Hipper* racing in again to run across his bows. From *Glowworm*'s afterdeck: a defiant bark, and an instant later the vicious flash of a shell high on the German's hull. Wreyford glanced questioningly at Truman.

" 'Y'-gun, sir. All we got left."

"Ossie Knowles—yes. . . ." He scratched at his right thigh, looked out at the enemy ship again and it seemed to Truman that his face grew thinner. 'Y'-gun barked once more, then a near-miss from the cruiser jarred the maimed destroyer from stem to stern and showered her with tons of spray. The Bridge shook, Truman and the two ratings still at their posts staggered, snatching for handholds, but somehow the Captain kept his balance.

Then, with the last of the spray whipping at them, Wreyford turned and looked again at Fielden's body—one move left, yes, David. And one at which I might with justification claim to be a master. . . .

He strode to the bulkhead, lifted the mike. His voice boomed out through the gunfire—

"Ramming stations! Ramming stations!"

Of those still living in *Glowworm,* only a few heard the Captain, for only a small part of the speaker system was still working. Nevertheless the command was passed on

with startling speed—bawled through cupped hands, relayed by frantic hand signals and carried by crouching,
weaving runners from post to post above decks, and where-
ever men could still exist below.

It was a drill they knew by rote. Throughout the ship
everyone, whoever he was, whatever he was doing, went
down, flat on his belly. Everyone but those on the Bridge,
and two others vital to the manoeuvre: Wally Hobson,
hunched half-asphyxiated over his throttles down in Emergency Control, and Bobby Boyce, hanging on the helm in
the dim, damaged wheelhouse, cursing off the waves of
weakness and the pulsing pain of his smashed arm.

Up for'ard Rosinsky made Lump and the others wedge
their lines with pieces of debris so that the water would
continue to play into the heart of the fire. It was impossible
to lie down here, because the plates were too hot—a few
feet away they were glowing a fierce red. Besides, he remembered a lecture at Dartmouth: in a ramming run, no-
one must be near the bows. . . . He waved his party back
and got them down beside Baker's crew in cover of the
jammed 'B'-gun.

The Midshipman bellied forward, raised his head and
beyond the fire and the tatters of spray saw the awesome
loom of the enemy cruiser smashing through the wild sea;
so close now he could make out figures huddled on her main
deck and grouped behind the sidescreen of her tall combat
Bridge. The immense turrets thundered and belched and
he pressed his face on his forearms as another salvo straddled *Glowworm*.

One of the shells ripped through the forepeak, tearing a
wide hole in the red-hot deck, and exploded deep inside.
The bows lifted, the whole ship trembled and when he
raised his head again the fire they'd been fighting for what
seemed hours, in the space of a single second had taken
hold of everything for'ard of the Bridge.

171

He could see only a roaring, blinding wall of flame.

To Mann, the British destroyer now appeared as no more than an atoll of erupting fire and greasy black smoke, surrounded by rearing plumes of water. His secondary armament—even machine-guns—had joined in the bombardment and again and again there were flashes inside the smoke as round after round struck home. He watched, wordless, and couldn't believe it—this battered, blazing hulk was still moving.

Directly towards him. . . .

His mind at first wouldn't accept the crazy thought—we are close, but she cannot keep coming, she is losing power, I can see her slowing by the second now. . . . No, she is no more danger, she had nothing left, not one gun still firing. She can live only moments more. . . .

But the moments dragged by and still the distance between them narrowed. And then von Scholtz moved close to the Admiral, touched his arm. "Good God, she's . . ." —voice low and shaky, face stretched by dread realization —"she's trying to ram us!"

Mann no longer could reject the possibility. He could feel the others around him tensing, stirring. "Port, hard over!"—and even as he spoke the possibility became a probability, and he knew he might have waited too long; that if the destroyer kept coming at her present speed *Hipper,* with her big turning radius, wouldn't have time to get out of the way. . . .

Truman ducked down as shrapnel whined through the Bridge. The Captain remained craning over the starboard wing so as to see past the smoke. *Hipper* was starting to turn—awake to the danger, trying to get clear.

"Starboard twenty!" Truman went to the speaking tube, relayed the order to Boyce. An age seemed to pass before he felt *Glowworm* begin to swing round. With the change of direction the wind now was dragging the smoke down their port side and he could see the enemy clearly, only two hundred yards away, heeling over hard as she strove to pull away. Her big guns had stopped firing—the range was too close, they couldn't depress sufficiently—but her secondary guns, all the port length of her, were ravening, pumping shells and bullets across the storm-whipped water.

"Midships, steady as you go!"—Wreyford called it loud and steady and again Truman relayed to the wheelhouse.

"Steady on two-nine-five"—the young Cox'n's voice was a distant rasp. And then Truman felt *Glowworm*'s straining heart falter under him: she seemed to wallow in a trough and when the next wave came she staggered sideways and slewed.

His own heart missed a beat—"Power's going, sir!"

Wreyford's eyes remained fixed on the enemy but after a moment he smashed a fist down on the rail and yelled, as no-one ever had heard him before—"Come on, old girl, come *on*!"

And it seemed to Truman then that *Glowworm* shook herself, picked herself up on to the humped back of the next big sea—and went slogging on.

Small calibre shell-bursts filled the air with shrieking shrapnel and flying debris, bullets drummed and whanged in ricochets. The big Chief Petty Officer lurched over to the Captain and with his good arm pulled him from the wing. Regardless of rank and dignity, he held him pinned with his back against the shuddering inner bulkhead.

Mann was utterly still. It *was* too late, his huge ship was too clumsy, she turned too slowly. Collision now was inevitable—unless the British destroyer stopped dead in the water, or blew up.

173

Fury hammered in him. Fury at himself, at his two escorting destroyers who'd failed to cope with the threat and thereby forced him into this trap. And yet he knew that what he was watching and enduring was a supreme act of heroism and seamanship.

A part of him was humble, recalling the legend of Sir Richard Grenville and the *Revenge*—'God of battles, was ever a battle like this in the world before?' He was too wholly a sailor not to be moved, and ashamed of the role Fate was giving him.

Everything below decks in *Glowworm* was disintegrating. Tides of flame swept through the passages, buckled and broke through the bulkheads, sucked and devoured the oxygen. Shells burst in her entrails, releasing floods of oil, water, and steam.

With every jarring impact young Boyce cried out as the wheel kicked viciously and the bones grated in his shattered arm. The heat and the fumes were choking him, shrivelling his flesh. Yet the needle of the magnetic compass somehow stayed hovering around 295 degrees.

Deeper still in the dying ship, Wally Hobson was on his knees, only semi-conscious. His lungs heaved in fumes, pushed them out in tortured rasps. In the foul haze he couldn't see the gauges but the vibrations going through his body told him the pressure was almost gone. He clenched his hands harder on the emergency throttles—feeling his palms peel, split, and adhere to the sizling metal like steaks to a dry griddle.

Those who'd taken cover behind 'B'-gun were driven aft by the intensified foredeck blaze. They crouched at the base of the Bridge structure and Rosinsky saw that most of the hoses his party had abandoned amazingly were still operating, but the blast from the latest hit had blown them free of their wedged positions. Some were wriggling about like snakes, squirting haphazardly. One, riddled by shrapnel, tossed up a thin fan of water, like a garden sprinkler. Others, slithering into the scuppers, threw powerful jets over the side in graceful arcs which the wind caught, bent, and scattered. Against the flickering glare Jackie thought they made a strangely beautiful display.

And then he saw a tongue of flame licking towards 'B'-gun—reaching for the ammunition-ready boxes. He broke out at a crouching run, snatched up one of the loose lines and trained the jet on the boxes, soaking the ammunition. Then he dropped the hose and dragged one of the steaming boxes behind the shield.

Bunty and the others were yelling at him to get down but he went back for the second box. Machine-gun bullets came probing, blindly, through the flames and smoke. A hammer blow, smashing his chest like a rotted cask. He was hurled against the side of the jammed shield. He leant there a moment, like a lost and bewildered waif, then his legs folded and he pitched forward on to the blackened plates.

From the Bridge Wreyford and Truman had seen the Midshipman fall. The Captain refusing to be restrained, by the CPO, had moved back to the for'ard screen and Truman reluctantly had come to stand at his shoulder.

The CPO swore with soft intensity. The Captain closed his eyes and lowered his head, his shoulders hunched up and his body bent forward as if he'd been stabbed in the midriff.

At the base of the Bridge, Baker's crew and the Damage Control men were limp with shock, helpless with anger. The boy's death was a personal thing for each of them. The Snotty had represented something, a green kid who belonged to them all, a kind of mascot. But to one man he'd been much more than that: Lump had appointed himself Rosinsky's bodyguard. Some gentle instinct in the simple giant had responded to the Midshipman's smallness and vulnerability.

Now Lump felt he'd failed completely—he should have stayed with the boy, stopped him going out there, but as usual he'd been too slow. . . . He uttered a moan, started towards Rosinsky's body. Tinker leapt at him, spitting curses, but the big man shook him off like a paper doll.

Crouching, arms swinging, like a great ape Lump ran up the littered platform to 'B'-gun. He picked up the slight figure in his huge arms and started back. The wind veered momentarily, flattening the flames and smoke behind him, and the others saw the towering grey bulk of the cruiser— only about a hundred yards away now.

Lump made several paces in a weaving run, then high on *Hipper*'s foredeck a machine-gun blazed. The line of bullets flared along the platform like a quick-burning fuse and stitched all the way up Lump's broad back. He lurched, but didn't go down immediately. He staggered to the edge of the platform. For a long moment he stayed there, swaying, mouth slack and eyes fixed, vacant. Then the ship slammed into a wave and rolled. He pitched to the water in an amazingly low arc, Jackie's body still clasped in his arms.

Bunty pressed his brow against the shuddering bulkhead. Tinker, beside him, gave a piercing screech, a frantic animal cry, and half-rose, glaring all around. Several yards for'ard on the starboard side he saw an unmanned Lewis gun swinging on its post—abandoned long before the ramming order, because it was perilously close to the fire. He launched himself from cover before anyone could grab him, sprinted to the front of the platform, jumped down on to the foredeck and, ducking and zig-zagging through the darting flames, ran nimbly to the gun.

He swung it round, levelled it high and, feet planted wide, opened fire, raking the German's superstructure and main deck. The wind was taking the smoke away from him now and his view of the huge target was unobstructed. The heat battered him, long tentacles of flame whipped at him as though trying to pluck him into the heart of the inferno. And he was completely exposed to the enemy gunners. Bullets zipped and whined about him but, teeth clamped in a savage grin, bawling obscenities all the while as the old Lewis hammered out its defiance, he was in this moment crazily exhilarated.

Every sense singing, every nerve throbbing, Tinker Bell poured out all his life's rage and hostilities. A delinquent released, a violent criminal for whom war had found a purpose.

He emptied the ammo drum, threw it away, and was reaching for another when the answering cross-fire from *Hipper*'s machine-gunners found him, knocked him out from behind the Lewis. He staggered blindly, clutching his belly, lifted his head and glared at the cruiser looming like a prison wall, only sixty yards away now. His lips snarled in final rebellion—"Faggin' bastards!" Then he pivoted and, still clasping his stomach, plunged head first through the great red hole in the deck, into the furnace below.

All this, too, Wreyford witnessed, gazing down, from his shattered Bridge. Truman saw the Captain's body quiver, his mouth open wide, and for a moment he thought he'd been hit. Then: a blinding explosion above them. What remained of the foremast, struck by a small calibre shell, crashed down across the siren wires. And above the tumult of battle the sirens shrieked like demons—an insane, deafening sound that chilled the brain and made any further speech anywhere in *Glowworm* impossible.

Debris skittered down. Wreyford glanced up quickly, then returned his attention to the *Hipper*. The for'ard section of the cruiser now was emerging to starboard of the deck fire as she began to cross the destroyer's bows. The

177

distance was down to fifty yards. The sheer steel cliff of her hull rose and fell, twenty feet and more, and tilted sharply from side to side as both ships pitched and rolled —and Wreyford suddenly realized they were still in the grip of a full-blowing storm.

The gunfire from *Hipper* had slackened off, almost stopped—the violent see-sawing was making it hard for the gunners, and as the ships closed some of them couldn't depress their weapons sufficiently. The wail of *Glowworm*'s sirens, weirdly amok, seemed to rise in key and volume.

Truman found himself instinctively edging away, staring in awe at the great grey barrier looming closer. He pressed his back against the inner bulkhead, stiffening his legs.

Wreyford stayed at the for'ard screen, put his palms against the splintered wood and braced himself for the impact. *Hipper*'s high Bridge slid out of the smoke and, looking up, he could see her officers grouped at the screen. Their faces were white blotches behind the salt-speckled perspex. He felt no enmity, no self-consciousness either— only a momentary, detached curiosity. He had never seen the enemy until now. . . .

Glowworm, shuddering and yawing sluggishly, slapped through a razor-backed wave, paused an instant on the summit. Then as her broken, burning bows fell she seemed to find a final reserve of power and charged down the long smooth slope of water.

Von Scholtz and Stenz backed away from the side-screen, hands fluttering out for support as the doomed destroyer— this suicidal fire-ship, with her sirens yowling—came hurtling down the steep hill of water towards them. Only Mann and Zeltmann remained on the starboard side of the Bridge.

The Admiral found himself staring down into the upturned face of the British Captain: a lone figure, bareheaded, in shirtsleeves, standing perfectly still at his command post above the rushing smoke. Looking up at *Hipper*'s Bridge. Fifty yards . . . forty . . . thirty . . . for long seconds, as their ships rushed into deadly embrace, each commander was aware of the other's gaze. . . .

Glowworm's bows were incandescent and as they ploughed through the freezing sea huge clouds of steam hised up. She rose halfway on another wave, butter through the crest, tilted over again—and smashed down into *Hipper*'s fo'c'sle hull a little abaft of the anchor.

A tremendous, sustained grinding and screeching of metal. Deep, deep the destroyer's bows drove—fourteen feet into the cruiser's vitals, splitting her open from beneath the waterline almost all the way up to the main deck. The last of *Glowworm*'s foremast came down with the impact and abruptly the sirens stopped wailing.

The great cruiser shook like a city block in an earth tremor —but she kept moving, dragging the destroyer with her, gradually slowing with the burden. As the locked ships rose and fell, out of rhythm, the grinding continued and *Hipper*'s wound opened wider.

Then from somewhere inside the cruiser: a dull, rumbling explosion. Thousands of gallons of water from her fresh-water tanks, high in the fo'c'sle, poured down in a wide cataract. Within seconds the raging fire in *Glowworm*'s fore-peak was extinguished. Dense clouds of steam rose.

Hipper, mighty engines straining, hammered on doggedly and *Glowworm*'s stern swung round, narrowing the angle between them to around forty-five degrees. More terrible rendings inside the cruiser and then, at the waterline, big black bubbles boiled up and spread rapidly to form a thick viscous, gluey carpet.

Oil. *Hipper*'s fuel tanks had been ruptured.

Mann tore open the side-screen and looked down at the gaping wound, the oil bleeding away, the mangled hulk of the destroyer clinging—tenaciously, like a hound hanging from the throat of a running stag. *Glowworm*'s foredeck and Bridge were hidden now in a vast pall of steam, but 'midships and aft the fires still raged.

"We've got to break away from her—before she blows up!" the Admiral yelled and never had his officers heard him raise his voice like this. "Captain, we will try turning into her! Hard starboard!"

Zeltmann was close beside him, glaring malevolent accusation. Mann ignored him. The Colonel spun on his heels, stalked to the other end of the Bridge and surveyed the main deck. Most of his men were on their feet, shouting in bewilderment. Panic pulled at their faces and showed in the way they were moving, bumping into each other. The Colonel started down the ladder.

Ernst pushed his way through the mob and joined Petty Officer Hart at the rail. They peered down at the British destroyer—a wallowing hulk amid the steam and smoke and spreading oil—and Ernst began to stammer a question. But Hart didn't seem to hear. He ran to a phone on a nearby bulkhead and wound the handle vigorously.

Ernst looked down again. The cloud of steam thinned away and he saw a figure on the destroyer's Bridge: a tall man in a white shirt, his head bared, leaning with his hands on the for'ard rail and gazing up stonily—there he is, there's the enemy, the first Englishman I've seen! Why is he standing there so casually, in the open, like somebody looking out of his window at early morning? Why the Hell doesn't someone shoot him?

Wreyford felt Truman grip his elbow—"We've ripped his oil tanks, sir! Wide open!"

The Captain nodded thoughtfully, glancing down at the heaving black grease. "Yes we have, indeed we have." He might have been commenting on a cricket score.

Then from somewhere high on *Hipper* a machine-gun opened up again, firing wildly, hysterically. The bullets whined harmlessly overhead. Truman looked up and found himself gazing into slack faces under steel helmets, lining the cruiser's rail. They stared down at him, almost vacantly. He touched the Captain's arm again—"Sir . . . we'd best move back a bit now."

Wreyford blinked at him, then allowed himself to be led away from the for'ard screen. They stood together, word-less and purposeless, in the Chart Room hatchway.

Ossie Knowles and Valentino crouched behind 'Y'-gun's shield—the only members of the gun crew left. All the others had been wounded and immediately after the ramming Ossie had sent them back to the stern—starboard side, away from *Hipper*, taking the Jockey with them.

More bursts of machine-gun fire from the cruiser sprayed overhead. Ossie glowered, nudged the Maltese and nodded at the ready-box—"Three bricks left, mate. I didn't 'ear nobody order 'cease fire', did you?"

The brown eyes regarded him reproachfully, then Valen-tino crossed himself. Together they rose, loaded the gun, trained it with the barrel fully depressed. The cruiser's hull was only thirty yards away.

Ossie fired. The shell punched a neat round hole in *Hipper*'s plates. From overhead German voices yelling shrilly. They reloaded unhurriedly.

Wreyford heard the shot, moved to the wing, and looked aft. He watched, expressionless, as 'Y'-gun pumped a second round into *Hipper*, then a third. Only two men left operating the gun, Knowles and—with a jolt he recognized Valentino.

Steward, civilian—the Captain was filled with a lacerating sorrow, a massive sense of responsibility, and a deep wonder-ment. What was it that had bestowed on these men such in-candescent will?—from the moment we took the bait and went after those two destroyers, each of them must have known it would come to this . . . but they faced it, and they've done their work splendidly, spiritedly even. And so, by God, has *Glowworm*. . . .

And now it's done, we have nothing more to give. We can only wait for the enemy to shake us off and blow what's left of us to flotsam. . . . The most excruciating part of it all—the waiting. . . . This is what I have brought them to, my ship is a slaughterhouse—and none of us will know if we've served a purpose or if it's all been senseless, tragic waste. What I have done here—can it *ever* be justified . . . ?

A great groaning and shrieking of rending metal: the two ships broke apart and *Glowworm* slewed round, powerless, listing to starboard, wallowing. Through her black and broken bows the sea gushed in. *Hipper* drew away, still losing oil, and with her fractured fresh water tanks emptying through the huge cavity in her side.

No sound now but the keening of the Arctic wind, the dull roar of the flames aft and the hollow rushing of water below. The Captain spoke very quietly and calmly—"Abandon ship, Chief."

"Ay ay, sir"—Truman's uninjured arm rose in a text-book salute, then he hurried to the starboard wing, leaned over. "Abandon ship! Abandon ship!" he bellowed. Immediately the cry was taken up on the decks.

The two ratings still on the Bridge hesitated, looking at their Captain. He nodded curtly. They saluted and solemnly started down.

No sooner had they gone than a grey and tattered figure came slowly up the ladder. Campbell. He stood for a moment, limp and drained, looking at Fielden's body, then approached the Captain—"Sorry I couldn't do better with the torpedoes, sir."

Wreyford nodded, almost affably—"You did your best, Jim. Conditions weren't exactly ideal."

Campbell peered after *Hipper*—"That's a pretty big hole

we made. He'll have to head straight back to base."

"Let's hope so." A short silence, then Truman came back from the wing. The Captain addressed both of them. "See that the wounded go first. Put them on the rafts and floats."

They waited expectantly. Wreyford's brows rose slightly. "Carry on, then." They saluted, Campbell with absolute correctness, turned, and left the Bridge.

Wreyford, left alone, took another look at *Hipper*, drawing steadily away in a gentle starboard turn. Already her big guns were swinging round, preparing to administer the *coup de grâce*. He turned his back on her and went over to stand by the body of his Number One. Lieutenant David Fielden, RN, officer and country gentleman—have you no apt last lines to quote for me now, my friend? No cynical, tender epitaph . . .?

He turned away, went into the Chart Room. The table was wrecked, maps and instruments were strewn all around, but the green-tinged light still worked. He searched in the debris and found the Logbook. Then he picked his way through the wreckage to his sea-cabin and rummaged in his locker.

He found a jacket and a cap and moved to the broken mirror on the bulkhead. The face that stared back at him was grave, the eyes were piercing, demanding. The face of a stranger, almost—somewhere there's a missing link, something still hasn't been explained. But what? David could tell me, but David's gone. What's the mystery, what is it I want to know?

The strange face frowned out from the jagged glass—it's he, yes *he* is the riddle! How could he do what he's done, *how*?

The ship lurched, the list increased sharply. She was settling deeper and he knew she would capsize. He slipped on the jacket and buttoned it carefully.

Mann couldn't take his eyes from *Glowworm*—the

foundering destroyer seemed to fascinate him. He was haunted by the image of that enemy Captain—hatless, dishevelled, alone on his mangled Bridge, perfectly still, leaning on his hands with his face uplifted—like a preacher praying in the pulpit. . . . And he was astounded by the cool impudence of the British sailors who'd stuck to the destroyer's one remaining gun and fired their last rounds while the ships were locked together.

A tactful cough beside him, he tore his gaze round. Stenz clicked his heels—"Preliminary damage report, sir. Seven fuel tanks destroyed. All our fresh water and the entire re-frigeration system gone. Extensive flooding below decks. Watertight bulkheads closed—and holding."

Von Scholtz and Zeltmann were just behind Stenz. The Captain spoke in a desolate tone—"We will have to return to Keil, sir. Immediately." The Colonel jerked as if he'd been slapped and his eyes drilled hotly into the Admiral's. Mann held his gaze a moment then turned to stare once more at *Glowworm*. The dying destroyer was low in the water now—even in these few seconds while his attention had been diverted the stern had settled and her starboard list had increased. The big waves besieged her, battering at her cloven bows, exploding into her belly—eager to roll her over into her grave. He saw again, in his mind's eye, that solitary figure on the smashed Bridge. . . .

"Stop ship!" the Admiral said.

An electric, stirless silence. He turned his head and scanned their stunned, unbelieving faces. "Stop ship, I said. We may be able to pick up some of these men."

Zeltmann stepped forward, tensed like a cat—"You cannot do that! The enemy ship is still afloat—she could attack again, while we were stationary!"

Once more Mann stared aft at the blazing, heeling shambles that had been HMS *Glowworm*. "No. She has nothing left. She has given it all."

Von Scholtz exchanged a dazed look with Stenz then drew nearer to the Admiral, "Sir, you said yourself, there are sure to be other British ships in the area. She *must* be part of *Renown*'s squadron."

"Then where are they, Captain? So far nothing else has been sighted." Glancing round at all of them, voice curling a little. "There is no need to run for home, gentlemen. Not just yet. Stop ship."

Von Scholtz, boot-faced, clicked his heels and moved off to comply. But Zeltmann held his ground—"Admiral Mann, you have Wehrmacht personnel on board." His face was bloodless, his voice cracked. "You have no right to expose my men to further danger!"

Mann looked bored. "I cannot put your troops ashore now, Colonel. The Captain is right—we must return to base. This is now purely a Navy operation. Your men will have to face the same dangers as the rest of us."

"But you must be aware, Herr Admiral, that the Führer has issued an order? No German ship shall stop on the open sea, not even to pick up our *own* survivors."

"I am aware, thank you, yes."

Now Zeltmann became shrill and the others turned to stare—"You are disobeying Hitler's personal order? You would jeopardize the safety of German soldiers to rescue a few Englishmen? God in Heaven, whose side are you on?"

Mann's eyes scythed round, fixed on the Colonel. "I . . .? I am on the side of the sailors," he said.

For several seconds Zeltmann held the hard stare, then he wheeled and strode to the other side. He stood there, a grey rod, glaring out at the raging sea.

As the cruiser slowed, beginning to heave to, von Scholtz rejoined Mann. The Captain was decidedly uneasy. As an aristocrat he secretly despised these brash new Nazi officers of the Wehrmacht, but it was perilous to offend them, even

185

for an Admiral. Besides: there was some truth in what Zeltmann had said.

Mann murmured in his ear—"So much to make up for.... Well, it can be done in different ways, Max. This time we are not going to run." Von Scholtz said nothing. "We will stand off here," the Admiral directed. "If the Englishman blows up, we will not be harmed at this range."

"That water cannot be much above freezing point," von Scholtz said doubtfully. "And with all that oil. . . ."

"Some of them should be able to get across. Warn the doctor, please. Ask him to be ready for survivors."

"Why have we stopped? Why?" Metchik didn't reply, he scowled and pushed the bottle of Schnapps against young Schiller's trembling lips. The boy swallowed a couple of mouthfuls then slapped the bottle aside, spluttering. He wiped his mouth on his sleeve and stared all about him— "Why have we stopped? What's wrong?"

Ernst came lumbering from the crowded rail and stood, legs straddled, gloomily confronting the three of them: the mean-eyed, knowing Metchik—now helping himself to the last of the Schnapps—the shivering, miserable Schiller; and Stummer, squatting, drained, blank—anthropoid.

Schiller wormed over to Ernst, grasped his leg—"Why have we stopped? Are we going to sink?" Ernst cuffed his hand away and snarled loudly—"Say 'Sergeant' when you talk to me, little boy! And stop snivelling, or by God I'll put you across my knee!" Metchik laughed harshly. Schiller re-coiled, stung and shamed.

"I'm sorry, Sergeant." Teeth chattering. "It's the cold, you see. I—I go to pieces—I can't stand the cold!"

Ernst spat. "Stay here," he told all of them in his grittiest rasp. "Don't move. There's nothing to be frightened of any more. The English ship is sinking."

He strode off. Metchik laughed again. Schiller turned to

him and on his bone-white cheeks now two spots of red glowed girlishly—"I'm not frightened, curse you! It's just this damnable cold!"

Ernst moved along behind the men flocking the rail until he found Hart. "What happens now?" he asked. The Petty Officer shot him an uneasy glance.

"I think we're going to pick up survivors."

Ernst surveyed the stretch of gale-threshed, oil-fouled sea between them and the foundering destroyer. The *Hipper*, her engines stopped, was rolling and pitching heavily, swinging round sluggishly into wind—her bows towards the enemy. "But, God in Heaven, man! How will you lower the boats in this?"

"We don't," said Hart. "We have no boats, only rafts and floats—but we won't put *anything* over." Nodding at the *Glowworm*. "It'll be up to them. We'll pick up those who can make it across on their own."

Glowworm's afterdeck was low in the water and sharply tilted, but it was the only part of her now not wreathed in fire. Under the supervision of Campbell and Truman the wounded were carried there by their mates—struggling along the rocking, canted deck, through the swirling smoke and squalls of spray, grisly staggering duets.

The injured men—many unconscious, some doubtless already dead—were lashed on to the floats and rafts and lowered into the water. The waves and the wind snatched the flimsy craft away, spinning and bucking, blackening them and their occupants with slimy spatterings of oil.

No man could live more than a few minutes in that sea, but it was all that could be done for them now. And they were the lucky ones—for soon there were no more floats or rafts and Campbell ordered Truman and those helping him to tie extra lifejackets on the helpless men still on board, and simply push them over the side.

Battle of the April Storm

As he toiled, Campbell swore steadily, virulently, fighting nausea and revulsion—he was supervising a macabre assembly line, bundling these silent bleeding creatures into the voluminous jackets, trussing them up like turkeys and then dumping them into the frothing cauldron. It was like methodical, mass murder, committing them with quick, callous heaves to the fury of the deep.

Some of the Carley floats were still secured on lines, bobbing crazily, at times almost standing on end. In each of them a wounded man was clinging to the line, instinctively unwilling to sever this last link with the ship. Truman felt the stern shudder, tilt again, settle deeper. Any moment now she could roll over. He drew his knife with his good hand, leant out and began slashing through the lines, closing his mind to the despairing cries as the floats were swept away.

Wally Hobson stumbled out on to the afterdeck, threw himself down and gulped the icy air. He was on the starboard side and waves washed over his smarting, blistered body. He gripped a davit and lay there for a while and gulped the freezing seawater too and he didn't care if he never got up, if he went down with the ship—he could comprehend no greater joy than to be free of the sickening fumes and the roasting heat. . . . He'd fought his way up from Emergency Control by sheer brute force and rage—clawing, tearing, heaving, ramming his passage through the mangled innards of the ship, ripping the hide from his hands, shoulders, and back, and leaving pieces of his flesh adhering, frizzled, to glowing hot metal.

Presently hands gripped him, hauled him to his knees. He shook them off—"I can walk." He hauled himself up to the port rail and worked his way to the stern. Wounded men were lying around the wreckage of 'X'-gun and others were tying extra lifejackets on them. One small figure lay apart, with neither blanket nor outer clothing. It was impossible to cover him without inflicting terrible agony, for his entire body was a mass of burns. It was a while before Wally recognized him.

He moved closer, bent, and was surprised to find the eyes open. "How's it goin' then, Jockey?"—a stupid thing to say, the first phrase to come to mind. The shrivelled lips moved but no sound came. Only the eyes spoke—an unmistakable plea. "Yeh, yeh, don't worry, mate. I'll get you off. You want to come with me, eh?" The Jockey managed a tiny nod.

Very little was left of the Jockey's lifejacket, only some charred chunks, fused to the blackened flesh. Wally found a spare one but the instant he tried to fit it on, the little man uttered a strangled moan—and fainted. Wally got the jacket fixed, picked up the tiny, blackened figure in his arms— 'struth he's light, he's like a little lump of coal. . . . He swung him gently over the rail and stepped into the water.

The cold dealt him a paralysing blow, piercing all his muscles, seizing up his lungs, his heart. A wave lifted him and his burden high, pulled him away from the ship, dashed him down into a trough and buried him in a white roar. He kicked desperately with his legs, broke the surface, struggled to keep the Jockey's head up. And now both of them were black—smothered in oil.

He swam for a long time, swallowing oil, breathing oil, until he was faint and choking. Then a raft bobbed near. He lifted the Jockey and felt others drag the tiny bundle up beside them. But there was no more room. Hobson clung on, treading water. The oil gummed his eyes, he couldn't see. It clogged his mouth, his nostrils. The cold was incredible, unbelievable—like an enormous weight dragging him under. . . .

Bunty Baker was propped up against the stern racks. He'd refused to go on a float until the more grievously wounded had been disposed of. Ossie lit a cigarette and put it between the pale, pain-drawn lips. Bunty murmured his thanks, then —"Anybody seen the Skipper?"

189

"Yeh, Bill Truman says 'e's all right."

" 'E done a good job, after all. Come up trumps, I reckon."

"That's a fact. 'Ere, let's get 'em water-wings on you."
But as Ossie began to tie the extra lifejacket on his mate
Campbell lurched over, grabbed his shoulder, and drew him
away. The Lieutenant was staring at the stern, and his voice
was a faltering croak—"Knowles . . . Knowles, for Christ's
sake! The depth-charges!"

Ossie turned and saw the racks of depth-charges, now
awash as the stern settled deeper. At once he recognized
the new danger—"God's grief, some o' them's still set to
'live'!"

"Why? They should've been put on 'safe' the moment we
went into action! That's the drill, dammit!"

"They jammed, sir, Nisbett tried, but 'e couldn't shift 'em.
Then we was too busy fightin' . . ."

They looked at the crowded rafts and floats and the men
treading water, clinging to them like insects.

"As she goes down, they'll start going off," Campbell
said. "Maybe all of them at once. . . . Holy Christ, they'll
blow everything within a hundred yards sky-high!"

As if to drive home the urgency, the ship lurched again.
Campbell began dragging himself aft—"I'm going to try
setting them back to 'safe'. Get everybody away just as quick
as you can—and tell them to get clear of the ship!"

"Right, sir!" Ossie hurried back to Bunty, to finish adjusting the extra lifejacket. But Bunty stopped him, gripped his
wrist and pointed, incredulously, off to port.

"Look . . . she's stopped!"

Ossie and others near him spun round. The *Hipper* was
hove to downwind, less than a cable distant, rolling ponderously. She had swung round, her port side towards *Glowworm*, her bows nearest. And all along her main deck figures
were crowding the rail, busily lowering lines and what
looked like huge spiders' webs.

190

Several cables further away, close by the last thin tatters of *Glowworm*'s smokescreen, the two damaged German destroyers were standing off—as if sulking, unwilling to intrude.

"They're lowering nets!" Truman yelled. "Jesus—they're going to pick us up!"

A surge of hope stirred all those still on board. The wounded raised their heads, straining to see for themselves, to be sure it was true. Ossie leapt on to the sagging searchlight platform at the base of the mainmast and bawled through cupped hands—"Make for the cruiser, lads! Fast as you can—make for the cruiser!"

The cry was taken up by the men in the water. The rafts began battling, slowly and grimly, across the five hundred yards of freezing, fouled, and furious water to the enemy ship.

Wreyford's cabin was a smoky ruin. One bulkhead was smashed in. Pieces of shattered, smouldering furniture, books and files, papers and personal belongings were scattered in massive confusion. The Captain opened the scupper to clear the fumes and surveyed the mess gravely.

The desk was littered and askew but still intact. He righted a chair, pulled it up to the desk, swept the surface clear and sat down. He opened the ship's Log, stared at his watch for a while, trying to estimate how much time had passed since he'd come down from the Chart Room. Then he took his Parker pen and made a neat entry:

> 0930 hours (approximately). Ship broke away from enemy. All power gone, settling. Ordered 'Abandon ship'.

While the ink was drying he rose, poked about in the rubble and found his code-books. Then methodically he

191

collected all the files and papers he could see. The lower drawer on the desk was jammed but he kicked and jerked at it until it opened a few inches and he could reach in and extract his big leather briefcase. He stuffed everything into it along with the Log, locked it, and put the key in his pocket.

As he started to leave his foot crunched on glass. He stopped, picked up the photograph in its smashed frame and as though induced by hidden music a thousand hurtful tendernesses wafted their frail airs into the remotest fibres of his being—Susan, dear sweet Susan, so gentle and so strong, and so unselfish: where are all the days of our sharing now? Where is the safeness of you? Always I could talk to you—you had a way of getting words, thoughts out of me I never guessed were in me. . . .

The wide glowing eyes of the photograph reached into him and lit up his brain—enlarged him. Thoughts long-imprisoned in the dark suddenly were starkly clear. He wanted desperately to make sense of them, and at once he found the phrases flowing—I wish I could talk to you now, Susan, and tell you of this day, this whole tragic farce on which the curtain is falling for ever. . . .

There are so many things I couldn't explain, things I can't explain to myself, however much I try. But if I had time—in the calm light of another day it would be good to review all that has happened here, dispassionately, and perhaps with your help I could find a pattern, a glimpse of the vast, mysterious interdependence of things that would end all the doubts. For now I have only questions. Is there some high purpose to this human suffering? Does it buy some reward, does it improve the species? Will something fine, undreamed of, spring up from this burned and dismembered flesh?

Up until today I tried to treat the coming of this war as a hiatus in normal life, a temporary suspension of reality. I

192

think I was a fairly good peacetime officer, but I couldn't harden myself for the killing ... suddenly I was a ghastly misfit, an impostor. I couldn't rid myself of a feeling of my own unreality, a feeling that made it impossible to commit myself, my ship, my men. . . .

Well now it's happened, it's all over, and there's no-one to judge or adjudicate. I've done it, killed my ship, killed my crew, and I'm overwhelmed by the proportions of the horror: the sheer ugliness, the incredible, pathetic courage of men in mortal combat, the shocking bloody waste—my God, if there's a victor here it's the cold and pitiless sea! All we have left is a vertical river of dead men, and only the wind and the waves will know where we lie, and how we met our ends. . . .

Here I am, then: the Lord High Executioner. I slay well, and I bury well. I make many corpses in a very short time and dispose of them quickly and tidily. Are you proud of me, Susan? Would you live with me, love me, after this?

Campbell sloshed about, up to his waist in a freezing flood, at times completely immersed in a rushing, dragging wave. The stern racks had been badly buckled by the blast and many of the depth-charges were swinging about, bumping each other, threatening to topple. He had to deal with these first, setting some back to 'safe', heaving them back on to their cradles and trying to wedge them against each other. A losing struggle: no sooner had he secured one than a battering wave tore others loose.

Many of the fusing switches were jammed on 'fire'. His icy, torn hands couldn't budge them. The terrible cold cramped his muscles, clouded his brain. Another wave gushed over him and he barely found the strength to hold on: he knew, absolutely, that the next would take him, carry him off, and he was half-inclined to give in and let this misery be ended.

He hauled himself back up the tilted deck and flopped down in shelter of the searchlight platform beside Ossie and Bunty—"It's no bloody good, Knowles. Get everybody away, quick as you can!"

Ossie kicked off his shoes and was bending to lift his mate when he saw a figure approaching from 'midships. The Captain, smartly dressed, his cap set square and his shoulders well back. He wore no lifejacket. The deck was steeply tilted, lurching and rolling, and the wind was gusting fiercely, yet Wreyford walked in a dead straight line, with a measured tread, and Ossie could have sworn not one drop of spray touched him. Under his left arm he was carrying his big briefcase as if on his way to a shore station conference.

Campbell scrambled to his feet and he, Ossie, and Truman came to attention. Ossie took the cigarette from his mouth and flicked it away, but he still felt clumsy, holding his shoes in one hand. Wreyford glanced over at Bunty— "You'll look after him, Knowles?"

"Yessir, we'll be all right."

"Fine, fine." Turning to Campbell—"No more floats left, Guns?"

"Afraid not, sir"—trying not to let his teeth chatter, pulling the words out one at a time, as if from the pit of his belly. "A good many were blown overboard and others were smashed up." Nodding out across the water, screwing up his red-shot eyes. "But at least the more seriously wounded have some chance of reaching the cruiser. The rest of us will just have to swim it."

Wreyford didn't look towards the *Hipper*. Lips pursed, he glanced once more at Bunty, then at the other wounded still on the deck. And now despite the correctness of his bearing and the calmness of his voice, they saw the suffering in his eyes and the cumulative fatigue in the taut mould of his face. "Surprising, isn't it—her stopping to pick up survivors, I mean. Well, get the rest of these men out of it just as soon as you can. And don't hang about too long your-selves."

On an impulse Ossie stepped forward, swept up a spare lifejacket and offered it. "Captain, if you don't mind—regulations y'know, sir...." A small smile strained to lift the tired lines. He took the lifejacket, swung it over his right shoulder. They looked at each other.

"The old *Glowworm* ... She done us real proud, sir," Ossie murmured.

"Yes." The small smile stayed. " 'Don't bump into any-one,' Admiral Whitehorn said."

"Yeh?" Ossie grinned back. "Well this is one bump we *can* be proud of, sir!"

"I hope so, Knowles.... Anyway, I think I'm pretty well stuck with 'Rammer' Wreyford now, don't you?"

"Yessir, reckon you are at that!"

Wreyford turned abruptly and strode away, heading for'ard. They stood a moment or two staring after him and Truman lowered his head, shook it in slow bewilderment: all this had the unreality of a dream—s'elp me, if I live through this lot to tell the tale, who's going to believe a word of it? After all the sneers and piss-taking, how're we going to make 'em see the old *Worm*, and Garry Wreyford, the way they was today ... ? The ship and the skipper have been a joke so long, what they'll never understand is the kind of cussedness that grew up among the older hands, until most of us stopped trying to defend ourselves, and even started boasting about the bumps and breakdowns and balls-ups, all the bumph and the bullshit and the fact that we'd never fired a shot in anger. Laughing stock of the Flotilla—we bloody well learned to live with that! *And* die with it....

Campbell glared after the Captain and snarled in sudden irritation—"Where the Hell's he going now?" Before any-one could venture a guess the ship gave another quivering lurch. Truman and Ossie went back to the wounded. Again

195

Ossie bent to lift his mate, hesitated, glanced round at Campbell. The officer was mouthing soft, tense oaths—and then he started after Wreyford.

Ossie called quickly—"Lieutenant Campbell, sir! Could you give us an 'and 'ere, please?" Campbell turned, then came over and helped him lift Bunty and edge him down the steep deck to the submerged rail. Before he stepped off Ossie looked hard at him—"Skipper said not to 'ang about, sir."

"I should have told him about the depth-charges!"—Campbell was angry with himself as well as with Wreyford. "I have to warn him." He lurched off. Truman looked over at Ossie, shrugged, and stepped off.

Ossie, with Bunty in his arms, waited, judging his moment. The stern dipped—"Right!" He bent his knees, flopped in. The shock of cold pulled the air from his chest and jerked every sinew taut. A wave raised him, swept him away, hurled him down into an oily trough and rubbed his face in the filth.

He kicked out with both legs, coughed some air into his lungs and somehow kept his hold on Bunty. Another roller lifted them and from its crest he glimpsed the distant cruiser. He pushed one arm through the straps of Bunty's lifejacket and struck out with the other.

Campbell spotted the Captain, a few yards for'ard of the 'midships fire. He'd put down his briefcase and was hauling a badly burned man out of a hatchway, lowering him over the side. It dawned on the Lieutenant that Wreyford was making a last tour of his ship, doing what he could for the wounded who'd been overlooked by the stretcher-bearers or who were only now managing to reach the deck from their posts below.

Wreyford went back to the hatchway and collected the briefcase. As Campbell started towards him, once again

Glowworm lurched—and then tilted very sharply. The Lieutenant felt his feet sliding. He snatched at a davit, missed—and slithered into the water.

At once he was plucked away, tossed around in a creaming smother, then dipped in a patch of oil that glued up his eyes, mouth, and nostrils. He threshed about, rubbing at his eyes, and when he could see again the ship was fifty yards away. A float bobbed near, men all over it, lying half in and half out of the water, paddling and kicking. Some of them called to him, beckoned, but he ignored them—no by Christ, I'm an officer, they're overcrowded as it is. I have to make it on my own. . . .

Ossie battled to keep his mate's lolling head above water—Bunty kept slipping into unconsciousness, a dead weight. He cuffed his face and wasted precious breath yelling at him. He had to rest. He rolled on his back, treading water, Bunty's head on his chest. Both of them were black with oil and Ossie was beginning to feel nauseated—he must have swallowed a pound or two of the thick grease.

A hunk of balsa, part of a smashed float, bobbed near. A man, so covered in oil he gleamed like a seal, was draped over it. Ossie kicked out with his leaden legs and managed to curl his free hand round one corner of the wood as it sped, spinning, to his right. He clung on, and presently the draped figure stirred, raised his head. White eyes stared out of the shiny black mask. He barely recognized Grannie Smith, half-drowned, unable to paddle or steer with his several wounds—bloody Christ, now I got two of 'em on me 'ands . . . !

His stomach contracted painfully: the first twinges of cramp. The wood was slippery but somehow he got his arm over it, heaved Bunty up and draped him beside Smith. He rested, trying to steady the balsa with his weight.

Then a wave reared, broke, and his hands slipped. The roaring foam battered him, pushed him under. By the time

197

he struggled to the surface the fragment of float was ten yards away, spinning and bucking as though trying to shake off its limp and helpless passengers.

White-lipped, Zeltmann descended to the deck and marched to the rail. The men around him, sailors and soldiers, didn't notice him : all eyes were on the water, and on those clinging to the nets below. He saw a space, moved right up to the rail. The fires faded from his pale eyes.

In the weird light oozing from the bile-coloured sky, the ocean was in convulsions. The thousands of gallons of oil haemorrhaging from *Hipper* had failed to quell the ferocious thrust and scend of the waves, the explosions of spray and the blasts of spume. The carpet of sludge had been ripped to fragments and strewn far and wide, and the alternate patches of black water and white foam created an unearthly scene. Only close in by the cruiser's hull, where the thick dark torrent still poured from the ragged wound, was the sea, a little calmer, smoothed out—heaving slowly, hideously, like undulating, breathing ooze.

Five or six hundred yards away the sinking destroyer lay almost on her side, with her stern down and the smoke from her fires stretching out over the water in a long cloud, teased and torn into curious curves, tors, and tendrils by the veering, slashing wind.

The stretch of sea between the ships was littered with tiny, tossing black blobs—men swimming, men heaped on floats and rafts, clinging to scraps of wreckage. They rose, flailing, on the crests and vanished in the bursts of foam and the plunging, sucking troughs.

Zeltmann was appalled, incredulous. He stood gripping the rail, swaying to counteract the wicked rolling of the stationary cruiser, and watched German sailors climb down the sagging, swinging nets—to rescue Englishmen. . . .

Some of them had lines looped around their waists, and

198

spare lines were being lowered, to be thrown to the survivors as they drew near. And even as he watched several of his own men dumped their weapons and packs, threw off their greatcoats and even their lifejackets, and went to help.

He opened his mouth to yell but a fierce jab of wind drove the air back into his throat. More and more troopers were flocking to the rail, snatching up lines, waving and bellowing encouragement to the nearest floats and swimmers. The Colonel realized he was powerless to stop them—it had gone too far, he'd lost control. The soldiers were men of action, they couldn't be expected to stand aside while the ship's crew risked their necks.

Now some of the British were less than a hundred yards from *Hipper*'s waiting nets, but the powerful wind was pulling them past, towards the stern. Zeltmann saw one lone swimmer struggle, stroke by stroke, ten yards nearer—and then abruptly slump forward, spent, crushed by the cold, beaten by the butting sea and the clinging weight of the oil. A wave snatched at him. He went under, and did not reappear.

A laden float came careening in, crazily tilted on a rearing billow. A man slid from it, clawed frantically at a shipmate's outstretched arm, then was swept away, buried in an ooze-clogged furrow. Zeltmann heard himself cursing, aloud, feverishly—cursing the Navy, the Admiral, the ship, the British, this vile and freakish weather, and this fierce and pitiless sea. . . .

Campbell fought his way out of a patch of choking sludge and turned on his back, rubbing the muck from his eyes, coughing the fumes from his lungs. The sea threw him up and down like a trampoline and he felt that his whole body, from the neck down, had shrunk, atrophied, turned to stone and must surely sink.

He understood now what had overtaken those he had

seen, swimming resolutely one moment, swallowed up the next: the cold had shrivelled them, stiffened the flesh, stilled the bloodstream, and stifled the mind until they simply gave up, allowed themselves to be extinguished—and now it's happening to me, I'm growing heavier, heavier by the moment; nothing this heavy, this rigid, can stay afloat. . . .

Another wave raised him, and he saw *Glowworm*. She was over on her starboard side now and the stern was completely submerged. A big sea dashed itself against the after hull and a giant genie of spray arose. Moments later the surface shook like an enormous jelly . . . swelled, boiled white . . . began to rise in a huge, broad column. He felt a massive blow, like a cricket bat in the belly, and the deep boom of the explosion battered at his eardrums. He saw a float, which had become bogged down in a pool of oil twenty or thirty yards off the stern, ascend majestically, high in the air, spilling out wounded men. Then the ravening wind snatched at the tall tower of spray and drew a curtain across the foundering ship.

Campbell knew too well the nature of this hideous activity: as he'd feared, the waves pounding at the sinking stern had torn away one of the 'live' depth-charges. And that first blast was certain to have ripped others from the racks.

He waited, counting off the seconds as the roller broke, dragged him down into a rushing black valley. A second explosion, much louder . . . another thudding body blow—and then a continuous roar, a long series of pummelling shocks. The blows jarred his mind out of its lethal lethargy, knocked the numbness out of his muscles. Another wave scooped him up, swept him on, and then he was swimming again, with measured, strong strokes. He did not look back.

Ernst Neuhofer was helping Petty Officer Hart and some

sailors lower another climbing net. The net was amazingly
heavy. Ernst turned his head and yelled—"Hey there,
Metchik! You others—rouse yourselves!"

Metchik, Stummer, and then young Schiller, a gasping,
glass-eyed ghost, came to lend a hand. They got the net
slung and then, toiling with a sudden sureness, like a well-
trained circus troupe, they broke out the life-rafts, secured
lines to them and lowered them into the water. Hart directed
them to pay out the lines and let the run of the sea take the
rafts out beyond *Hipper*'s stern so that survivors who were
swept too far might still be saved.

Ernst became aware of Colonel Zeltmann coming towards
them from the Bridge ladder, shoulders hunched, chin on
his chest, glowering. Quickly he passed his line to Metchik,
jerked to attention. For some twenty seconds the Colonel
stared at him then he turned his angry gaze to the water.

"Carry on, Sergeant!"—a low, slow growl, dragged from
him like a shameful confession.

Valentino moaned as a gust of wind trepanned the crests
and dashed the freezing spray in his face—rhythm, one must
keep the rhythm. . . . He could hear his father's voice boom-
ing out, sternly instructing the naked, flailing children, and
he glimpsed the stocky brine-browned figure standing in
the stern of the little fishing boat anchored in gentle blue
water off Gozo, pushing them off with the blunt end of a
boathook each time they grabbed in panic for the gunwale
—you know the strokes, my little ones, perform them as I
have shown you and you will lose all fear, you will ride the
sea like resting gulls! Remember the rhythm, count it out—
one a–n–d two a–n–d three a–n–d one! Do not hurry it,
keep the rhythm, the rhythm is everything . . . !

He tried to count and his limbs moved in a jerky, anxious
breast-stroke. Even with the lifejacket he seemed to have no
buoyancy, he had trouble keeping his head up and was

201

swallowing water—I was a poor pupil, dear Father, a great disappointment to you. . . .

A bursting wave knocked him out of the careful rhythm, half-smothered him. As he rose again his hands touched something solid: a float. He clung on, shook the water from his eyes and found himself looking into the smudged faces of Baker and Smith. They were sprawled, motionless as corpses, on the tossing, spinning scrap of balsa.

Valentino rested, then pulled himself up until he had his chest on one end and began working his legs in a frog kick, pushing the float on towards *Hipper*—one a–n–d two a–n–d . . .

After a little Grannie lifted his head. His blue lips moved.

"Good ol' Malt. Make us a cuppa char, eh, mate?"

The first survivors reached *Hipper*: Hobson, pushing the helpless Jockey on a float. Both were gleaming black with oil. Wally was semi-conscious, the movements of his limbs were automatic. Vaguely he heard frenzied shouts, saw the huge bows looming overhead. He kept swimming, pushing, he could think of nothing else to do. A line came snaking down nearby, but he couldn't reach it.

Hart bent over the rail—"Move along to the nets! The nets are easier . . ." The little float butted the bow plates and for a moment looked like capsizing. Hart was frantic— "The nets, the nets!" he bawled. Other voices took up the cry. Someone on the foredeck threw another line but it fell short. Hart turned to Ernst. "They don't understand!"

Schiller squeezed between them, leant out, and began yelling hoarsely in English. But still no effect: the float was being carried aft . . . it drifted out . . . it was being swept past the nets. . . . Sailors hanging on the nets threw line after line and some fell across the float. But the exhausted Englishmen made no effort to grasp them. The sea was carrying them off.

Ernst couldn't stand it. Without plan or conscious decision he tore off his heavy webbing equipment. Metchik and
the others watched blankly as he climbed over the rail and
started down the net. Zeltmann watched too, erect and
motionless as if on a parade ground, wondering why he
wasn't screeching at the Sergeant, ordering him to come
back, threatening to have him courtmartialled—what was
the fool trying to do anyway? He moved to the rail again,
peered down.

Ernst clambered past a German sailor hanging on just
above the high water level. The sailor bellowed something
at him and grabbed at his arms. Ernst shook him off, continued down. A big, black-slicked wave came racing along
the hull from the bows and in an instant he was completely
submerged. The knifing cold and the weight of the rushing
water almost plucked him from the net but somehow he held
on. The water fell away and he saw the float sliding towards
him, only a few feet out from the hull. The ship rolled, the
net swung outward. Ernst stretched out his left arm—
reaching, reaching. . . .

As if in a dream Hobson saw a hand. Extended, coming
closer, to within inches of his face. A big, powerful hand
with rounded knuckles, stubby fingers: calloused, chafed
across the palm. *Whose* hand?—what's it doing there, what
does it want . . .? It wants to help, it's for me . . . His right
arm was like lead. He forced it up inch by inch.

The two hands met. Gripped.

Hobson's hand was slippery with the oil but Ernst
managed to work his fingers out and clasp the wrist. He
pulled, got Hobson on to the net, then reached out again
just in time to grab the float. He clung there, praying that
someone would come to his aid before another wave arose.

Schiller stared down from the rail and a spasm of shivering seized him. Emotions warred within him: fear of the
Arctic water's piercing, paralysing cold; a choking, tearing

compassion for those frozen, filthy wretches floundering down there, and a shamed envy of Neuhofer's courage and physical strength. He forced the trembling from his body and began to throw off his webbing. Metchik watched him for a moment, amazed, then he too snatched at buckles and straps. Together they went over the rail and down the net.

Zeltmann watched in a sickly trance. Then all along the deck his troopers were swarming down the nets to assist the seamen in the perilous rescue. The thing was incredible— German soldiers were not supposed to show initiative....

Beside him now there was only Stummer: slouched, immobile, grey-faced and expressionless as ever. He knew that if he barked an order the man would be galvanized into action and blind obedience—if he told him to dive from the rail the dolt probably wouldn't hesitate.... For the first time in his military career the Colonel found himself wondering about the old Teutonic principles and the whole system of discipline on which the Wehrmacht machine was built.

Ernst grunted curses through gritted teeth as he felt his grip on the greasy, bucking balsa begin to slip. The seamen had come all the way down the net now to take care of the man Ernst had pulled from the water, and somehow they'd survived two more icy, tearing immersions. But the other Englishman was still on the float—a black bundle, small and slight as a child, so terribly burned Ernst would have been sure he was dead had he not seen one charred hand moving, groping for a better hold as the float tilted sharply and swivelled round—almost tearing Ernst's arm from its socket.

The ship rolled. The net swung out, then they were slammed back against the hull. The big Englishman struck the side of his head and would have fallen if a sailor hadn't held him, with one arm around his back and a leg crooked over his hips. The Englishman stirred, pawed at the ropes like a spent butterfly beating feebly in a web. This couldn't last: Ernst knew the next wave would wrest the float from his weakening grasp. . . .

And then Schiller came down the net. Rapidly, agile as a trapeze artist descending after a performance. He twisted round to face the float and launched himself in a flying dive. He surfaced outboard of it. For a despairing moment Ernst was sure the boy would be swept away, but he got one hand hooked over the balsa and pulled himself against it then pushed it in against the net. With the other hand he grabbed the burned man's arm and, working himself round, dragged him to the inner end of the float. Ernst let go the wood, got a good grip on the limp arm. Schiller lunged, caught at the net. Together they lifted the second survivor up beside his companion.

Now Metchik and two other troopers came scrambling down the net. They looped lines around the injured men and within moments they were being hauled to the deck.

Ernst and Schiller climbed clear of the waves, wedged themselves in the net and rested. Ernst looked at the kid: '*if you ask politely maybe the Admiral will stop for a while and let Schiller take a dip . . .*' He was shivering violently, his skin was bright, blotchy pink and streaked with oil, but after a moment he pointed at the water: Ernst saw several blackened heads bobbing between the racing crests—more lone swimmers, fighting closer. . . .

Schiller squirmed, doubled up in the tangle of ropes and began to pull his boots off.

Ossie had been lucky this far: somehow he'd missed the thickest patches of sludge and acquired only light spatterings of oil. He'd suffered stomach cramps, the concussion of the depth-charge explosions had almost battered him senseless and the cold had penetrated deeper and deeper until it was like a lance through his heart, but still his lungs and limbs kept functioning—at times it seemed quite independently of his flagging will.

Now suddenly, surprisingly, the cruiser's bows towered over him. He let the sea pull him along the hull, caught the first trailing line that came within reach and looped it around him. The line went taut, he felt himself being lifted in small firm jerks. He put his feet against the steel plates and began to 'walk' up the ship's side.

Far above he saw men crowding the rail, shouting, gesticulating: he realized they wanted him to move sideways, aft on to the nets—"The nets are easier!" But some unquenchable defiance made him ignore this advice. A Petty Officer of the Royal Navy did not take orders from the enemy ... Besides, there were the wounded, coming in on the floats: the nets were their only chance. So he gritted his teeth, gripped the harsh rope, forced his numbed legs straight and kept 'walking' until several hands gripped him, pulled him over the rail.

Then his knees gave way, he sank to the deck of the ship which, only minutes before, he'd been doing his best to destroy. His face was inches from a huge, black boot. He studied it: a German boot. It moved, shuffled closer—and then merged into a greater blackness. . . .

Ernst, making his way back down the net as another float bobbed closer, saw one of the Englishmen rise on his knees to grab at a thrown line. The float tilted. The man was pitched into the water, swept away. Even as Ernst cried out Schiller flashed past him, hit the water in a flat dive. This time he had to swim about thirty yards, ploughing through huge, racing waves before he caught up with the Englishman. He took him by the shoulders, turned him on his back expertly, fighting wind and current, and slowly hauled him in. Only an exceptionally powerful swimmer could have done it.

Ernst and Metchik clambered aft from net to net to meet

them. They lifted the half-drowned Englishman and passed him up to the men above. Then Metchik caught a dangling line, coiled it, passed it to Schiller as he climbed back on to the net, quaking with cold—"Here Johan, tie this round you, man."

Zeltmann was still staring down from the rail at the struggling men, at the clambering, clutching, shouting, toiling sailors and soldiers—*his* soldiers. He'd seen Neuhofer repeatedly risk his neck, drenched by icy waves, and watched Schiller go into the water twice to save enemy lives.

Now the Colonel's chin jerked up and his eyes focused sharply on the blank, motionless Stummer—"What's the matter with you, trooper?" he snarled. "Get down there and help the others!"

Stummer's heels thumped—"Very good, Herr Colonel!" And he began unfastening his webbing.

Further along the deck *Hipper*'s Medical Officer, a middle-aged stooping man with greying hair, was moving among the British survivors with his orderlies. To the wounded he administered morphia. Gently, in thick and faltering English, he repeated to each of them a small incantation—"You are safe now. I am giving you something to take away the pain."

The orderlies wrapped the shivering, filthy, exhausted men in thick blankets. A plump steward appeared with an enormous tray: huge steaming mugs of coffee. He served them to the unhurt survivors and the less seriously wounded.

Ossie opened his eyes. He was lying in shelter, under a blanket. He got up, slung the blanket over his shoulders like a cape and shuffled to the rail. Anxiously he surveyed the water, then the nets, hoping to see Bunty.

He felt a hand on his arm: a medical orderly. Firmly he led Ossie back into shelter by a gun turret and made him sit down. The steward handed him a mug of coffee. Then a Petty Officer appeared, stood over him, studying him with open curiosity. To hold the coffee mug Ossie had to let the blanket slip from his right shoulder and he saw the German's eyes fasten on his badge of rank—'sright Fritz, opposite numbers . . .

Hart fished out his cigarette tin. He lit one, bent and held it close to the Englishman's lips. Ossie took it in the corner of his mouth, nodded.

"Thanks, mate."

Hart moved on. Ossie inhaled deeply.

Another float, bucking savagely, was alongside. Bunty and Grannie were draped over it like old coal sacks. Valentino was in the water, still kicking rhythmically to hold it against the nets—one a-n-d two a-n-d . . .

This time Ernst was able to step right on to the float and secure the line. With Metchik, Schiller, and Stummer helping, the two wounded men were passed up safely. Then Ernst reached for the man in the water.

The float rocked. Ernst lost his balance and fell.

The first massive sting of cold flattened his lungs, he felt himself being swept away—he'd never been a strong swimmer. . . . A wave burst over him, he was inhaling water. He began to fight, flailing, kicking—no, this is not the way, it is not to happen like this! I am a *soldier*—Sergeant Neuhofer, E., Iron Cross second class, master of fieldcraft, unarmed combat, and automatic weaponry—specialist in sabotage and demolition. . . . Veteran of Poland, proven under fire, not afraid to die for the Fatherland; ready to face bombs, bullets, bayonets—to go down fighting, leading my men, and sleep in the good brown earth. . . .

But not this—not to die all alone in the cold, feeble as an infant! Having my breath stopped up, suffocated by this dirty grey water. To sink and be lost for ever, my body bloated and spongy, drifting, decomposing, in the deep darkness, fodder for scaly scavengers—God in Heaven no, please, not this way, *save me for a soldier's end*!

But the harder he struggled the more water he swallowed, inhaled. The rushing, crashing waves pulled and pounded him until his muscles were locked and quivering and there was a tightening steel band around his chest and a strange drowsiness weaving a cocoon around his mind and stilling his desperation.

Schiller dived from the net. When he surfaced he couldn't see the Sergeant. He had the line around his waist and Metchik was paying it out. He began swimming towards the stern.

Metchik, on the net above, spotted the Sergeant's head, fully fifty metres from the ship. He pointed and shrieked at Schiller. The Bavarian swam in that direction and soon, raised on a wave, saw Ernst threshing weakly on a rushing crest.

Schiller hurtled down into a trough then climbed a steep, heaving hill. Again he saw the Sergeant—only ten or twelve metres away now. . . .

But then a menacing cliff of water arose, and ran at Ernst. Schiller saw him raise his right hand, almost as if in salute, then he let his head fall back. The wall of water exploded down on him. Engulfed him in a welter of foam.

Schiller swam to the spot and stared frantically about him: only the heaving, wind-scored sheen of water. He shouted breathlessly, pointlessly—"Sergeant! Ser-geant!" Until his heart and lungs were thumping painfully, until the cold cleaved his skull like an axe and his voice would come no more. He turned and began fighting back to the ship. Metchik and Stummer hauled him in on the line.

Ossie couldn't stay in shelter, he had to see what was happening. He got up again and went to the rail. The wounded survivors were being lifted on to stretchers. Among them he saw the Jockey: his face a black mask, his body

209

smaller than ever—shrivelled up like a twisted cinder. The grey-haired Medical Officer was bent over him, adjusting a wad of dressing.

As Ossie drew closer the doctor straightened, looked at him. Ossie's eyes held the question: the German answered with a tiny shake of the head.

Ossie drew harshly on his cigarette and turned away. And then he saw Bunty, next in line for treatment—the sea 'asn't got us all then, some old matloes live to tell the tale ... ! He knelt down by the stretcher, looked into the thin, coarse-stubbled face—"Wotcher, me ol' cock! Reckon we'll be able to scrounge some blades an' 'ave a decent shave now, eh?"

A very young German sailor was hanging on a line aft of the first net, his feet braced against the plates, an arm stretched out towards Campbell. With a final effort the Lieutenant pushed closer, gripped the hand. But the cruiser fell away sharply in a trough. The sailor couldn't take Campbell's weight. He was plucked from the rope and both of them splashed down.

The sailor couldn't swim. Campbell tried to hold him but the boy panicked, pulled them both under. Campbell got him to the surface, then a wave broke and they were torn apart. With a wailing cry that Campbell would remember to the end of his days, the German was borne away by the next roller, lost amid the ragged peaks and heaving oil patches.

Ironically, the same wave threw the Englishman in against the net. He felt an arm supporting him, then the rough rope rungs against his palms. Voices rang about him, strange, guttural sounds. He was being raised out of the sea's icy clasp—up, up, up. . . .

Schiller was curled up like an infant in his blanket, against a bulwark, shuddering. Metchik and Stummer stood over him, drained, silent, shivering occasionally as the wind jabbed through their soaked clothing. Schiller looked up, his bloodless lips twitched out the words—"I tried . . . but I couldn't reach him. He went so fast—you saw?" Metchik nodded quickly, almost irritably. "I swear to God, I tried . . ."

The Corporal went down on his haunches and gripped the boy's shoulder, hard. "You did your best. Just take it easy. The doctor is coming to have a look at you."

Schiller closed his eyes, moaned softly. "It was the cold that beat me, Metchik. The damned awful *cold*. . . ."

Ossie searched the tumbling, seething sea for more of his shipmates: only three solitary swimmers now, unrecognizable black blobs struggling the last few yards in to the nets and lines. Further out, nothing but the evil oil stains, empty floats, and rafts bobbing, tilting, whirling in a malefic ballet. . . .

He turned and counted the survivors on deck. Including himself, there would be about thirty-four. But the Jockey and two or three others couldn't last. So, out of a ship's company of 125—no, he'd forgotten the Midshipman, Rosinsky; the lad had made it up to 126—probably thirty would live. Among them were Bunty, Eddie Nisbett, Valentino, Grannie Smith, Wally Hobson, Bill Truman. Only one officer: Campbell—funny it should be 'im, newest we 'ad. . . . Odd sort o' cove, too—kept 'imself to 'imself and nobody knew 'ow to take 'im. But 'e done all right when it come to it, I saw 'im on the tubes an' 'e done 'is level best an' I shall say as much if ever anyone asks me. . . . Still, funny it should turn out this way, every one of the others gone. . . .

He moved slowly along the row of stretchers. Bunty was straining to raise himself, staring out—"Look! She's capsized!" Others tried to sit up, even the German medics straightened and were still.

The wind had dragged away the last gauze of spray thrown up by the exploding depth-charges. *Glowworm* had rolled completely over and was settling by the stern. She seemed to have drifted closer. Her fires were quenched, only a light haze of smoke seeped from her now—sad mist stretching out across the waves. . . .

And then, as the smoke became thinner still, they saw him: a tiny, solitary figure amidships, sitting on the hull with his back against the keel. The Jockey lifted his head, his shrunken lips moved and somehow he croaked out— "The Captain . . . it's the Captain!"

Wreyford felt his ship tremble beneath him as her bows rose and her stern slipped deeper. *Glowworm*, hapless orphan of the Flotilla, very soon would sound the desolate depths of these Arctic waters and find her grave in eternal darkness and silence. A sunken sepulchre for scores of the men who had fought and suffered with her—men, like her, unblooded until this day. . . .

Another body floated past, face down, arms and legs spread wide—like a child's first drawings of the human figure. One of those killed by the depth-charges, or trapped below decks and released only now as, gurgling and bubbling, the upturned sinking shell disgorged her flotsam, farting it out through a hundred jagged holes.

A wave lifted the body, flung it down then fell upon it, roaring, and devoured it. A scrap, a morsel, a little bundle of cells reclaimed by the element from which they had emerged blindly, measureless millennia ago.

Poor, feeble, finite Man, the planet's crust-crawler; for all his absurd and pathetic pretensions—nothing but a puny assembly of bones, flesh, and fluids, so easily destroyed! And by weapons invented, developed by himself to incredible

212

sophistication—Man in his genius one day fashioned a flint into a tool, and was doomed ever after to become a tool himself. . . .

Wreyford sat there, alone, islanded in a vandal ocean, clutching his briefcase, and stared at the enemy cruiser. Beyond her now he counted four destroyers, lying well off in a wide arc—two more escort ships had come up from the rear to join the damaged *Paul Jakobi* and *Bernd von Arnim*. He stared at the enemy force and wondered again how many of his men had reached *Hipper*. Not many, he feared—but the fact that the cruiser had stopped, and lowered nets, astonished and confused him. Completely unexpected, certainly against all the rules. . . .

He remembered the tall figure of the German commander, the fine-boned face, the grey eyes trained down on his in the final moments before the ramming—you and I, what sort of men are we? What compels us to continue and compound the tragic follies of our forebears? Can you, sir, explain what we have been doing here today, in the middle of the North Sea, in the middle of the Twentieth Century A.D., setting our young men upon each other to kill and maim methodically as no other species on Earth ever has done?

The ship shuddered again, huge air bubbles burst up from the stern and the keel plates jolted against his back. He glanced at the bows: higher now against the scudding cloud-rack. He lifted his briefcase, fat with the Log, codebook, and the ship's papers, and tossed it into the water. He kicked off his shoes and got to his feet, steadying himself against the vibrating keel. He took off his cap, looked at it a moment then threw it after the case. He paused, checking the tapes of his lifejacket and taking long breaths, counting up to five with each inhalation—as he'd been taught as a schoolboy athlete, to store up oxygen before a race. Then he moved with small steps down the barnacled slope.

213

And slid without fuss into the sea.

"*There* 'e is!"—Ossie leant far over the rail and stabbed a finger at the swimmer, surmounting a raging peak, beating through the foam and dropping swiftly, slantingly, down the almost sheer wall of the wave to vanish once more behind the closer crests. He was more than halfway across but it seemed to Ossie that he was being swept too far to his right, towards the stern. The wind had risen again to a steady whine and more flurries of sleet were thrashing the water.

Bill Truman's voice broke the silence—"She's goin', lads. . . ." All eyes swung to *Glowworm*. Only her for'ard half remained above water. The jagged bows were rising, streaming white wisps. The sea around her frothed, reached up to enfold her. Slowly, smoothly, she slid under, leaving a wide stain of purest white.

Wreyford fought on, trying not to hurry his strokes or his breathing, but the terrible cold clasped him tighter and tighter. His chest was constricted and his muscles stiffened and ached as though pounded by mallets. He felt as if his whole body were being squashed between giant slabs of ice. But he was drawing near the cruiser: through the writhings of sleet her grey flank loomed over him, rising and falling and leaning, and all along the length of her the water was glossy with oil—a behemoth wallowing in her own blood. . . .

As a wave lifted him he looked up and saw figures crowding the rail, others halfway down the nets. Some of those on the deck were swathed in blankets and although he couldn't discern their faces he knew them for his men—I shall talk to them, tell them the truth I've discovered about myself. I was afraid, always afraid . . . 'This is the Captain speaking. . . .'

Nets. Lines. Only a few yards now—but they were rushing past him, to the left. From above: confused shouting. He realized he was being swept to the stern.

Mann opened the side pane and leant out. The swimmer had missed the nets and was being carried aft. The men were surging to the stern. More lines snaked out. The swimmer made a last effort, ploughed over a huge roller and thrust through a clogging pool of oil. He caught one of the lines and clung on with both hands.

The Admiral beckoned Stenz—"Go down there. The English Captain should be received by an officer. When the doctor has seen him, if he's fit enough bring him to me." Stenz, wall-faced, clapped his heels and went. Mann called to von Scholtz—"As soon as he is on board you can start engines. Have the destroyers stand by."

"Tie it round you!"—"Loop the line round your chest, sir!"—"Captain, pass it under your arms and make fast! Captain!" German and British voices roaring against the wind's moaning and the sea's thrashing. "Captain, do it now and we'll haul you up—*don't try to climb*!"

But Wreyford heard only a distant confusion. He'd swallowed some oil. He clung to the line, retching, giddy. His mind kept wandering. The cold was burning now, burning into his lungs, into his head, cauterizing his brain—this is the Captain speaking. . . .

At the stern rail Ossie, Hart, and two brawny seamen held Wreyford's line. They'd pulled him in against the side, almost under the bulge of the stern, but they dare not start hoisting until he'd looped it securely around himself. All the men were yelling themselves hoarse, gesticulating, but still the Captain simply hung there, gripping the line with both hands, head lolling. Waves lifted him fifteen, twenty feet, and let him fall again. Waves crashed over him, tried

215

to flush him out, suck him away.

Ossie realized the Captain was only half-conscious. He let go the line, flung the blanket from his shoulders, and swung a leg over the rail. But hands gripped him, held him— German sailors and soldiers were bawling in his face, shaking their heads. There were no nets here, and the overhang of the stern made rope-climbing difficult and dangerous. Besides—there was no need for anyone to go down: the English Captain was only resting a moment, recovering his strength and breath before looping the line around himself. . . .

Ossie tried to argue—then abruptly the shouting changed, everyone was crying in alarm and despair. He looked down.

Wreyford was starting up the long, slender, swinging rope. He'd made no attempt to secure it around himself. He was moving his hands together, holding with his feet while he changed the grip. His progress was painfully slow. His head rolled back, the mouth wide, eyes staring up and blinking, twitching with strain. His sodden hair and clothing fluttered feebly in the wind.

Hart growled an urgent order to the seamen anchoring the line. Slowly, evenly, they began to haul in—raising Wreyford gently and carefully, reducing the length of climb. An officer in what Ossie took to be an SS uniform pushed through to the rail and stared down. His face, only a foot away, was wrenched in anguish. Then a plump Navy officer bustled up behind him, followed by two blanketed figures: Campbell and Truman. No-one spoke.

The Germans, falling back to make way for the officers, had released Ossie. Instantly he snatched at a spare line dangling from the rail, swung himself over and went down, fast, hand over hand. His aches and weariness were gone. He heard himself bellowing—" 'Ang on, skipper! Stay where you are!"

Wreyford stopped climbing. He clung there, head thrown

216

back, chest heaving. The men above kept hauling and he continued to rise slowly as Ossie descended.

Ossie stopped just above him and saw that now the Captain's eyes were tight closed. The men on deck stopped hauling. Ossie reached towards him, but the lines were too far apart. He put his feet against the plates and started to work his way across.

The great ship lifted on a mammoth wave, rolled ponderously. Wreyford swung outward, then back in against the side. His left shoulder thudded against the plates. His whole body jolted. His grip loosened. He dropped about four feet—then braked himself.

Ossie moved swiftly down his line and at the same time worked sideways until they were on a level—"I gotcha, Captain!" He pulled up the loose line from beneath him and stretched out to loop it around Wreyford. But the ship rolled again and both of them swung far out over the racing, reaching water.

Wreyford's eyes opened. Across six feet of spray-laden air he fixed Ossie with a calm stare. Then they swung back. Ossie managed to stick out his legs and hit the plates with his feet but the Captain began to spin on the inward swing and again his shoulder and left arm slammed against the solid steel. It knocked the breath out of him. He began to slip.

Ossie let go the loop of line and made a frantic lunge. With his right hand he grabbed at the Captain's lifejacket . . . missed . . . caught his left wrist. Wreyford took his hand from the line and Ossie felt the fingers curl around his wrist, trying to lock. He waited for the Captain to bring his right hand over, so that he could draw him close and hold him until others came down. But Wreyford's wrist was coated with oil. He began to slide from Ossie's grasp.

Ossie screeched—"Your other 'and, sir!" Wreyford's head sagged, his whole body went limp—and he came off

217

his line. For an instant Ossie's failing grip held him suspended, then he fell, in a slow forward somersault.

The sea took him quickly. He was plucked away, face down, a limp bundle, and in moments was lost among the towering, tumbling waves.

Ossie felt his own grip weaken. The grief and rage drained him, the cold and the exhaustion invaded him again. He knew he'd never climb back to the deck. But other lines were snaking down around him, voices rang in his ears. He managed to get one line around him, made it fast.

As they hauled him up he began to sob.

Mann closed the side screen. Slowly.

"Start engines!"—von Scholtz's voice was strangely muffled.

Mann didn't turn immediately, he stood with his shoulders hunched, his legs wide apart, and his hands clasped over his pelvis, looking out at the greyness—well I wanted them to come, I hoped and prayed for the British to come out of Scapa and challenge us. *So much to make up for ..."* But I did not bargain for this—to be held up, turned back, by one ship; to be brought to such long, hard battle by just one little destroyer ... and then to have to watch a brave adversary perish within reach of safety....

How am I to report this, what will Berlin say? There is nothing to be ashamed of. I shall tell them the truth, exactly—how gallantly the English captain fought his ship ... how he stayed on his Bridge, exposing himself to our concentrated fire until the very moment when he drove his bows into our guts. I shall tell them how I looked down at him then, looked into his eyes, and knew the kind of man he was ...! I shall tell them of the terrible punishment we inflicted, yet the enemy ship refused to die, her crew would not give up....

They will ask me why I took it upon myself to stop and

pick up survivors, and I shall tell them simply that as a naval officer I respected the enemy's superb seamanship and deliberate self-sacrifice. And so did my men, *and* the Wehrmacht personnel—some gave their lives to pull the English from the sea. . . .

If I can, I shall see to it that the English Captain's heroism is recognized, and remembered, by his countrymen—perhaps a report can be sent through the International Red Cross. . . . There is one officer among the survivors, I will talk with him later, ask him about his Captain. I must know his name, where else he has fought, in what other engagements he distinguished himself before this final supreme act. I must learn all that is possible about such a man. . . .

It is important to make our leaders understand all that has happened here today: Germany is overwhelmingly strong and this far we have had easy victories; but if the war is to go on, if we are to attempt the conquest of England —then we must understand the nature and full measure of our enemy. Men like those will be hard to beat, however outnumbered, however hopeless their situation. Men of high skill and experience, with something more than mere courage—a strange, unexcited, entirely English brand of fanaticism.

Men like that Captain, with the cold, calm eyes. . . .

He felt the ship stir beneath him, vibrating to the steady tramp of the engines. He lifted his left hand and consulted the big Swiss watch on the inside of his wrist: 0958 hours. Von Scholtz was intoning his orders—"Half speed ahead. Steer two–three–zero. . . . Make to destroyer escorts: 'Returning to base, resume stations. *Jakobi* and *von Arnim* to report damage and casualties.' "

Mann turned and saw Stenz and Zeltmann come back on to the Bridge. Their faces were pale and pinched, somehow smaller. Spots of sleet glistened on their coats. They looked over at him, pulled themselves upright and Zeltmann saluted in the Nazi fashion. Mann acknowledged, Navy style, and waited for the Colonel to come to him with words of censure and dogma. But Zeltmann moved quietly to the far corner of the for'ard screen and stood looking down, expressionless. Stenz went with the Captain to the charts, to work out their course for the Skagerrak and Kiel.

The Admiral walked over to stand beside Zeltmann. On the deck sailors and soldiers were working together, quietly, hauling up nets and lines, stowing floats and gear, gathering scattered equipment. Stretcher-bearers were carrying the last of the British wounded below and a Wehrmacht guard party was marshalling the others into a rough line.

The captives moved in a mournful file, coming towards the Bridge. With their blackened skins and rumpled, voluminous blankets they resembled a group of nomadic African tribesmen.

But one of them had discarded his blanket and contrived to wipe some of the oil from his face. His sodden wrinkled tunic bore officer's braid. He stepped out of the line, raised his head and called sharply. The others straightened, pulled their shoulders back. None wore shoes. But, feet padding wetly, they got into step and marched through the sleet.

Campbell fell in at the rear of the file, asking himself why he'd felt compelled to call on the men to smarten themselves up—a thoroughly theatrical gesture. But all of them knew it was what their Captain would have wanted.

Poor, punctilious Wreyford—his loss, within reach of rescuing hands, had stunned them, even now it was hard to accept that he was gone. All the petty paperwork, the fussing and the foibles and the maddening bullshit—the whole strange tyranny of the man—now were endearing, an intriguing part of what would always be for Campbell a sublime mystery. "There's a right way and a wrong way to salute, you know. . . ."

As they passed the Bridge on the port side the ship's bell began tolling: 1000 hours. Campbell turned his head to look at the bell and the smart German rating sounding it. The chimes were deep-toned, impassive, hanging in the cold dank air, defying the tearing wind. The bell was large, finely engraved, glowing in the gloom. And he decided: I will have that bell, one day I will take it home. For *Glowworm*, for those who are gone, and for Garry Wreyford. . . .

The guards opened a hatchway and herded them below. As he went down ladder after ladder, deck after deck, Campbell was convinced he still could hear the bell.

Kiel, Germany/V-E Day + 2

THE BELL, propped up in its frame in the back of the truck, gave out an occasional soft-throbbing chime as the wheels lurched over debris. McCallion drove slowly to the dockyard gates. Allied servicemen and German workers turned their heads to stare, baffled, strangely awed.

The Canadian MPs lifted the gate boom and waved them through. Campbell took his right hand from his pocket to acknowledge the Sergeant's salute then hunched down in his seat again. He was still cold, he'd been cold for five years. He doubted if he'd ever be warm again.

McCallion picked up a little speed. The streets of the ruined city were quieter now. The food queues had gone, the work gangs had moved off the roadways to dig and sift among the tottering shells and massive mounds of rubble which had been tenement blocks, warehouses, office buildings, and shops. The tyres jolted over ruts, broken bricks, and humps of litter. The bell pealed plaintively and the sound echoed away, weirdly, through the gutted buildings on either side—I have the bell, I've claimed the prize, but it shouldn't be me, I wasn't one of them, not really—I have the least right. . . .

The bell pealed again—I remember, at the Admiralty, a little courtyard . . . in Summer a warm, shady place, in Winter always very quiet; sheltered, a kind of sanctuary where storms may not enter. And in April the bluetits and the first swallows flit among the eaves and arches, and fill the air with their chatter. . . .

I'll suggest they keep the bell there. Set it on a plinth, in the centre, still in its frame, with a plaque underneath, listing the names . . . Wreyford, Fielden, Trenton, Rosinsky . . . Bell, Longmore, Grant, Boyce, Clark—the bell shall be their memorial, in that well-sheltered little courtyard in the very heart of London, where the traffic noises can't be heard, and in April the swallows come singing. . . .

The truck drew near the bombed-out church. The old man and the little boy were still poking about in the remains of the tenement opposite. They turned to stare again at the alien vehicle. They were much closer than before. Campbell stared back. The child's eyes were as old as his companion's years and the old man looked bewildered, lost—like a little boy. . . .

The truck drew abreast of the burnt-out, roofless church and again the wheels juddered over a patch of rubble. *Hipper*'s bell sounded a pattern of clear, deep notes that sang in the still sharp air. And like an aching cave the great, hollow shell of the broken place of worship seemed to snatch the notes, echoing and magnifying them as though they were its own, so that they sang on and on in the shattered black steeple long after the truck had passed out of sight.

The old man and the little boy stood amid the nightmare landscape of their ruined city: two lean and dusty figures, stilled in awe. They looked up at the jagged stump of the church steeple and listened to the chimes singing on and on where no longer hung a bell.

FOURTH SUPPLEMENT
TO
The London Gazette

Of FRIDAY, the 6th of JULY, 1945

Published by Authority

Registered as a newspaper

TUESDAY, 10 JULY, 1945

ADMIRALTY.

Whitehall.

10th July, 1945.

The KING has been graciously pleased to approve the award of the VICTORIA CROSS for valour to:—

The late Lieutenant-Commander Gerard Broadmead ROOPE, Royal Navy.

On the 8th April, 1940, H.M.S. Glowworm was proceeding alone in heavy weather towards a rendezvous in West Fjord, when she met and engaged two enemy destroyers, scoring at least one hit on them. The enemy broke off the action and headed North, to lead the Glowworm on to his supporting forces. The Commanding Officer, whilst correctly appreciating the intentions of the enemy, at once gave chase. The German heavy cruiser, Admiral Hipper, was sighted closing the Glowworm at high speed and an enemy report was sent which was received by H.M.S. Renown. Because of the heavy sea, the Glowworm could not shadow the enemy and the Commanding Officer therefore decided to attack with torpedoes and then to close in order to inflict as much damage as possible. Five torpedoes were fired and later the remaining five, but without success. The Glowworm was badly hit; one gun was out of action and her speed was much reduced, but with the other three guns still firing she closed and rammed the Admiral Hipper. As the Glowworm drew away, she opened fire again and scored one hit at a range of 400 yards. The Glowworm, badly stove in forward and riddled with enemy fire, heeled over to starboard, and the Commanding Officer gave the order to abandon her. Shortly afterwards she capsized and sank. The Admiral Hipper hove to for at least an hour picking up survivors but the loss of life was heavy, only 31 out of the Glowworm's complement of 149 being saved.

Full information concerning this action has only recently been received and the VICTORIA CROSS is bestowed in recognition of the great valour of the Commanding Officer who, after fighting off a superior force of destroyers, sought out and reported a powerful enemy unit, and then fought his ship to the end against overwhelming odds, finally ramming the enemy with supreme coolness and skill.

The KING has further been graciously pleased to give orders for the following appointments to the Distinguished Service Order and to approve the following Reward and Awards:—

For great gallantry in H.M.S. Glowworm's last action on 8th April, 1940. H.M.S. Glowworm attacked the German heavy cruiser Admiral Hipper and, after inflicting damage, was sunk with colours flying.

To be a Companion of the Distinguished Service Order:

Lieutenant Robert Archibald RAMSAY, Royal Navy.

The Conspicuous Gallantry Medal.

Engine Room Artificer Third Class Henry GREGG, P/MX.51369.
Petty Officer Walter Thomas William SCOTT, P/J.113793.
Able Seaman Reginald Thomas MERRITT, P/JX.154145.